BRING YOUR LEGS WITH YOU

Drue Heinz Literature Prize 2004

Bring Your Legs with You

Darrell Spencer

UNIVERSITY OF PITTSBURGH PRESS

Published by the University of Pittsburgh Press,
Pittsburgh, Pa., 15260
Copyright © 2004, University of Pittsburgh Press

Printed on acid-free paper
First paperback edition, 2013
10 9 8 7 6 5 4 3 2 1

Library of Congress Cataloging-in-Publication Data

Spencer, Darrell, 1947-
  Bring your legs with you / Darrell Spencer.
    p. cm.
  "Drue Heinz Literature Prize 2004."
  ISBN 0-8229-4242-9 (cloth : alk. paper)
  1. Las Vegas (Nev.)—Fiction. I. Title.
  PS3569.P446B75 2004
  813'.54—dc22   2004013590

ISBN 13: 978-0-8229-6248-9
ISBN 10: 0-8229-6248-9

This one is for Kate, as always;
& for Maxine & Willie

CONTENTS

BRING YOUR LEGS
WITH YOU

Bring Your Legs with You

My brain is not wired for chess, so the Tuesdays me and my dad Gus got together he punked me good, game after game. "One move at a time," he told me. "Don't be counting your chickens." All that talk about calculating ten, fifteen plays ahead, Gus declared it crap. Be his guest, you're such a pistol. You're such a genius, you can calculate infinity? Because that's the number of plays is possible. It ain't like making doughnuts. "Go ahead, ace," he said to me. "Tell me where I'll be one play from now." Trouble was I bogged down on the board, and he took me apart.

Tonight he cooked linguini and tossed a seven-layer mile-high salad. He baked breads. Poured wine, a port, and me and Gus, the two of us in front of the TV we cheered on the Utah Jazz, loving their game, the many ways they embarrassed the showboating Lakers, all the time Gus talking about the years he was acquainted with the mobsters who ran Las Vegas when Grandpa Jersey owned one mortuary rather than the twenty Gus now let run themselves here in the city. Story I hadn't heard before was how Grandpa Jersey chewed cigarettes when the cops brought in a body they found in the desert, one that had been stewing there a week or two in a shallow grave. Tobacco killed the stench. Allowed him to breathe. Grandpa Jersey laid out the problem for an air conditioning guy named Phillips, who designed a system that pulled fresh air down across the body and out of the room. Phillips got rich. Grandpa Jersey caught his coattails and bought land cheap out near Red Rock and along Paradise Road. Turned nickels into gold.

Gus grabbed a bottle of wine, studied its label, mustered up a face, and said, "Portugal. Supposed to be what the gods imbibe." He set the bottle aside. Said, "Tommy, you want a real drink? Whiskey do you? Bourbon?" I shook him off. On the TV, the Jazz ran the Lakers dizzy, which is what you get when you think money can buy you what only busting your butt can do. Sports, at a pro level, is 99 percent mind. One percent agility. It's a given you're quick and strong. Question is: What's in your chest? Do you have the fire? Second question is: When your big guy thinks he's Aristotle, how far are you going in the playoffs? Gus poured himself bourbon, neat, and said, "You know this Brit calls himself Prince?"

I told him I saw the man box on HBO, Friday Night Fights.

Gus said, "What, and you didn't call?" He took me by the elbow and was walking me and him through his billiards room toward the backyard.

"How'd I know you'd want to see it?" I said. "It was close to one in the morning."

Gus said, "I'm old. I'm roaming the house all night."

I said, "The man backs up his mouth. Hits like a sledgehammer in the night."

"They say he's the second coming," Gus said.

"I got to admit he had me sitting up in my chair," I said. The ringside announcers, a couple of poets in their own right, talked about fistic thunder in Prince's hands and a three-punch rhythm, left, left and right, equal weight and speed. He brought his legs with him blow after blow. The man was a headhunter bell to bell. A show and a half.

"A knockout?" Gus said.

"Right here." I showed Gus where Prince bopped the other fighter on the crown of his head. Where he thumped him. He stunned the guy, who was a lanky piece of barbed wire, a treacherous puncher from Scarborough, England, who was putting up a cockfight of his own. Threw darts himself.

Gus opened the slider to the patio. Stalled. He said, "Am I going to see you fight?"

I stepped aside and said, "You go ahead. I'll catch up with you. I need to see a gent about some land."

In the john off Gus's bedroom, I took a leak and went hunting for Gus's cocker spaniel, Vegas Vic. He came to Vic or Victory. He was standing on the bed in the guest room, perched at the foot of it, calculating the distance he would need to travel to reach an ottoman shoved up against the baseboard for him to use. Vic was fifteen and wore sadness like an overcoat. He had seen that life was a carnival ride at its best. Gus got him as a puppy, one more dog sold out of a cardboard box on Fremont Street. Vic suffered from what the vet called paperfoot, which was the least of the problems the man had diagnosed over the years. There was a heart murmur. Vic had gone deaf in one ear. Lost teeth.

"Show me what you got," I said to the dog.

He blinked real slow. Baleful. Had a look in his eyes that said he had spent some of his nap time chatting with St. Peter and the message he was bringing back wasn't quite what we expected to hear. The other side didn't differ much from this side. You got flats on heavenly highways and the nectar of the gods soured if you left it out. Fruit rotted. Hearts got broken.

Vic made the big jump, came off the bed, hit the ottoman, stumbled, then righted the ship of himself, putting forward the effort the old make to get up from a sofa.

"You did it," I said.

He still had to get to the floor, so I airlifted him. Vic did his pins and needles walk down the hall, me at his side, the two of us pals. Outside, we took the flagstone steps to where Gus was sitting on a lounge chair by the pool. Gus tipped his head back and polished off his bourbon. Heard us behind him. He said, "You think you'd be on his list?"

It was clear to him I didn't catch his meaning. He was completing a conversation I hadn't followed.

"The Prince has a list," he said. "He's checking names off and knocking everyone out."

"Once upon a time I'd have been on it," I said. Prince boxed featherweight, which was where I did my amateur fighting. As a pro I moved up through the weight classes, and in the end, I retired from the ring holding two belts. Never lost. Not once. Thirty-one wins, twenty-nine by knockout. Now I roofed houses, not out of need, but for the love of a task physical enough to keep me sweaty and light-footed. My doing so made no sense to Gus. His argument was: *Who notices a roofer on the roof unless it leaks, and then you're only a noise?* He shakes his head at my walking away from the money, the fame, the celebrity.

"You'd've been the top of his list," Gus said.

I said, "Number one, number two, and number three."

"You'd've knocked his frigging head off."

I had enough of the boxer left in me to think so.

Gus in tonight's Bermudas and sandals was a disturbing picture. Beachcomber Gus. My dad was looking like he took a detour that was leading him too far out of his way. If he had been a sign he would have been missing some letters. Maybe the u from his name. Would be just G . . . s. I was growing up, he was Armani suits before Armani came to Las Vegas. I once saw Gus wear a white linen jacket and trousers and wide-brimmed Panama hat at a funeral. You could have used the shoes Gus bought as collateral on a loan. He wore nothing but silk ties a lady, one of those personal shoppers, chose for him.

"I'm thinking of a plan," he said. He was frisky, jittery, grinning, flashing his newly bought-and-paid-for choppers, teeth so white against his tan they made you think of death riding a tricycle. I pulled up a chair. Vic flopped on his side and rolled in the grass, wiggling himself around, cooling off. Gus said, "It's about your mother." Edna, she died seven months ago—cancer, quicker, sneakier, and more vicious than the worst scenario you can imagine or have ever read about. Ain't no words for what can happen to a body. If there is such a thing as a soul, cancer's got its number. Trust me. Edna was fifty-seven. She could have been a tree stump by the time she let go. Looked that bad.

I said, "You going to do something behind her back, is that it?"

"Not possible," Gus said. "Nobody got nothing past her dead or alive."

I could see he could use another drink, so I hoofed it up the steps and carried home the bourbon. Poured till he signaled stop. Halved his tumbler. He stared at the drink and said, "I met her mother's mother once and that was it."

Met was the wrong word. Our family drove to Ely, Nevada, in time to be told Edna's mother had just died in the hospital. I don't think I was in high school yet. An Indian girl named Naomi, chasing a dog down a hill, ran into Constance, my mother's mother, and broke her hip. Then Constance, the day she was to go home from the hospital, fell from her bed and rebroke it. She never was released. No one phoned Edna until after the second break. Too late, like I said.

4

We drove through the night, went straight to the hospital, and Constance was dead. Second time around on the hip, internal bleeding. Edna refused to stay for the funeral, and she didn't try to reach her family. Not even Gus ever learned what the trouble was, if it was a feud, who had offended who and in what way, how deep it ran. He never shook anybody's hand—not her dad's, not brothers' or sisters'. Not one of them. We had a couple of photos left was all.

"It's time to solve the mystery," Gus said.

Vic moseyed over to the pool, and I got up to keep him from toppling in. I turned on a hose and filled one of the bowls Gus kept on the patio. The dog wandered over, pawed at the water. Huffed off.

Gus said, "I'm going to Ely." He sipped his bourbon, said, "You up for it?"

"When?" I said.

Gus said, "What's wrong with right now, this minute?"

———

I walked Vic and his fleece pad next door to the Kimballs, good people and dog lovers. Gus located my sister, Ginger, at her fiancé's. Let her know she was on her own for a couple of days, and we were packed and gone by midnight. It was one dark ride up 93, a two-laner that took us through Alamo and Caliente. No moon sitting pretty in the blue-black sky, just Gus sawing logs.

Out of Pioche, on a long stretch, the sun appeared. Popped up and gave me a boost. I felt the way you do when you open the blinds in the morning after a sleep on your pal's couch. The desert lay to our left and right, gorgeous in its soft haze. Sagebrush, then a dry lake, and a range of mountains, different shades of blue and purple like a jigsaw puzzle. Middle of June and there was snow on a couple of peaks to the east. It could have been five miles or a thousand to the foothills.

"Obdurate," Gus, eyes slits, said. He was leaning for a slow look out the passenger's side window.

Sure, I thought. No pity. Hard hearted. But not only. You limit your vocabulary and you miss the beauty. You turn the desert's rigor ugly. You miss its point. You forget what resolute can mean.

Gus realigned himself and buzzed his seat up, then down. We were driving his Cadillac. "Coffee?" he said. We had a thermos in the back. I pulled over, and we stood on the shoulder, the sun already burning color into the desert. Reds. Pinks. Yellows. The blue-green sage. Gus said, "Do you know how far?"

"Another hour," I said.

He filled our tin cups. "My plan runs out once we get there," he said. "Then we play it by ear." Up ahead, where the road cut through a ridge, five coyotes drifted toward the highway. Not more than fifty yards away. "Sweet Jesus," Gus said.

I said, "You want to talk about obdurate."

They moved easy, relentless. Body fat 0 percent. Rangy and unyielding. They glided, loped, turned north. Try talking one out of its desire. Good luck. Creatures like that, if they got hungry enough, would, on the move, tear off a piece of their own chest or leg muscle and chew on it.

Gus said, "You don't see that every day."

———

Ely, Nevada, Gateway to the Great Basin National Park, the crossroads where US Highways 50, 93, and 6 met. We topped Connors Pass, swung through the grasslands and past Comin's Lake, and there it was. Our room at the Bristlecone Motel sat on us heavy as a root cellar. Gus showered and volunteered to locate some breakfast. He had put on fresh shorts and, this time, a Hawaiian shirt, a flora-and-fauna print to it.

Edna's family name was McCarty. Edna McCarty. Only one McCarty in the book, P. T.—Paul, Gus said, her father—and we found the address in five minutes, a one-story house on one of the avenues laid out into and along a hill. The houses on the low side dropped away so that you could see beyond them to Highway 93 running north to McGill. It was clear from where we parked in the street the McCartys hadn't replaced their roof in forty years. Shingles were missing. Others were curled, and the felt and wood showed through. The sidewalk in front was ragged, the slabs tilted, off-shot. Weeds grew in the cracks. There was a four-foot retaining wall running the length of the entire street. A set of steps led you to the McCartys' walkway. The handrail was plumber's pipe, galvanized, painted silver. The wall in front had been whitewashed. The house itself didn't match its surroundings. It was brick, the color of red wine, was the house you would see in a neighborhood crowded with trees. There ought to have been shrubs and gooseberries surrounding it, rose bushes bordering the yard and in bloom. Maybe a dogwood. It had arched windows, an arched porch, arched doorway. Reality here was that the front yard was hardpan. Not one blade of grass. Not a tree. The driveway was gravel except for two narrow strips of concrete.

We reached the front door, and a man came around the side of the place. He was carrying a punch bowl. Had to be crystal. He was holding merchandise worth five thousand dollars, I was thinking. He could have been seventy given the way he moved, which was a little like he'd been forced out onto a diving board. His face said ninety— there was that much detail to it. Not a hair left on his head. No lips to speak of. Bitten eyes.

"What you peddling, gentlemen?" he said. He was dressed in a black suit I would have bet he wore for one hour in the 1950s, maybe to his own wedding half a century back.

Gus said, "We look like salesmen?" He swept a hand over his shorts, his Hawaiian shirt, his sandals.

"Peddlers come in all shapes and sizes," the man said. "You know as well as I do they say you don't judge a package by the package."

I said, "We're not selling anything."

"For sure you're not giving it away," he said. "No offense, but no one is." He crossed the yard and set the punch bowl on a porch chair. He had jammed a ladle into his back pocket. He set it inside the bowl. We followed, and he came at us to shake hands.

Gus said, "We're trying to find P. T. McCarty's."

"Art Worst," he said and we shook. "Worst of the Worsts is our joke," he said.

"Is this McCarty's place?" Gus said.

"Is," Worst said. He picked up the bowl and said, "Was." He started down the walk, stopped to punctuate what he was about to say. Said, "Surprising, isn't it, the turns life takes?"

We tagged along, Gus saying, "You've got our attention, Mr. Worst."

"Call me Worst," he said. We stalled at the top of the steps to the sidewalk. He handed the ladle to me and said, "You mind watching over this, if you're coming along?" It had been sliding around inside the bowl, making a racket. I took it, and he said, "This fine crystal is for the funeral. Mr. Luther McCarty's passing to the other side, which, I'm guessing is why you're on my doorstep."

Gus said, "We didn't know."

"I was thinking you're family," Worst said. He hustled as best he could down the steps, talking, telling us he was running late. "Hands to shake, babies to kiss," he said.

So Worst filled us in. Luther McCarty was P. T. McCarty's younger brother. There was an older sister named Emerald. P. T. died ten years ago. Prostate cancer he didn't have an inkling of until he was too late and one month from the grave. P. T.'s name was left in the phone book for privacy reasons.

"Whose privacy?" Gus said.

Worst said, "Patience. I'm getting there."

A year after P. T. died, Worst married his widow, a woman named Selma, who had been P. T.'s third or fourth wife, Worst wasn't recalling exactly, him and Selma both over seventy at the time, both of them still good in the feet and the head, pals more than anything else. She died, cancer again, the twentieth century's undertaker. Her passing left Worst alone in the house. "You know what they say," Worst said. "You live long enough, and, hell, your body's going to take matters into its own hands." So Selma died, and Worst stayed on. Luther McCarty came to live with him, fell off a ladder, broke his hip and never recovered, hip death—so the logic went—being a family curse.

"You lost me," Gus said.

"Point is," Worst said, "house is mine. I'm family by the law."

We followed the hill down a couple of streets, Worst talking a blue streak. Gus told him he had married Edna, P. T.'s daughter. We reached a stretched-out, flat building, looked like the low-rent place you'd sell insurance from, the building that might house the post office temporarily, where you'd go for a notary. Across the front were Venetian blinds hung in elongated windows. Worst handed Gus the crystal and unlocked the door. He took the bowl back and stepped aside for us to go ahead. It was freezing inside. One hundred on the dirt out front. Sixty in here. Worst said, "I'm thinking I didn't know Edna."

"Edna McCarty," Gus said.

Worst said, "Isn't a name I recall."

Inside, at one end of a hall was a casket, a pot of carnations at the foot of it, yellow day lilies near the head. There was a banner that said *Luther "Luke" McCarty/God Rest His Soul.* In a corner was a Yamaha keyboard, not quite a piano, but the kind of music maker you see in some family's rec room. It had foot pedals. A short boxy speaker sat on each side of it on the floor. A padded bench was waiting for the musician. Worst placed the punch bowl at one end of a long table, next to a box of Dixie cups. I laid the ladle by it, heard Worst say to Gus, "She sister? niece? what?"

"Edna was my wife," Gus said. "P. T.'s daughter, like I said. Constance was her mother."

Worst said, "First wife? Second?"

"I thought there was only one," Gus said.

"None of it rings a bell," Worst said. "Except P. T.'s name." He shifted paper napkins so they were next to the bowl. They were blood red. Worst said, "It's all in one day we'll be doing the ceremony. We got the viewing starting at five, and then we load Luther up and it's ten minutes to the cemetery. I'm saying five words at the grave site and that's all the service there will be. You're welcome, the two of you, if you'd like to come along." He laid out silverware, saying, "Luther's dying wish was to be under the ground within forty-eight hours. It was all he asked for, a pine box and quick burying, and I'm killing myself to oblige."

––––––––

Gus talked to Worst, and I wandered outside. Across the street, there was a garage sale going on. A woman holding a papillon was sitting in the shade of a tree, the pair of them on one of those plastic chairs you buy at gas stations, the kind you stack. This one dark green. She had covered three card tables with knickknacks. Clothes hung on hangers along the edges. There was a row of vacuums next to her. There were floor lamps. She was selling a mower she hadn't bothered to hose off. It was caked in grass and mud. An extension cord snaked out of a window of her house and plugged into a fan at her back. It stood tall and rotated 180 degrees. On an end table at her elbow was a CB walkie talkie, its antennae extended.

She called to me. Said, "You family?"

I walked toward her. "You know the McCartys?" I said.

She was wearing wrap-around sunglasses, the lenses big as the ears on her dog. Her clothes made me think of a garden of sunflowers, one badly watered. She wore a scarf for a hat and had on her feet wrap-around shoes that fit like bandages. I waited until I had crossed the street, until I'd gotten the squint out of my eyes, and I said, "Edna McCarty was my mother."

The woman had white paper dots stuck to the backs of her hands. Prices on them, $4, $.50, $5, $6.50. She saw me staring and said, "It's how I keep track of what I sell and whether or not I've removed the price if it's a gift wrap." She pointed at a paper sack full of jewelry boxes, most of them white, some gray.

I said, "Did you know Edna?"

"If Edna was your mother," she said, "then that would make that other gentleman the gangster she went off to marry, if he's your father, I mean, and I'm thinking he is because I seen bits and pieces of him in you from where I'm sitting."

"Sharp eyes," I said.

She said, "The way you put your shoulders is one example." She showed me what she meant, and I recognized me and Gus in the way she held herself. The woman said, "She flew the coop still wet behind the ears."

This, of course, was not the story I'd been raised on. The gangster part had to be small-town foolishness. Was stupid gossip. The story I knew was Gus met Edna in Las Vegas at a Frank Sinatra show on the Strip. A man named Lenny Shafer introduced them, rubbed his hands together like that matchmaker he was being, and said, "I hear wedding bells." Their courtship was flowers and Perry Como songs, was long and slow and romantic. It involved boating on Lake Mead, and they loved the movies.

I said, "The gentleman is my father. I'm Tommy Rooke, and he's Gus. If he's a gangster, you've got a scoop."

"I'm just saying what was being talked around, and we're going back thirty, forty years, or so." She licked a finger and held it up. Testing the wind. She said, "Maybe not so long as that." She said, "i. e. God." Said, "Tick tock. God's lips to your ears. Throw away the key." And she did. She zippered up her mouth, locked her lips and tossed the key over her shoulder.

"That's one sorry-ass way to run a funeral," Gus said. We'd gotten back to the car, and he had the air conditioning on high. Gus slapped his dark glasses to his face. He said, "Let's find some decent clothes."

I said, "We're going to the burial?"

"There's got to be some family there, right?"

I said, "The woman running the garage sale tells me the word in Ely is that Edna ran off and married a gangster."

"Me?" he said.

"She tells me so."

We pulled out, Gus saying, "She could have. Who knows. Anything can happen in this world. She never told me one word about her life before we met. That subject was off limits, completely, no negotiation."

"You talked some about it?"

"Your mother was an incomprehensible woman."

"But you would have known."

"You'd think so."

———

Gus bought himself some duds, downtown, Ely, Nevada. Slacks a goat would have worn only if it didn't have any say at all. We did our best at Penny's and had an afternoon to kill before the service, so it was back to the McCarty home. No one answered our knock, and Gus walked right in. It was like we stepped into one of those boxes they use to ship bottles. Rooms the size of cells. You wanted to move so you didn't touch the walls. Off the short hallway entry to the left was a kitchen. A squat table, one of those with bowed legs and the chrome sides, that style that's popular again, was shoved into and squared up with a corner. No way could you have sat across from someone. You had to sit kitty-corner. There was a napkin dispenser, like you see in cafes. Salt and pepper shakers, cat motif. The floor was linoleum, acid green mostly, but the tiles speckled like a bird's egg, and white squares here and there, no pattern to them, replacements. To the right was a dinky family room. The floor was hardwood, ancient oiled six-inch-wide planks. There had been water damage near the window. Dead center on an oval rug sat two ladderback chairs facing a thirteen-inch TV on a crate. It was hooked up to cable. The chairs looked like contestants. On top of the TV lay a hammer, a few nails next to its head. I wandered over to a cluster of photos. My best guess was they were all of Worst—Worst as a kid, Worst in his twenties, Worst middle-aged, Worst somewhere around fifty, where they stopped. The grouping formed a square.

I found Gus in one of the two bedrooms. It was empty, except for a cot, and was not much bigger than a walk-in closet. A window looked out onto the backyard, which was narrow like an alley, like it was here only to shuttle you from yard to yard. Its dirt looked hard as concrete. There was a T-bar clothes line. No wire or cord to clothespin things to. Straight back, the yard ended at a cinder block fence, ten- maybe fifteen-feet high. It had been painted white and patched. A crack—a scar—zigzagged down it. One block had fallen and broken. Two heavy-duty poles were angled into the ground and wedged into the wall. To keep it from collapsing was my guess. You could see there was lettering under the paint. A big window on the other side of the room framed the neighbor's garage.

Gus said, "So you wake up every morning, and you see what I'm looking at. What do you do?"

"You die a little," I said.

"You're fifteen. You're sixteen. You're seventeen."

"You're staring at your future."

"Like there is one. Like you have any choices."

I said, "The garage-sale lady says mom flew the coop."

"With a gangster."

I said, "There's a door that must lead to a downstairs."

"Cellar," he said. "They call it a cellar."

Then there was nothing to say. This was where my mother grew up. She had a couple of brothers. Gus knew one of their names. Clint. Clint McCarty. Sounded like a gun fighter. There had been a baby sister who died. We think there were two other sisters. The next bedroom we located had a brass bed in it. There were a couple of throw rugs on the floor and a chest of drawers in a corner. Clothes in the closet. Worst's, we figured. We couldn't get the door to the cellar open. There was beer in the refrigerator, and we took a couple. Gus set a five-dollar bill on the rack inside. We stood at the kitchen sink, and a square window showed us Ely, Nevada. We could see a drive-in movie screen alongside the highway to McGill.

Gus said, "I don't know when she left."

I wasn't sure what he meant.

"She could have been fifteen years old," Gus said. "She could have been twenty."

I said, "I'd have left at ten."

"It's creepy, isn't it?" Gus said.

"It's hard to imagine it being livable, even in its prime. Every minute you'd be within three feet of someone else."

"You think it sounds like much of a family?"

I had no idea. Shrugged so.

"It's no kind of a family," Gus said. He turned his back to the window. I did too. We could see the two chairs in the living room. Heartless. Forsaken. "She graduated from high school," Gus said. "I know that. But I don't know where. She was in Las Vegas a long time before I met her."

"The garage sale lady might know," I said. "You got to be a certain age to leave to marry a gangster."

Gus polished off his beer and opened the cupboard below the sink. Cleaning supplies, but no waste basket. He set his bottle on the counter. "I don't want to know," he said. He looked directly at me—first time since we walked in—and he said, "Do you?"

"It doesn't really matter," I said. "You had your life, the two of you." I set my bottle next to Gus's. Said, "Was there ever a day when she wasn't smiling?"

"She slept in that room and woke up to that wall. There's no question about it," Gus said, and he headed for the front door. Just like that, he was leaving. I heard him say, "You see what I saw? Fucking cinder block wall shoved in your face every fucking morning you wake up?"

I caught up with him out front. He was glaring at the house and was beat up around the eyes. Had gone eleven rounds of a twelve-round bout, and in three minutes, if he could stay on his feet, if he could keep from hitting the mat, he would be decisioned. That was what he had to look forward to. His one hope was to counterpunch, was to walk the other guy into a big left hand. To cut him off and time a knockout blow. Only the other guy was too smart. He had nine, maybe ten rounds in the bank, so he was hitting and stepping out. He wasn't even showing Gus his face.

Gus took a long hard breath. "You spit in the ocean," he said. "End of story." We took the steps to the street. Gus fired up the Caddie and said, "This is a nightmare. This is a one hell of a goose chase."

———

Like Gus said, our plan ended when we got to Ely. We rolled dice from that point on. We still had a couple of hours before the service. A sign told us the Railroad Museum was open, but the door was locked. We ate Mexican and shot pool at the Outpost Bar, nine ball,

Gus on my turf, and I took him for fifty bucks, trapped him, as payback for our chess games, in a niggling battle of safeties, me kicking the ball two, three times off the rail shot after shot until I ended his misery with an impossible massé, curling the cue ball around the six and dumping the three in a side pocket. Skill? Sure. But the make required luck you understood you would some day have to pay for. The gods don't give it away. I ran the table out. Cruising Ely took us twenty minutes. Waves of heat shimmered above the intersections, and the day was fry-your-brains hot.

At five, we drove over to the building Worst had taken us to. The garage sale was still going strong. There was a family picking through the clothes, and a guy in a dusty Jeep was pulling out, a floor lamp next to him in the passenger's seat, belted in. He was wearing a do-rag and a nose ring. I waved to the lady running the sale.

"You sure you don't want to talk to her?" I said to Gus.

"Maybe rough her up," he said.

Inside it was like a wedding reception. The crystal bowl was bubbling, some kind of pink punch. There were paper plates and those Dixie cups. Finger sandwiches and cookies that had red and green fruit bits stuck to them. Leftovers from last Christmas was my guess. A woman was playing the keyboard. Loud. Obnoxious as hell. "Rock of Ages," and stuff like that. You had to pick up your voice to talk.

Worst met us at the door. "Please," he said, "sign the book." We did, and he said, "Luther would appreciate your presence." There were three names above ours. No McCartys. We were probably it, as far as the family was concerned. Worst escorted us toward the refreshments. A man and a woman sat at a table, and two boys were running wild, were racing tin cars across the floor. The man wore a mustache, thin, like in the movies forty years ago. Sign of a personality defect to my way of thinking. They turned out to be Worst's people.

"Eat up," Worst said to us. "Waste not, want not."

I said, "Is there family coming?"

"There's been no communication," he said.

"Which means?" I said.

He said, "What it means."

Gus said, "Did you know P. T.'s family at all?"

"The one wife, Selma," he said. "We was—I told you—married."

"Besides her, I mean," Gus said.

"There was me and Selma. Then there was me and Luther, and we didn't pry after each other. Your business was your business. Where would snooping get us? Can you tell me?"

"You didn't talk about family?"

Worst said, "I can't say we did."

"Selma have any children?"

"Never laid eyes on any."

"We're not after you for anything," Gus said. He tried to square himself up to Worst, to cut down on the man's constant two-step. Gus needed to look him in the eye. He said, "We don't want jack from you, Mr. Worst."

Worst said, "You don't, then you're a rare bird for sure. You're a first." He dipped himself a drink and said, "Ain't one thing you can get your hands on even if you hired yourselves a lawyer."

Gus moved closer, and I sort of got between them, was afraid of him lowering himself into that peekaboo squat he had been working on and letting one fly. I could hear him breathing at my back—puff, puff, puff, like he was rowing a boat.

"House, land and mineral rights is in my name," Worst said.

Gus said, "You hear me?"

Worst cupped a hand behind his ear and said, "I'm old but I ain't deaf, dumb or stupid."

"Jesus," Gus said.

I took his arm and walked him over to where we grabbed paper plates and a couple of sandwiches. Tuna fish and white bread. The crust had been cut away. The music got inside your head and made you want to find a cave. Gus and I wandered over to the casket, and there was Edna's father's brother. Screwed up as he was in his coffin I saw her in him. Particularly the cheeks and the set of the eyes. Me, I think you see relatives in distant blood, in kin, in the brothers and sisters, aunts and uncles, more than you see the parents themselves in the children. Gus said, "Could be anyone." He settled his plate on a table and said, "I'm telling you this is no way to run a funeral." He reset Luther's tie, a stiff K-Mart piece of cloth, diamond shapes on it.

The door opened behind us and let a triangle of light in. The heat followed, rolled in. A tall couple met Worst, and he hugged the woman. The man shook his hand. No way to hear over the music what they were saying.

I said to Gus, "Family?"

"Not likely," Gus said. He looked over at Worst and said to me, "Was there a family or just the rumor of one?" He circled me. "If there is anyone, they're not coming," he said, and he stepped us away from the coffin, saying, "You saw that house. Would you bother with it if you'd ever lived there?"

I checked the signatures on our way out. LeRoy and Stella Brown. Gus got the Caddie's door unlocked, and we heard the garage sale lady. She whooped, like she was hollering down a horse. She got to her feet and walked her papillon half way across the road. She said, "Hold on," and she bent and gathered in the dog. She was carrying her walkie-talkie and had to do some juggling. The dog yapped, lifted one foot, then the other one. We waited for the woman to reach us. The dots on her hands had grown to about fifteen or twenty. She had had a good day. She said to me, "I couldn't get your face out of my mind." She breathed hard, short and insistent, and I reached for the dog. It growled. "She bites the hand that feeds her," the woman said. "Don't be offended."

"I like that in a dog," I said.

She said, "You're Tommy Rooke."

"Like I told you."

"Well I didn't put the name to the face."

"No reason for you to."

"My husband, Errol," she said, "he got cable just so we could watch the fights. He was a boy who growed up in New Jersey."

Gus said to her, "Tommy tells me you knew Edna."

She shifted the dog. Got a grip on it, about lost the walkie-talkie doing so, said, "I knew her business was all. The way it is in a small town."

"She left to marry a gangster?" Gus said.

"They say she did."

"Did this gangster have a name?" Gus said.

She said, "Tommy here tells me you're the gangster."

"I'm the one she married."

"What kind of a gangster are you?"

Gus said, "Only in my heart."

"Edna was a fighter," the woman said to me. "She wanted what she wanted. You had to know she was that kind of girl. She had a mouth on her." She released the dog on the dirt, and it was dancing right away. Too hot. The woman looked directly at me, and she said, "My husband said you had murder in your hands before you quit fighting."

I said, "I'd put it another way." We were walking with her back to her chair.

She said, "You got it from Edna." She stooped for the barking dog and said, "She was, like I said, a fighter. She had pluck. That's where you got it. My husband says you fight with what's inside you." Her walkie talkie squawked. "That'll be Errol," she said. "The husband," and she pointed toward the house. There he was, a face in a window, looking like one of those photos on a T-shirt. Errol pulled a curtain back and talked into his own walkie-talkie. We didn't hear him on this end. The woman said to me, "He forgets to push the button." She shook her head, sad, like the world wasn't as difficult as Errol made it. She said, "After you drove off, he was telling me if you came back to the funeral to see if you would shake his hand. He wanted you to understand it would be an honor."

I said, "It would be my pleasure."

She got on the walkie-talkie. Said, "Errol?" There was a squawk. "Errol?" she said.

"Over," Errol said.

"Over my ass, Errol."

"Ten-four."

She said to him, "The man says it would be a pleasure."

We had all of us sought out the shade, Gus examining some pottery on a table. Errol said something I couldn't make out. Then the woman said to me, "You'll have to go over there. He don't come out. Hasn't for twenty-three years now."

I looked at the window. Couldn't see Errol. I said, "Over there?"

"If you would."

I followed a rock path to the door, then crossed to the window, careful of a square plot of marigolds. The window came open—I heard it more than I saw how—and out shot Errol's hand. Felt like I put my buck worth of quarters in one of those fortune-teller games. "Errol?" I said, and I accepted his shake. "I'm pleased to meet you," I said.

Nothing. Not a word. His hand was a big as his face, and it was dry. I think he had clapped talc on. He let go of my hand and the window came down.

Errol's wife—I'd gotten back to the street—she said, "He can talk. He just don't, much."

Gus's dad, Grandpa Jersey, he met Jack Dempsey in the hallway to a restroom in a cafe somewhere in Montana. They stepped aside for each other, and then Grandpa Jersey recognized Dempsey and said, "Holy shit" and stuck out his hand. Dempsey shook it, kicked the door open, and walked out.

There you had it. Holy shit.

What more do you want? What more is there to say?

"Errol says you never ducked anyone," Errol's wife said to me. She was wrapping an ashtray in tissue paper, one from the Copper Queen Hotel and Casino. She had stuck the price to her wrist. Seventy-five cents. Gus paid for it. She said, "He says you took on all comers. He tells me he's proud of you."

I said, "You tell him how good it was to meet him."

She said, "You can count on it."

———————

Me and Gus, a more stubborn pair of competitive personalities you'll never sit down to dinner with, so come midnight, the two of us in our tiny room here in Ely, and we got into a nit-picking quarrel about what looks easy to do but isn't if you try it. Gus, to my way of thinking, was being small minded, so I fed the pot, neither of us quitting until we were all-in, raising and re-raising, double popping. Our one-upmanship was the result of a TV ad for tonight's upcoming movie, *Rio Bravo*, John Waynesday, Turner Classic Westerns on TNT, the Duke himself one-arm cocking a Winchester rifle, butt over barrel and then back again, and Gus saying, "That's harder than you think it looks."

We had the set on mute, it being halftime of the basketball game we located, the Jazz again, taking on Sacramento and its gang of nitwits, and we didn't want to listen to the ex-jocks, to hear how the has-beens know what some guy is thinking when he bricks a free throw or doesn't run his lane on the fast break, like having played the sport at that level gives them the right to another man's brain.

"My bet is it's a stunt double," I said.

Gus said, "To cock a rifle right in front of your eyes?"

"Everybody with legs can see it's special effects."

"What, a stunt arm?"

"You know what I mean."

"Tommy, Tommy, he's in front of your face," Gus said. "The Duke, he was doing that back then when they couldn't do to a film what they can now. Nobody was trying to fool you. He had to do it for real. A little practice and I could."

So I countered with the everyday, with the down to earth, with what I told Gus was real life harder than it looked if he or the mouse in his pocket dared take at shot at it, which was shingling around a mid-roof chimney, flashing and counterflashing one, a subject whose real purpose was to irk Gus, him, as I said, not understanding how a boxer could quit at the top and take jobs roofing houses.

"Flashing is no picnic," I said.

"Tommy, Tommy," he said. He threw left and right jabs from where he sat. "But, Tommy," he said. "Tommy Gun. Tommy rot." He punched. "Rat-a-tat-tat," he said. He threw an upper cut. Said, "Fighting is an honorable profession, Tommy."

Result was we ended up on our feet where he liked us to be, me showing Gus how hard it is to be the boss inside the ropes and how easy you got to make it look. Gus now in khaki shorts and a bowling shirt, gray mostly but a butter-yellow yoke, black piping, bowling pins embroidered between his shoulder blades, a ball hitting them, the pins flying. He was wearing those thick sandals you see on college kids, no socks. He set his fists the way I had shown him a hundred times, Floyd-Patterson peekaboo style.

"Don't let me in," I said. I redrew that invisible line between us. I said, "I'm coming in your house. The doorway's yours. You own it." I came at him, said, "You letting me through?" He jabbed, and I tapped him on the chin. "You hang your head out there, I'll knock it into October," I said.

He retreated, all defense, covering up. Not bad footwork. He achieved a good angle.

I said, "Don't allow me to put it together. I throw, you break it up."

He let go an uppercut. Rotated his shoulder, turned his hips. Spun on his toe.

"Protect that handsomeness," I said.

He took stock from behind his fists. Squinted. Gave me his scowl.

"You come through the doorjamb, don't retreat," I said. "Don't be wiping your shoes off, all polite. I'll murder you. You come through the door throwing, you keep coming. Put it together yourself. Come on in and turn the room upside down. You don't need no warrant."

"You got to be in it to win it," Gus said. Huffing, puffing. Gus was over sixty. Unyielding as hickory and just as hard-nosed. "Fighting dumb's okay," he said, his breathing choppy. "But fighting without fire's not." He snapped a left I took on the chin. It landed, and he did a mule's version of the hallelujah shuffle. He threw his hands up. Jitterbugged. His nose whistled. "Whew," he said, and he dropped his arms, plopped into a wingbacked, saying, "Whose house is it?"

I said, "You tell me."

He said, "Who's the boss?"

I said, "Who *is* the boss?"

He said, "The one who throws or the one who catches?"

I said, "The one who catches?"

He said, "The one who throws."

We sat through *Rio Bravo*. Midnight, and the credits were running. "Plan C," Gus said. "We wing it."

I said, "We had a plan B?"

He said, "Somewhere in all this it got lost."

Plan C was basic. We got some sleep.

"You'll slap me if I ever get another bright idea?" Gus said.

I said, "You bet."

I woke around five. No Gus. Not in his bed. Not outside.

McCarty's.

I left the car in the parking lot and walked. Ely was a ghost town this early. The sun, just up, yellowed the air. I never think about birds—who does?—but today, there they were. You couldn't ignore them. They had their commentary.

Gus stood in McCarty's back yard. He was staring at that wall. Challenging it. He spotted me and said, "You wake up every morning and this is what you see."

I said, "You don't know for sure, Gus."

But he did, and so did I.

We looked at the window of the room Edna slept in, and there was Worst squared-up in its frame. He wasn't more than ten feet from us. The house was his. The yard was his. We were trespassing.

I don't even know what a mouth harp is or how they work but it hit me that the man ought to be playing one.

Gus turned to the wall. He said, "Tommy, it's seven months now, and it's like I made Edna up." He was shaking. He said, "Did she live?"

"Without a doubt," I said.

"Jesus, Tommy," Gus said, "if I made her up, did I put this wall here? And the gangster? Did I add the gangster to the mix?"

I said, "Gus, be logical," and he said, "I am, Tommy. I am. You see, that's just it. I am. I can't touch her. It don't matter what I do, I can't touch her. You want proof she existed. I can't give you proof. You going to tell me you had your own eyes, and she fed you, and all that other stuff she did. That ain't proof."

Remember, this was a mortician talking.

He said, "Photographs? Might as well eat bullshit for breakfast for all a photograph can really mean."

I reached for my dad, and he put up his dukes there in McCarty's back yard. Over Gus's shoulder, there was Worst like a store dummy in the window. Gus dipped into the peekaboo I taught him and said to me, "I'm coming through the door."

I said, "My door?"

"All yours," he said. "I'm coming in."

I said, "Gus, don't stop to wipe your feet."

He said, "Polite's out the window, the baby with the bath water."

"This is ten rounds of hell."

"Ten rounds of bloody hell."

The Sweet
Science

Where we kicked back, you got to talking, the bunch of us sitting around, cooking up half-baked hypotheticals about everything under the sun, particularly about ladies and the wonder they are, our BS rising like flood water, swift and with weight and consequence to it, intent on damage, and if you wanted another beer, you interrupted the deluge and said, "Don't give me theory, give me the answer." A cold Coors was in your hand before you finished the sentence.

Our gang went back to the sixth grade, John S. Park Elementary here in Las Vegas, Nevada. Now, none of us quite thirty years old yet, we came together a mixed bag of riffraff. Two ran the companies their dads built from sticks and stone into enterprises, and we had a couple of talkers who tended the bar they partnered half a block east of the Strip. Two of us were lawyers, me being one of them. There was a certified public accountant among us. Seven all together, three divorced, two cheating, one in limbo and one a widower, his condition the result of a fire, a badly built house (something not up-to-code about the attic and a fire wall), and burglar bars on the windows of the ground floor. His wife found herself trapped in a back bedroom, their cat and a dog too. The thought of the theater of such tragedy enough to spoil sunshine. His name was Rick, from Frederick and him hating anyone calling him Fred. You called him Freddie, say your prayers. He had installed the security bars himself. Took him a week. Measuring. Drilling. Bolting. Fifth grade, we nicknamed him Toot, which had to do with a trumpet his daddy played at the Four

Queens down on Fremont Street. He buried his wife and we kept him on meth. Now he was clean and sober, except for beer. Still, he never felt up to doing much.

I'm your public defender and twice divorced. Unlucky in love. Lucky in love. It's a coin toss.

All of what I'm telling you was what I explained to the baby in the crib in the living room of the house where I woke up on a couch. Clueless as to where I was. Hungover. Concrete for brains. Bang-bang music somewhere outside, punishing me. A Vikings-Packers game was on a television. Muted. First quarter, the Vikes rolling. Randy Moss on the lope could catch arrows in a forest. This was big screen TV, like you could walk right in and join the goings-on.

For myself, I had a question, a two-parter. Part one, had I lost only a couple of days or had I lost an entire week? NFL on TV, sunlight squared up on the hardwood floor. It was Sunday. I began partying on Friday. Was that two days ago? Or a week and two days? Had I slipped into another month altogether?

Part two—this I asked out loud—was, *where am I?*

"You listening, Huey?" I said to the baby.

And into the room, like I made her up because even a drunk needs beauty, came a woman.

"No, I'm not," she said before I got out what my face was already saying, which was, *Hey, you're that movie star.*

But she *was*, was a dead-ringer for that cutie-pie whose curly smile flip-flopped my heart. The kind of woman who kept her nails short and wore no polish. You saw her only in cotton shifts one size too big so they slipped like a miracle along the collar bone they were riding and slinked toward one shoulder or the other. For dinner, she showed up in a black dress so fundamental and elegant in its line it made you imagine your life as a perfect circle. You caved in if she winked. Eyes, well, eyes—not big, and forget your almond shape, your sloe-eyed, like some guys get off on. Look up the word piquant in *Webster's*. And they were that brown that kills me—rich, unapologetic. She talked to you, and she wasn't flirting over your shoulder. There was no one else but you at the party. Wish upon a star, here she was. What she had to say was genuine. Direct. Forthright. Her appeal, of course, was that I wanted to dirty her up. My goal was to make her so pissed she would use the word pissed. I'm told she made a movie where she was a hooker, which was a bubble burster I wouldn't go near. I wanted the maiden chaste and in a pickle I could rescue her from.

So I said to this lady, "Yeah, sure you are."

"Hair's wrong," she said.

Well, not as sandy, but *wrong* was an overstatement. Like it should, her hair said I'll-just-run-a-comb-through-these-snarls-and-we'll-be-on-our-way.

I was completely dressed, wrinkled head to toe, laces double-knotted. Shirt untucked. I noted—there's a feel to it—I had no socks on. The taste in my mouth was like I had eaten rotten fruit. My fingers, ruddy and swollen. I said, "Who else would you be?"

"You're hoping."

I asked her where the music was coming from. Its bass pounding away made my eyes throb.

She said, "The neighbor kid's working on his car."

"In the next room?"

"His driveway."

"Will he for god's sake turn it down?"

"It depends on your approach."

"A bribe work?"

"I doubt it."

I nodded at the television. "You a fan?" I said.

"My ex is," she said. "He likes you, I'd say."

An adios line if I'd ever heard one. Getty-up. Time to mount my stallion, locate a side entrance, and gallop on out of here. I said, "Your ex likes me?"

"He didn't say he didn't."

"I know your ex?"

"He brought you here."

I got to my feet. Took inventory. Legs? Two. Ten fingernails, so no torture. No open wounds. No body organs extracted as payment for debts or past events. One unsettling fear I carried like a crowbar was the day I would come to and find an ear chewed off, ears being my most appealing feature, which is rare, but ladies noticed. Ask them about ears. You'll get your world rocked. It's one of those best kept secrets. I said, "Do I have to guess who?"

She said, "Tommy Rooke."

Could have floored me. How many years had it been? I said, "Tommy Gun," à la those *Rocky* flicks, and I took a fighter's stance, not that I understood squat about boxing. I threw a punch and pulled something near my ribs, left side, high up. Doubled me over and cut my breathing to gasps, left me struggling to get air in and out. Hurt like a branding iron would. I had to sit down. Tommy and I, we grew up together, his house behind mine, a six-foot cinder block fence and oleanders between us. We scaled it like it wasn't there. Elementary school on through high school, it was basketball, Tommy at guard, me at forward, him tough and pushy and quick as electricity itself. And there was football, where he was opportunistic. Ubiquitous. God, he had hands. He played wide receiver and corner. Cover and catch. Zip. Zip. Zip. Not to mention baseball, his arm and his glove. All the time him boxing on the sly and none of us paying attention. Then, boom, high school was over, and Tommy Rooke was in the newspaper. He was on the TV. Took him seven or eight years to win a couple of titles. Light heavyweight was the last one. I saw the fight on closed-circuit. Pay-per-view. Tommy hit like a fucking Mack truck. Lefts, rights, uppercuts. Thud. End of story. I think he quit undefeated and with almost nothing but KOs. But the magazines were saying he had hurt one too many fighters. Were claiming he was unlucky that way. Tommy bailed, reports said, before he did more harm. There was a news conference, bits and pieces of it on ESPN and the TV Sports, Tommy there on the screen sad as hell around the eyes, trying with words to square what he did to some nineteen-year-old Cuban. At that minute the kid was still in a coma.

His ex, here in front of me, she said, "Me, I'm Jane, if you were about to ask."

"Jacob," I said. "It's been almost ten years."

"He said something like that."

"Where is he?"

"He'll be back soon," she said. The baby squawked, and she checked it.

"You're divorced, you and Tommy?"

"Only legally."

"What does that mean?"

"You'll see."

"Girl or boy?" I said.

Her back to me, the weight of the baby in her own body, her lifting it out of the crib, Jane said, "You up for lunch?"

"Could eat a house," I said.

Tommy Rooke and me flying along Tropicana Boulevard, Tommy at the wheel of a pickup he must have bought at a junkyard auction, in its bed roofing shingles, plastic tubs, and gear. I tried accounting for myself, worked at putting the coordinates together. Last memory was it was a Friday. There was plenty of beer, like a college kegger, and it had gotten late. Definitely night, and there was a woman calling herself Gypsy or Gypsum, sharp clothes and pumps on her feet, me drunk and talking out of a thick pool of dark gloom, like being under water, Gypsy or Gypsum answering me out of her own same pool, only she was somewhere to the side of me. She had kneecaps and a handbag, a tiny gold clasp to it. The two of us were debating Clinton's culpability. These are the last facts I recall. I was lying on my back. There was a tile floor underneath me, and to my right a carved leg of a table? A bedpost? Maybe a chair? I reached out, stretched some, and touched a throw rug, the kind where they weave a hundred rags together. Very last thing Gypsy-Gypsum said was, "Just suppose she'd had the dress dry-cleaned." Somewhere in that line resided the epitaph for the last decade of the twentieth century here in the United States, if only the right person had been around to record it.

Tommy and I exited the gated and guarded community where Jane-his-ex lived, and he clarified their relationship for me. "Only on paper," he said after I asked if the look-alike movie star was really his ex like she said.

I said, "What? Why? The IRS? For tax reasons?"

"Irreconcilable reasons."

"Differences?"

"You're the lawyer."

I said, "What I do is recon work," and I lit a cigarette which he told me to put out, so I tossed it. "Baby yours?" I said.

Tommy said, "Ours."

"That clears it up," I said.

And it did, enough for me, so here I was motoring through the Las Vegas heat, alongside my man Tommy Rooke, windows down, the air blow-drying my brain. Me sweating beer, head to toe, from my fingertips. I hadn't asked Tommy where he collected me, and I wasn't about to, my old pal circumspect enough not to bring the details into play. Don't ask. Don't tell. Stand me in front of a trial judge and I couldn't have accounted for my whereabouts. Tommy did clear up the big question. I'd lost only one whole day. Put a Saturday in the forfeit column. File it under misfiled. Tommy's pickup thumped along, didn't so much turn corners as bust through them. It was a geezer of a truck, wired, bolted, and welded together from parts found in the desert. My knees ached like bad weather was on its way. Gout was after my big toe, left foot. Left arm hurt like I slept on it too long. It was going to be hard work cobbling the body together for one more shot at one more day.

I said, "Great ride you got here," and offered Tommy my cheekiest grin, my quid pro quo wink.

"Will be," he said. "Restoring it."

The beast had no swing or sway, just drove like a wooden crate. It was soapbox derby time. One door was blue and one white. The hood was primer gray, and the fenders, left-side black, right-side red. The front bumper took up space like the grillwork on a vintage Caddie. Was restored original equipment. Big as a cattle guard. The side panels were rusted bad, and the tailgate rattled.

"One stop," he said. "You mind? It's on the way."

Course I didn't mind. My buddy from the pubescent years was giving me a lift home—I had a condo in Summerlin—and he was gentleman enough not to clarify my position for me.

I said, "Christ's sake, Tommy, you still look seventeen, only like you're made out of steel."

"This is a compliment?" he said.

"Jealousy," I said. "Look at me," and I gave him those hands that say, *Check this out*, meaning my overall appearance. I said, "Bloat. Jowls on their way. There's a chance I have scurvy." I opened wide for him to see. I said, "Whose belly is this sitting in my lap?" I grabbed two fists full of fat. I said, "Not to mention my soul wherein something unnamable is swarming."

Tommy said, "You're a lawyer," and he tapped his forehead.

Brains? Is that what he was saying? The law was sloganeering and vocabulary. Was he thinking my job required intelligence? It was grunt work. I said, "You want to see some of the old gang?"

He glanced over at me for the first time.

I said, "Leo. Rick. Stanley."

He said, "Larry, Moe and Curly."

"Sure."

"Why not?" he said.

I said, "You still play golf?"

"I've been known to."

We set up a time, and I got into his glove compartment, found a pen, and gave him my number. Wrote it on a card he got out of his wallet. Hit me that I hadn't even considered my own wallet, that I understood in my bones I had lost another one. A jacket went with the pants I was wearing, and it was missing in action.

Cal's, a pool hall on the Boulder Highway where Tommy introduced me to Carl Thomas Plugg—this was Tommy's stop. I had seen Plugg in newspaper photos, at Tommy's side. Couldn't tell you what he did. Didn't think he was a Don King type, wasn't a promoter, and he wasn't a trainer. Seemed too old to be a pal. Maybe he worked Tommy's corner. Was a cut man. Definitely was a minor functionary in some way.

"You and Tommy, you were tight?" Plugg said to me.

I said, "High school. Sports. We did sports together."

"You didn't box," he said.

"No one did." Tommy had drifted over to a counter. I said, "Except Tommy."

"I say this," Carl Thomas Plugg said, "because I was the bird dog who spotted his talent."

I said, "You can be proud."

He said, "Snooker?"

"Just a game I've heard about," I said. "I hear the word, I think England."

He looked me up and down. "You don't fight. You don't shoot snooker," he said. "You a friend or the enemy?" He created a smile, the one he would use after he swallowed me whole.

Tommy was back. "Done," he said.

"One hand washes the other. It's a gentleman's world," Plugg said directly to me. He was dressed in order to influence. Wore a vest, a hand-painted silk tie, a coat—lightweight, the color of gun powder. This morning—you could count on it—he perched himself on top of one of those shoeshine stands, displayed the beauties he wore, and had them polished. He could tell you the color. Cordovan. Black Stallion Black. Thatcher Brown.

At the condo, I invited Tommy in, and he took a rain check, said, "I've got a roof to do."

I said, "You roof yourself?"

"Yes, sir."

"On Sunday?" I said. A question—it was clear—not worth his answering. He had said what he had said, so I said, "You'll let me know about the golf."

"Sounds like a plan," he said.

It wasn't. He didn't call. I told the gang I bumped into him, and we raised a beer to Tommy Rooke. "To the health of Tommy," we sang. The bunch of us, we were a choir.

Leo said, "To Tommy Gun."

"Rat-a-tat-tat," the seven of us shouted together.

———————

"Drinks," I said. "Liquor." Definitely a statement, not a question.

Tommy's Jane, the baby in a pouch strapped to her, the two of them face to face, she cupped its head. She covered the baby's ears. Such talk at ten thirty in the morning. Her boy didn't need it. She pointed me to the booze.

We—me and Rick and Leo—had finagled our way through the main gate and come to see Tommy. I handled the convincing. Had called at 9:00 A.M. Had cajoled, coaxed and snow-jobbed Jane, me on a cell phone, a security guard at my shoulder. Big dude. "NFL?" I said to him, and—take this to the bank—he says, "Everyone's not a cliché." You don't want to face so much hostility too often and you without a drink in your hand. He wore a pistol there at his hip. Tommy, Jane explained on the phone, was off bidding a roof and then was going to the gym. He would be back at ten or so. Okay by us. We reconvened at ten, and Jane told the guy at the gate to let us in. Tommy hadn't returned yet. *Pals,* I said to Jane on the phone. *Guys Tommy would want to see.* I told her Tommy and I talked about playing golf and Tommy hadn't connected with me. Maybe I missed a message, I said. An e-mail. A page. A note. A fax. It had been over a week.

"You call his place?" she said.

I said I didn't know he had a place.

She said, "He does."

"He'll wish you let us in," I said.

So she did.

Now, Wild Turkey in one hand, Johnnie Walker Black Label Scotch whiskey in the other one, I said, "Leo? Rick? Jane? I'm taking orders."

10:30 A.M., and still no Tommy.

"We'll toast the better times and present circumstances," I said. "We'll raise our glasses to the world because it can turn on a dime, and in a flash you're ass-over-teakettle on the downhill side."

Rick buried himself deep in a sofa, sinking, vanishing, the way he did in crowds since the fire. He carried so much pain today I thought he might tip over. Leo was acting like it was high school and we were dealing with somebody's mom. He studied photographs in boxy frames on a wall in one corner. He drifted between sofa and chair and coffee table, his elbows tight to his body, his hands clasped behind him, riding his butt, feigning interest in watercolors and cut glass. There was a picture of Tommy and Muhammad Ali, signed. There was one of Tommy with Yogi Berra. We had already gone through the *isn't she a dead ringer* talk, right in front of Jane, Rick and Leo agreeing I was right and Jane peeved, recognizing that she had made a mistake and let flies in her home. She should have kept us on the porch.

"Scotch?" I said. "We'll make it simple."

Leo said, "Let's do this another time." He said to Jane, "Tell Tommy we dropped by."

I said to her, "Are we annoying you? If we wait, are we a nuisance here? We are, we're gone. You say the word. We're history." I refit the bottle of Scotch to its place in the liquor cabinet and said, "We keeping you from what you were doing?"

She shook me off, kissed the baby's brow.

"Tommy's on his way," I said to Leo. "Relax. He wants to see you. He told me so. The old gang, sure. He were here, he'd say, 'Pull up a chair. Take a load off. Stick around.' Tommy would be the one breaking out the liquor." Leo refused to sit. Was loitering. "We've come to see our boy," I said to Jane.

Three windows that ran floor to ceiling made up the living room wall that showed us the front yard. Past the palm trees, we could see the cul-de-sac and up the road. Any minute, Tommy and that old banger truck, here they would be. The sound of thunder coming first. I said to Jane, "Vermouth? Sugar? Limes? Lemons?"

"What we have is what we have," she said. The baby was fussing, was tired of its pouch.

I shuffled the bottles in the cabinet. No vermouth. I located a bottle of gin. There was crème de menthe. I grabbed it. Heard Leo say, "So Tommy is a roofer?"

Jane said, "He owns the business."

"But he puts roofs on?" I said, and I made like I was nailing down a shingle.

"Sometimes."

"Why?" I said. I arranged bottles on the kitchen cabinet and said, "Cocktail glasses?"

"I don't speak for Tommy," she said.

I said, "A practice I admire."

She stroked the baby's hair.

I said, "There's a wish for all of us—we'll drink to it—that my exes, the pair of them, felt as you do." I raised a bottle and said, "That they had worn the cloak of rectitude as willingly."

No one responded.

I said, "That they had kept their mouths shut."

Jane opened a cupboard and showed me regular glasses and a couple of tumblers. I took an eight-ouncer and double-checked to see who was joining me.

Leo said, "I'm passing," and Rick said, "Me too." He sunk another six inches into the couch. The top of his head was now even with the cushions. He hugged a toss pillow. I looked to Jane, who said, "I don't drink and mother." Fair enough. Chalk one up for her. Jane one. Me zero. I located a lemon in the refrigerator, saying to the crowd, "It's not polite or politic to let a man drink alone."

"I'm putting the baby down," Jane said, and she left for the other end of the house.

The ice maker chugged ice into my glass. "This drink has a name," I said. Loud enough for Jane to overhear. She needed to know she was dealing with a man who had skills. A drunk—well, okay, but a schooled one. A dash of bitters, and I was humming show tunes. I measured a teaspoon of the crème de menthe. I was your boardwalk man, your slicer and your dicer. Rick pulled himself out of his chair and headed for the front door. It shut behind him, rattled the big windows. Would have made me worry about the construction if it were my place. "Shake well," I said, and I did. "Serve with a cherry," I said.

Leo said, "I'll meet you in front." He was fleeing the scene of the crime. Rick, out there, leaned against my Lexus. If he scratched it, I would sue him. Toot would think the loss of a wife was a picnic by comparison.

"Cherries anywhere?" I called to Jane. I walked down the hall, drink in hand, was, out of courtesy, announcing my presence before my arrival. Found her in the bedroom.

No answer. Dead quiet in the back of the house.

She turned to look at me.

"Cherry?" I said. I showed her my glass.

She said, "You're Tommy's friend, is what you tell me." The baby fussed, and she turned to it. Spoke at it, but was talking to me. "Tommy brings you here once. Okay. A rescue, for old time's sake," she said. "Right now, you're a guest in *my* house, and I don't want you in this part of it. Here is off limits. You weren't invited beyond the kitchen."

I raised innocent hands and spun on my foot. I had my own agility, wasn't a total has-been yet. Dexterity and I were not complete strangers. Who knows who could box or not? How many try? Headed down the hall, I said, "Hard hat area." In the kitchen, I checked the refrigerator. Sure enough, way back and behind a jar of pickles, a bottle of cherries, which didn't seem to matter since I couldn't remember what they called what it was I was drinking. Who needed the ingredients if you couldn't come up with the name? Out front, Leo had joined Rick, the two of them roasting in the ninety degrees, framed in that wall of windows. I took a sip. I heard a door softly shut somewhere down a hallway. No footsteps. Deep-space silent. I was standing in Tommy Rooke's ex's house. His baby was in its crib, and you could be sure his ex-wife was cooing the sweetest words to it, bent over the baby, gifting her boy with that curly smile, knocking the kid's socks into next week, the two of them in the geometry of sunlight. The kid didn't understand yet, but this moment and one or two like it could hold his world together until he was seventy, if he chose to hang on that long.

Lovely.

Never leave a stone unturned or a drink undrunk, so I polished mine off. Set the glass on the counter and exited stage left.

————

I am a complete horse's ass, so I phoned two days later.

"What, you can't accept an apology?" I said to Tommy's Jane. I had messengered over a pin earlier, the 18-karat gold bluebird of happiness, five hundred dollars on my MasterCard. One of its kind, signed, some guy out of San Francisco. On the other end of the phone she said nothing. I swear I could hear her fussing with the baby. "It's a bauble," I said. I had included a note. *They tell me I was rude and crude and out of line. For such offenses I offer my apologies.*

"Where can I return this?" she said.

"It's in your hands," I said. "Put it on. It goes with your hair. We tried it, me and the sales girl. I told her all about you and the movie star you're the dead ringer for."

Profound silent treatment.

"You're a tough audience," I said. "A rough crowd."

"So you'll know," she said, and then there was the sound of her opening what must have been a cupboard or a door. "What you're hearing," she said, "is me getting into the broom closet, and I'm about to drop this bauble into a trash can. You won't hear it. The can's half full, but trust me it's on the way. I'm counting to ten."

"Forgiveness is not one of your virtues."

Silence. Then, "Five . . . six . . ."

"Someday," I said, "we'll laugh about this."

"Ten."

I didn't hear anything, and I told her so.

She said, "Tell me where to send it."

"You want directions to my place."

Nothing.

"I can draw you a map. Better yet, I'll pick you up. I'll show you the back roads, how to avoid the traffic."

More nothing.

The lady didn't know to let her fingers do the walking through the phone book? She couldn't dial information she was so hell bent on looking a gift horse in the mouth?

She took my call. She didn't hang up in my ear. These efforts I counted as signs of interest. Of attention being paid. I said to her, "Have Tommy return it."

"Tommy doesn't run your errands," she said.

I said, "It's not my errand. It's yours."

"Believe me, it's yours."

"I respectfully disagree."

I heard what might have been the sound of a 18-karat pin dropping into a can half full of garbage, and the phone went dead in my hand.

Dialing, beep after beep, I said, "She loves me. She loves me not. She loves me."

From the outside Cal's had the demeanor of a trailer home. But it was cinder block and completely whitewashed. Driving by, you didn't notice the building or the football-sized CAL'S in green neon. The narrow, sideways-set windows across the front were so high up you couldn't see in them, not without a stepladder. You tooled up the Boulder Highway headed into or out of Las Vegas and paid no attention. If you had a map, you would still have to struggle to find the place.

Inside was a different story. Believe me. You walked on terrazzo floors. A fortune right here under the heels of your shoes. Art deco design. The rooms were big, and there was the one for snooker—where I met Plugg the first time here. There were house tables for the gamers and the hustlers, rec tables for the locals. Up front was a bar. There was a short-order grill and booths right out of a James Dean film, only in Technicolor, that burgundy leatherette and chrome look. Even had the music players where you flip through the songs.

Carl Thomas Plugg spotted me five seconds after I walked through the door. He put on a jacket and then came at me with a big handshake. The man an ambassador. He was resplendent in his clothes, today white linen jacket and pants, sky blue shirt. Necktie. Sounded like he wore taps on his shoes. He was as thin as the cue stick he held.

"You in the neighborhood for Tommy?" he said.

"Sort of," I said. "I was thinking I might run into him."

"Drink?" he said.

"I'm buying," I said. "Scotch?"

He said, "Call me Plugg. Two g's."

I told him I could do that.

"Do it," he said.

"What?"

"Call me Plugg. Go ahead."

I tried. Flubbed my chance.

"Two g's," he said. "You know like two grand."

It was four in the afternoon and my tank was dry. I stepped away to get some hollering distance, and I gave his name another shot. Came up short. He frowned, said, "Plug-g." Two g's, like he claimed.

I tried again. Could tell by his face I failed. I said, "Let me get a couple of drinks under my belt."

He said, "So it goes," and he offered to give Tommy a call, to let him know I was here.

———————

Tommy, Plugg told me, was on his way. We carried our Scotch room to room, Plugg showing me around and the two of us small-talking, me on the thinnest of conversational ice but, in good faith, holding up my end. We got to the house tables, and he said, "I'm not believing you don't play."

I said, "You going to hustle me?"

"Hustling is a waste of time," he said. "I'm seeing you as a man who can't resist a wager. You bet on the game, sure, but you're the guy who asks odds and wagers on how green the grass will be by the end of April, on how many crows the rooster will give us come sunrise. It's the World Series, and for you it's *fuck the game*. With you, it's you put money down on whether the pitch will be inside or outside, high or low. I'm betting you're the guy who loses the car, the house, the kids, his inheritance. Your credit cards are maxed. You're the fellow who truly believes two and two, when put together, do not necessarily add up to four. There are always variables, possibilities, alternatives, other avenues to pursue."

"I'm game, if that's what you're saying," I said.

"It ain't a matter of winning or losing with you," Plugg said.

What could I do but shrug.

"Let's knock some around," he said. He racked the balls, handed me his stick, a work, even I sensed, of art. Ebony butt, inlaid ivory. It had weight you noticed. Your local gum-chewer would have understood that if Stradivarius made pool cues Plugg's would have been one. You got it in your hands and you wanted to dress better and comb your hair. He said, "Any pocket."

I skunked a few, but otherwise did okay, and he said, "In all honesty, you own a nice stroke."

"Don't hustle me," I said.

He got out of his jacket and said, "Personally, it's not my nature to do so." He racked the balls. "I would tear my own heart out first. Those movies you see, hustling is just a word they use." He stepped away from the table, took his stick from me, and indicated I should use one from the wall. He signaled for me to break. I did, badly, and Plugg said, "You, you're a friend of Tommy's. You go back to a time before I know him." He re-racked and showed me where to place the cue ball for the break he wanted me to try, and he said, "Give you money, this I'd do, out of own my pocket. Cash and the shirt from my back, these are yours. You don't even have to ask. If, as you say you are, you're a friend of his."

Either he was double-talking me or I was already feeling the Scotch, the repose it always gave me. I broke, and a couple of balls fell. "Maybe I'm the hustler," I said.

"Cue ball's moving too far. Stand taller."

I did.

"On the break," he said. He handed me a new stick.

"Lower the butt," he said.

I missed a length-of-the-table, straight-in-the-corner gimme.

"You're not breaking now. Stay down," he said. "Pull the trigger." Plugg showed me. He pocketed six balls, and my heart beat once.

I corralled the balls, racked them, stood back, and said, "So, do you think boxers these days are stealing money? I'm talking about these guys hugging each other through ten rounds. Doing the waltz."

"Talk or shoot," he said. "Don't do both." He side-stepped into me, so I couldn't draw the cue stick back. I turned to him, and he reached across and tapped my shoulder. He said, "You want to know about fighting, do you? About the sweet science."

I straightened up, and he tapped my chest. This guy was going on sixty was my guess, and he had quick reflexes. I said, "I am curious why Tommy quit, only I wasn't really asking you."

"Ask him." He touched my other shoulder.

I said, "What?" and he tapped my chest, said, "You asked about the sweet science. Fighters keep busy." He touched my cheek, a baby slap. I said, "Okay, Pops."

"A fighter's in the ring," Plugg said, "and he's not throwing so he's keeping busy is all. It's like a Q and A, his touching you is. It's as sophisticated as *Meet the Press, Face the Nation*." Plugg poked my shoulder again. He said, "Q," and he swayed, touched my chest, said, "And A."

"Got it, Pops," I said.

"Pops?" he said. "No. No. No. Is this a movie you're living in? Pops? It's Plugg. Two g's, like I told you. Tears my fucking heart out you don't recall."

I said, "Okay."

"In the ring, within the confines of the ropes, if they're not punching," Plugg said, "fighters, they keep busy. They're touching you, they're measuring the distance from them to you. Mathematics is involved. The complexity of trapezoids and parabolas." He went for another slap and I used the cue stick to whack his hand away. "Tommy's friend," he said, "you disappoint me." He picked up a pool ball and said, "Use the balls, Tommy's friend. This is my second lesson for you." He faked throwing the ball at me, not like he would actually do it, but like he was just showing me how, and he said, "You get shoved into a corner in a pool room, there's one rule. Use the balls."

It was then I saw Tommy behind Plugg. He was in the doorway, a couple of drinks in his hand. I didn't know how long he'd been there, how far he would have let things go. "Let's talk," he said to me. To Plugg he said, "You're an impressive specimen," and Plugg said, "I'm riding cloud nine." Tommy said, "Got a rocket in your pocket." Plugg was chalking his cue stick and recreating that smile of his. He said, "Got me a skyrocket in my pocket."

———

Tommy and I sat in a booth. Our drinks, club sodas. Between us, in a box I recognized, was the pin I'd sent over, that 18-karat bluebird of happiness. Tommy set it there, didn't say a word to acknowledge its beauty. Instead, he said, "Plugg giving free lessons?"

"Two," I said.

"It's always two with him."

"He tells me I get in a fight in a pool hall I should use the balls."

"It would be wiser yet," Tommy said, "not to get in the fight." He was dressed like he had come from roofing a house, T-shirt, Levi's, boots.

I said, "What's with the roofing?"

He said, "Let's change the subject." He got into his wallet and pulled out the card I had given him, the one I wrote my home phone number on. He tore it up, opened the gift box, and sprinkled the pieces inside it, bits of paper snowing on the bluebird of happiness. Truly sad. He said, "You asked if I still play golf. I do, scratch. Me and some pals—one's a criminal lawyer you might know, a Mr. Wayne Steiner—we have a standing tee time at Shadow Creek. They wave the green fees because of who I am and because of the way I hit the ball. Me and the people I play with, we put up a grand a hole plus on top of that another five thousand a side. Add to those terms another ten thousand for low score. It's all cash up front, and we tend to break close to even during the year, all of us not bad at the game." Tommy sipped his drink, set his glass to one side, and said, "Did you want to get in on that? Because I can ask, if you'd like. You being a lawyer. One of us can't play, I could give you a call. Would you want me to do that?"

I shook my head. No.

He fetched another card out of his wallet, and he wrote Jane's phone number on it. He said, "You being a lawyer you probably re-member calling this number." He showed it to me. "I bet you're so smart you've got it memorized," he said. "You programmed it to be fast dialed." Then he tore that one up and mixed the pieces in with the others. "You being a lawyer," he said, "you've got a memory like a fly trap. They tell me that's what you need to be an attorney. To serve the law. You have to have a memory for the specifics. For the facts."

I hadn't touched my drink.

Tommy tapped his head the way he'd done in the truck, and he said, "Am I correct on this?"

"On what?" I said.

He gestured at the bluebird of happiness covered with scraps, and I nodded yes. At what, I wasn't quite sure. He said, "The cat hasn't got hold of your tongue, has it?"

Actually the cat had.

He said, and he was still tapping his head, "They also tell me lawyers have selective memories. They can forget what they need to. Not bring up in court what shouldn't be brought up. Some fool forgets to light a lamp, and there's a wreck. People die. But we don't need to talk about the lamp. Maybe a blinker was on the fritz. Don't bring it up. The practice of the law. Forgetfulness. Like a phone number, just to illustrate."

I nodded again. Like I had been paid to.

"We're old pals, Jacob. You and me. Hell, we were neighbors. We'll get along now, won't we?" he said, and he was on his feet and gone. Was walking away. I heard him say, "Carl T., I'm feeling I got a game of nine ball in me that is the mother of all nine-ball games." I sat for a minute, listening to the click-click-click in Cal's. Then I left my drink sitting on the table. Club soda was for pussies was what I was saying. I left the blue bird of happiness where it sat. Let the janitor take it home to the wife. I could send a message with the best of them.

Our gang's watering hole, DeHaven's Race and Sports Bar, Tropicana, near the Strip. The boys had gathered, collectively put our feet up, the colors from a bank of TVs flicking across our faces. Leo, me, Rick, etc. Monday Night Football, our money on the Jets.

Me confessing my sins. Talking Plugg, talking bluebird of happiness, 18-karat gold. Talking Jane. Talking Tommy Rooke talking to me. Embarrassing me.

"So I lost myself in drink," I say to the boys.

"Surprise," they shout. The choir. "Bottles high," they sing in perfect harmony. "Here's to courage in a bottle," they say. "Here's to solace in a can."

I say, "I came to consciousness days later on the road to Tommy's ex's. Who knows how long it had been?" I accept a cold Coors and say to the gang, "Cell phone at my ear, and I'm dialing one-handed."

"Don't give us theory," they say. "Give us the answer."

"Set 'em up," I say to a waiter. "On me."

Bottles high. Bottles high.

I say, "I'm a lawyer, this you know," and I touch my head where all the thinking takes place and right where Tommy tapped, and I tell the boys I'm here to remind them there are two ways of looking at anything. There's north and there's south. There's east and there's west. There's inside out, and there's outside in. There's your *on the one hand* and there's your *on the other hand*. There's longitude and there's latitude. There's always *however*. There's Fahrenheit and there's Celsius.

The band of merry men says, "So you're on the road to Tommy's ex's and you're dialing, you claim, the cell phone one-handed."

I say, "I'm on Flamingo, and I'm maybe twenty minutes from Tommy's ex's, and I'm dialing."

They say, "One-handed."

I say, "One-handed."

"And it's ringing," they say.

I say, "Hold on to your hat," and them that was wearing them did. Baseball caps, already on backwards or sideways, upside down, rally caps. We're all in shorts and grunge shirts. There must be fifty or sixty TVs in here. We're betting football, sure—and winning, but also baseball, the Yankees, because we're not stupid. Screw the underdogs of this world. I say, "Tommy's Jane answers. 'Rooke residence,' she says."

"The movie star," they say.

I check to Leo. He's my movie star witness. He's the expert. He's the man who's been to her home and seen for himself. He can vouch for Tommy's Jane. "Very hot," he says. "She's a burner." We turn to Rick. See if he can dig himself out of the grave he's flopped himself into. He tugs at his beer. Kills it. "Rick?" the boys say. He was with us, all morning. He was in her house. He does that hand gesture, the one that says *too hot to touch*. Half-hearted, though. Rick is still wearing his mouth open in despair. "Yeah?" they say. The gang's rooting for him. They're willing, if Rick's able, to breathe life into his body. He lost his wife. His dog. His cat. Let the dead bury the dead. We say, "How hot, Rick?" We pretend to sizzle our hands on a stove. Then Rick, he goes for his groin, does a dry jerk-off, like he's pumping a baseball bat, and we sing our follow-up question, which is, "That hot?" Leo shouts, "Bottles high." Stanley chips in. "Bottles high." And everyone is jerking their beers off in their laps.

"So," I say, "I hear 'Rooke Residence,' like she isn't his ex," and I say, "Tommy's Jane?" I can hear the baby. It's crying. I say, "I never got the kid's name."

"Who are you calling?" she says, like I'm telemarketing.

"Doll," I say, "it's the cocktail man." No recognition. I say, "It's the bluebird of happiness calling." She isn't going to give me the time of day. "You know," I say, "Tommy Gun's friend. Your ex-husband's pal. A fan of his."

Phone goes dead in my hand. I'm a couple of miles away now. Traffic is slowing me, but I'm devoted. I'm running a red light and dialing. She picks up, which tells you something Freudian must be going on. She's playing along. There's some desire in her voice. Lilt. She wants to fight. "Don't cut me off," I say.

"Tommy's jumping rope," she says.

"Seven to one says he can jump and talk at the same time," I say. She says, "He doesn't have to."

I say, "What's the boy's name?"

"Hector."

"Jesus," I say, "what kind of spic name is that?"

Leaves me with a dead phone, and I'm stopped eight-cars deep on Decateur. I'm resourceful. I'm a lawyer. All together now, tap your head. I redial. And she picks up. I say, "Touchy. Touchy."

Get no response.

"Yell-o," I say.

Nothing, and I'm turning up the street to her gated community. I whisper into the phone, "Seconds, and I'm at the front gate." Dead air. "I'll huff and I'll puff," I say. I'm beeping the horn for the security guy to open up. "Can you hear me?" I say into the phone. I step out of the car and keep honking. I don't know what I look like to the guard who's come out of his booth. He's got to be hot in his uniform and I tell him so. He fits his cap to his head, and I try to commiserate with him. I tell him I'm sure he remembers me from before, that I'm a friend of Mr. Tommy Rooke's, and I'm on the phone with his wife right now, but the line has gone dead. "Could be the battery," I say. The man is six-foot-five, two-hundred-eighty pounds. I say, "A couple of weeks back, me and Tommy in his truck, you might recall us?"

"Mr. Rooke is on his way," he says. He unsnaps the strap that holds his gun in his holster. You've seen real cops do that.

I say, "Let's save him the trouble."

"It's no trouble," the guard says to me. "It's a pleasure."

I've still got the phone to my ear. I speak into it, say, "Tommy's

Jane, where are you?" Wherever she is she's not on the other end of the line.

Tommy parks his old banger, the bed full of rolls of felt. He steps out looking like he's been to a wedding. Tuxedo slacks, the ones with the shiny strip down the seam. Starched white shirt, bowtie loose at the neck. Shoes fit for dancing. The guard opens a side gate, and Tommy slips through.

"You jump rope dressed like Sammy Davis, Jr.?" I say.

"You smoke?" Tommy says.

Is this a trick question? He doesn't recall he stopped me from lighting up in his truck? Did our time together mean so little to him? He's got a pack of Luckies, and he withdraws a cigarette, puts a match to it, and offers me the result. He says, "Have a cigarette, sir." It's not a question.

I inhale like I'm hearing philosophy, then speak through the smoke, saying, "I never could tie a bowtie."

He says, "Of course we know now that smoking kills, only not real fast." I look at him like he's got a point, and he hands me the pack of Luckies, which I accept. He says, "Problem is sometimes it's not fast enough, given certain obligations."

"Obligations?"

"Obligations. You're the lawyer."

———

"So," I say to our gang, "what do you think I did?"

"No explanation," they say. "Answers."

I buy another round. Jets are winning. Yankees are winning. The world is awash in grand emotions. The TVs color us in reds and blues and greens.

"What would you do?" I say to my pals.

Leo says, "Get in my car and leave."

"I didn't," I say.

Our CPA, a guy whose name is Tony, he says, "Give him a hundred bucks for any damage I may have inadvertently caused, then get in my car and leave."

"Rick?" I say.

He stirs. "Act," Rick says, "like I'm getting in my car, and when he turns to go, I bushwhack him. I get him in my wheelhouse and coldcock the son of a bitch. I lay the six-foot-long two-by-four I carry in my pants up the side of his head, the motherfucker. I poleax Mr. Tommy Rooke."

So it's then I remind the band of merry men that I spend a lot of time at jails. "First thing the cops do when they haul in the criminal element," I say, "is determine whether or not they're nuts. They assess you according to the laws. They got a list of questions." I take a drink. Bottles high, I'm thinking. Bottles high. I say, "Number one thing they ask everyone who's booked is, 'Do you want to kill yourself or someone else today?'" I raise my beer, to DeHaven's and all these televisions, to the Yankees, to the Jets. My pals join me. I say, "I sit on a bench, rubbing shoulders with the reprobates of this world, and every time I'm waiting on some loser I've got to defend in a court of law, and I hear a cop say, 'Do you want to kill yourself or someone else today?' I think, Yes and yes. Yes, I do want to kill myself. Yes, I do want to kill someone else. In no particular order."

My pals and I, we touch beers. Bottles high, we're all thinking. Bottles high.

What I did, when Tommy tells me cigarettes kill too slowly given certain obligations, is I did what a prosecutor is sworn to do. I kept the faith. Unpacked the book of logic. I spoke up for all of us who need it most. I did my job. I said what had to be said in defense of all the reprobates of the world.

I spoke up for you and me.

I put Tommy in his place. You know I did.

Death Care
World Expo,
Reno, Nevada

Here's what I owned. The jaw I gave my boy Hector and the two professional weight-class belts I never lost. Boxing, middleweight division and light-heavy. Headed for the cruisers, I quit. Retired. Now I roofed houses for the clarity of the job. I owned the business.

My gift? Calm in a storm of fists. You try to put something together in the boxing ring or out of it, and I don't blink, not ever. I won't let you manufacture a combination. I undo what you try to get done. I have hands and the accompanying footwork a bird dog named Carl Thomas Plugg spotted from the bleachers at the Bonanza Rec Center here in Las Vegas, Nevada. Ten years ago, me and my pals playing basketball, five on five, full-court, summertime rag-ball, and in the middle of a fast break, there was Plugg standing on the floor, five feet the other side of half court, looking for all the world like someone you'd call Slick or Puck or Charlie, asking me did I comprehend—truly comprehend—how much palookas would pay for hands like mine. God almighty, he said. He claimed electricity, head to head, would lose to me. He wondered did I have feet to match. I showed him, in high tops, on the hardwood, there at the center jump circle. He shut his eyes real slow and listened. Hummed.

My shortcoming, if you can call it that, was a killer instinct that won't quit. I gather on an opponent, close the distance, and don't retreat.

You sold on me?

My ex-wife, Jane, wasn't, not yet, even though it was 7:00 A.M.

and the morning of the third night in a row I had spent at her place. Out her kitchen window the sun was sitting on top of Sunrise Mountain. Cross your fingers, blow on the dice, things were looking up for us. Divorced almost a year now, we had been married eight years, and these days we were talking about new vows.

Jane in the bathroom, I had gotten up to grab the phone and been greeted by my kid sister, Ginger, calling to tell me our dad was trying to get hold of me from Reno. He had phoned her.

"At seven in the morning?" I said.

"Six for me," she said. "I called your place. You weren't there. I didn't think you'd want him calling Jane's so early."

Jane walked in and held up Hector. Put our baby on display. Here in front of me was my chin and Hector in black gym shorts and a UNLV T-shirt, that Rebel mascot and its wide mustache taking up the boy's entire chest. His socks were black to match the shorts. So cute they would have fit my thumbs.

Ginger was telling me Gus wanted me to know Nevadans were opting for cremation. We led the entire country. He had the statistics in his hands. Fifty-five percent of Nevadans chose the furnace. Twenty-something percent in the next closest other state. Gus, the Godfather of mortuaries in Las Vegas, he was building his first one in Reno, had driven up there to check out the construction and the Death Care World Expo.

I asked Ginger if he said why, and she said, "Why what?"

"Cremation," I said.

She said, "You'll have to ask the dead."

I didn't want to argue either the logic or the futility of talking to ash and bone.

Jane was feeding Hector. There he sat in a high chair. We were calling him Sweepstakes, the boy being such a lottery pick and a miracle. I asked Ginger to be sure to ask Gus where he was staying if he called back, and I got off the phone. I said to Jane, "So, you want to marry me this morning?"

"And repeat myself?" she said.

Three nights in a row, and I was feeling expansive. I spread my arms wide for her to behold the entire package, me in my roofer's togs, in steel-toed boots you could rely on, in a baseball cap. I had a strip mall to finish, clay tile a football field long. There was a wink in my heart. My hair, wet and slick, said I was a catch. I was, after all,

Hector's dad. A man who could produce such a child, can you go too far wrong in his arms?

Jane spoke to Hector, said, "Where do you stand on this issue, young man?" He got Jane's eyes, brown and smart and unyielding. He had lucky eyebrows—mine. Jane's nose. My jaw. "What do you think about stepping into the same river twice?" Jane said to our boy, like he really had a say in the shenanigans of grown-ups, like he had a vote.

"It's an offer you don't want to miss," I said.

She spoon-fed Hector, saying, "So you're giving me my second chance of our lifetime?"

"Or we could live together," I said. "I'll move in."

She said, "Did you ever move out?"

"I'll take that as a compliment," I said. My truck was loaded, and I had to get going. I was half an hour late. I said, "Gus calls here, get a number. Tell him I'll phone later."

————

A subcontractor I was using on a house outside of Boulder City was a joker who had given me reason not to trust him. His name was Tuttle. I stopped by on my way to the mall job. I could see from where I stood in the yard he was ripping off the customer. Roof was half done, and his crew—bless their little pea brains—was going to be redoing all of it if I had to hover above them in a helicopter. The customer was paying for two layers of thirty-pound felt. Tuttle's crew had laid fifteen-pound felt, one layer, and halved the overlapping. Plus the felt, where it met at the eaves and rake, was showing wrinkles, and there was only a single course. They were cheating at the step flashing around two chimneys. The owner's lifetime roof was going to last about ten years at best. The year 2010 rolls around, he would be calling me, and my bet was there would be no Tuttle in the phone book. Word around would be he flew the coop, address unknown. Probably swimming in his Olympic-size pool outside of Phoenix. A new roofer would be out here, lifting the tiles, removing the battens, and replacing the felt. The Nevada building code called for nails on every tile, not only on the three courses up from the eaves, in from the rakes and down from the ridge. Tuttle was relying on lugs and gravity, which might hold in a vacuum, but which weren't going to protect squat in the wind that could huff, puff, and wail and knock over buildings here in southern Nevada. Where Tuttle's crew bothered to nail they drove them too tight and broke tiles. It was an even bet they were using a coil nailer to save time. Up on the roof, I was holding a cracked tile, and a guy in a ponytail stepped from the house onto the back patio. "We help you?" he said.

"Coming down," I said. "You work for Tuttle?"

He said, "Every single day."

The crew was taking a break. Five of them altogether. I introduced myself to the man in the ponytail, and he said, "We heard of you. The fighter, right?" His name was Neil. I got his last name, for the record I kept in my head. Pelham it was. Neil Pelham. Not one I would forget.

"You hearing of me," I said, "in certain ways that makes my task easier."

Stumped him. *Task?* he was thinking. One of his crew, a kid, maybe nineteen, but not yet twenty, got to his feet, set aside his coffee, and said, "Shake your hand?" His name, he volunteered, was Steven Bunt, and I told him what I told Neil, that I was Tommy Rooke, which, the kid said, he already knew. We shook, and he said, "It's a pleasure to meet you," and I said, "Probably not on this occasion," which offended the kid who was just trying to grow up. He said, "I saw you fight."

I said, "Gentlemen, you all been introduced to Mr. Hunt?"

Steve, the kid, said, "I don't know who he is." He rubbed a tattoo on his forearm, hard enough to smudge it if you could. It was of a snake twirling a basketball on its forked tongue. On a better day I would have asked him about it, about what it meant to him. You could see he played the game. We would have compared notes. Vertical leap. Where our jumper felt most comfortable, left or right of the key, or looking down the barrel. Could he shoot with his off hand? The knowledge of our tribe. But not today.

"My guess is you have, Neil," I said. "Met Mr. Hunt, I mean."

Neil said, "This is his house."

"It is," I said. "Lloyd is his first name. You're putting the roof on a house Lloyd Hunt paid close to one-point-five million for."

"Where we going with this?" one of the guys sitting on bags of cement mix said. He was enjoying the hell out of a Coors. Every crew has its hard ass, one guy who doesn't know any better.

I walked over and hunkered down near him, crowded him, and I said, "Lloyd has a remarkable wife named Nancy. She'd turn your head, yours, and Neil's and Bunt's here. Nancy's a real wet dream." I was five inches from Coors man. He wore a goatee. I said, "Lloyd and Nancy, they have two children, a boy and a girl, whose names escape me right this minute." I took a chunk of ice from the cooler at this guy's elbow and chucked it into the desert. You knew numbnuts thought he would have served with honor in Vietnam if he had been old enough at the time. I spoke directly to him, said, "They're paying for a high-quality roof that they're not getting. I believe the word *lifetime* was in the contract. Fifty years was mentioned." I stood and said to the man in his goatee, "I don't mean to suggest the failure is in any way directly contributable to your drinking on the job."

Steven Bunt was rubbing his tattoo to the bone.

Neil said, "You got a—"

He stopped short. I was shaking my head, saying, "My problem's not with you, Neil. Not even with this man drinking his Coors." I walked back over to Neil and said, "My problem is with Mr. Tuttle. It's not with nobody in this outstanding group of roofers." I looked at the Coors man, who said, "We do our job." He raised his beer to me, and I stepped over, snagged it out of his hand, and tossed it into the sagebrush behind the house. He started to get up, and I kicked his feet out from under him. He scrambled, and I heard Neil say, "Stay put, Perry." He made a gesture that told Perry to calm down. To me he said, "You made your point. We got it."

I said, "No. I haven't. Not quite." I got a pen out of my pocket and ripped a ragged piece of paper from a bag of cement. I gave it and the pen to Steve Bunt and said, "Would you do me a favor and write this down?" He nodded. I said, talking real slow and right next to Perry, "Mr. Hunt is paying for two layers of thirty-pound felt." Steve wasn't writing. I said, "Write it down, Steve. Write *Mr. Lloyd Hunt is paying for two layers of thirty-pound felt*." He wrote. Printed, I could see. I said, "Now write, *Mr. Hunt is paying for nails on every tile*."

"Should I write Lloyd again?" Steve said.

I said, "Please. It's polite."

I waited on Steve, then said, "Write this. Write, *Tile alone does not keep the weather out. It's what's underneath that waterproofs a house*." I suggested to Steve that he fold up what he wrote down, put it in his shirt pocket, and make certain Mr. Tuttle read it when he arrived. I told the crew they had two choices I could see. They could quit, which was fine with me. Get in their trucks pronto and drive away. Or they could undo what they had done on the roof and then do it right. I said, "You know, 'Tote that barge. Lift that bale.'" I told Neil to tell Tuttle I would be back in the morning and I didn't want the tile in place before I inspected the felt. If the tile was down I'd be asking him to remove every single piece himself, tile by tile, and if he hadn't done the job exactly to my liking I would hire a crew and he'd pay for it.

To Perry and his goatee I said, "What is the overlap on felt?"

If looks could kill.

I said, "Measure it if you have to. You know, snap some lines." I popped a fresh Coors, offered it to Perry, and said, "I have a temper." He ignored the can. I said to him and the rest of the crew, "It's not personal, gentlemen," and I hauled the can of beer to my truck and poured it into the street. On the way across town I phoned my pal Buzz Gaulter, who had recommended Tuttle to me. Not in, so I left a message. Warned Buzz. Keep an eye on Tuttle, I said. Tuttle was roofing another subdivision Buzz was building out near Red Rock.

––––––

I found Ginger at Gus's, sunbathing. Her fiancé, Snyder, was below the pool shooting hoops on a square of cement Gus put in years ago for me and my friends. Snyder worked the lane, baby hooks left- and right-handed. Quick. The kid had a great first step and recovered in a flash. Six-foot-seven, two-twenty, he had a future. Basketball was his ticket, and all he needed to do was get it punched. He was thinking two, maybe three years of college hoops, then the NBA. Snyder was one hell of a swingman who could put the ball on the floor and nail the three. University of Utah up in Salt Lake City signed him to a full ride. Duke courted him. North Carolina. Kentucky. UCLA. He chose the Utes when they showed up in the NCAA finals. He liked the brutal way they protected the paint and re- bounded. Played, he said, like they were Peterbilt.

"Hot," I said to Ginger.

"Hairspray," she said. "It's wiping out the ozone."

I said, "You think so?"

Ginger got up on her elbows and said, "Gus is creeping me out."

"He can do that."

She said, "He's all, we got to provide choices for the people. Customers want caskets that express themselves and how they went about their lives. He said death shouldn't be a downer. People are looking for ways to celebrate the passage to the other side." Vegas Vic had followed me through the house and into the yard. Music rolled in from a neighbor's. Deep-rooted anger in its beat. Vic limped, his paper-foot acting up. The way the dog moved made me think of a sad-in-the-back whiskey-drinking old duffer at a piano picking at tunes no one sings anymore. I bent down and splashed water on Vic, and Ginger said, "You're not supposed to do that."

"What?" I said.

"Splash water on a dog," she said.

"He's hot."

"The chlorine," she said. "Bad for him, wouldn't you think?"

There was a time when Vic swam in the pool, but who wanted to argue? So I said, "You using sun block?" and Ginger said, "Whatever." I guided Vic into shade next to the pool house, the two of us listening to Ginger, who was going on about Gus acting like a ghoul. She didn't want to hear about see-through caskets in neon colors. He had phoned twice since his first call, and I wasn't here, or at my place, or Jane's, so Gus mouthed off to Ginger. He told her burials need themes, like Disneyland or Dolly Parton's world. Like game shows. The death business wanted to be uplifting.

Ginger was wearing a soft hat. She never got in the pool, never actually swam, just fried herself. Snyder moved outside the three-point line marked with strips of electrician's tape, and he started burning the net, throwing up shot after shot, heat-seeking missiles every last one of them. Release, the flick of the net, the bounce of the ball on cement, its echo in the yard. Ginger said to me, "Our father won't shut up for two minutes about cremation." She squinted at Snyder and said, "I tell Gus I'm off limits, and he talks right over me." She had hung up on him.

From where we sat the air above Las Vegas was filthy. It looked like the city had coughed itself into a dust storm.

Snyder hollered over. "Show me your stuff?"

"Got none," I said.

He said, "True. You're an old man who jumps like an elephant."

"But I have wisdom."

"So the story goes." Snyder went back to impressing the passing clouds.

I said to my kid sister, "I like Snyder."

"You would," she said.

"You're on one today," I said.

"Gus describing his own funeral to me," she said, "is that something a father should do to a daughter? It's abuse. I could have him arrested."

I said, "He's all alone up there, away from home and caught up in the moment."

"He wants a record player in his casket. You know, one of those old ones you stack real records on."

"Cut him some slack."

"*You* cut him some slack."

"He's thinking sideways about his life."

"Yeah, whatever," she said. "He wants Sinatra, Bing Crosby, Dean Martin. Long-playing records. He gave me the store name where we can still buy vinyl. He said *vinyl*." She looked at me sideways and said, "Who puts the records on, keeps it going in the grave?"

Ginger told me where she had written Gus's number down, and I went inside and phoned. No answer.

————

At my place, a message from Gus was on my machine. "Tommy, Tommy," he said, "my boy, we're behind the times and the eight ball. What I'm seeing here, on display—so many booths you need a golf cart to get around—I should bury my head in the sand for all I don't know. What does it say on all our buildings? Mortuary, Tommy. Rooke Mortuary. Mortuary. It's old hat. It's the oldest hat. It's not good business, and it only upsets potential customers. And all that about location, location, location. Not so true anymore. Now they tell me it's image, image, image. We say in person, when we're face to face, we say *home*. Our girls, they answer the calls, and they say, Rooke Funeral Home. This much we're up on, only we haven't changed the buildings for anybody to see when they drive by. It's like we're walking around with our pockets turned inside out. I should be responsible for this? What do I pay people for? I hire—" His message ran out. There was a second call. "Tommy, Tommy, where are you? I phone here and there, and you're nowhere. You're not there. You're not here. You're at Jane's. You're not at Jane's. I called Plugg. Plugg has no idea where you are. You're across town. Where are you? Do you ever go home? What's up with you and Jane? You can't return a message I leave and people write down?" He was staying at the Tahoe Hilton. "Call me," he said. "We got to get things rolling."

I needed to remind Gus I didn't work for him. Never had. His money was not my money.

I took Carl T. Plugg with me to baby-sit Hector. Jane had asked for a couple of hours to clear her head, to see if she could converse with another adult, to check her powers of locomotion. Could she still walk a straight line if she didn't have to account for Hector's weight? Jane handed Hector over to Plugg and led me back to the slider off the bedroom. Tuttle, she told me, had called here. Part of the message she was stamping backwards on my forehead was *don't give out this number*. The slider was sticking, got bumpy a foot into its opening. She left me working on it, where I could overhear her and Plugg.

"Hector's got his mother's beauty," Plugg was saying. "Day after day he grows more handsome." I could tell he had drifted into the kitchen, could hear Jane putting a few dishes away.

She said, "Tommy's coloring, though. Tommy's hair."

"Peekaboo," Plugg said. He said, "Oh."

Jane said, "He's got his father's punch. He hurt you?"

"Fire power," Plugg said.

I reached the kitchen door. Plugg was hoisting Hector to his shoulder and checking his own lip. He saw me and said, "Left, left, right, and he was gone. The kid did damage and took an angle in his retreat. He gave me a fat lip." Plugg fingered a tooth.

I said, "He knock one crooked?" I was headed through the kitchen to the garage, hunting some WD-40. Would pick up silicone later. The slider track wanted lubricating was all.

Jane kissed the top of Hector's head, put two fingers to her lips, then to Plugg's and said, "You're healed."

He followed her down the hall to the front door, and I headed for the garage. Then I was back, standing in the kitchen in time to overhear Plugg saying, "You see his stride is off. His back is bent, always the bundle of his unhappiness on his shoulders. High noon, and all is lean and sad. Eclipse, and you don't want to look directly at it."

Me, he was talking about me.

"What is he without you? Without Hector?" Plugg said.

Plugg was counting on Tommy Rooke and Jane remarrying or his world would continue to wobble in its orbit.

"Thomas," Jane said, "your heart is in the right place."

Plugg said, "Rabbi Tarfon—"

"No, no," Jane said. "Not Rabbi Tarfon."

He said, "It's a short one I'll make shorter even."

Jane stood where she was, and Plugg said, "Rabbi Tarfon, one day he notices his wife's sandals, which are old and brittle, and so worn they drop from her feet like ashes. The leather has turned to dust. What remains crumbles in your hand. What's left would fit in a sandwich bag. The straps crack like a dry lake bed and tear, break in two. But there is nothing can be done but go to the market. Cross the square, the courtyard. To the best shoe repairmen she drags the sandals, which gets her in return a shake of the head. The shysters, they sing only one greedy song after another greedy song, the sales pitch blues. Buy buy buy. There's no money for herself, and still she must shop. The household is to be fed. There is food to be bought and cooked and on the table. To market she must go barefoot. Rabbi Tarfon, he gets on his knees. He puts his hands down so she can walk on them. All the way he is in front of her. He is crawling and putting his hands so she can walk on them. His bare hands. She tells the Rabbis the story, not leaving out the smallest detail. She says her husband honors her beyond what the law asks. Pray for him? She asks the Rabbis. The Rabbis, in their wisdom, they tell her, Had he done a thousand times more for you only one-tenth of the law would he fulfill."

"Give me the moral," Jane said to Plugg.

Plugg said, "Tommy. Your Tommy, he would lay down his open hands on the ground for you. Palms up, all the softer. Here in Las Vegas, on the hot concrete where you can cook an egg the sun is so hot. You come to the street, and he's there, on his knees, hands ready. Step. Palm. Step. Palm. Step. Palm. He's ahead of you."

Jane said, "His love, I know, is big."

"Bigger than big."

"And wide."

"Ah, lovely Jane," Plugg said, "the indiscretions of youth, the mistakes a handsome man can't avoid on the road to wising up."

She said, "Time will tell."

"So?" Plugg said. "You're saying, book the chapel? Call the newspapers? We got a scoop?"

"So," she said, "keep your guard up, Thomas. Hector's quick as lightning. You said it, left, left, right, and gone. The boy has his daddy's fists."

Jane was taking an exit was all. *Left, left, right, and gone* meant *God Bless, and bye bye Thomas.* She said to him, "Thomas, you look so sharp today you could be dangerous to the ladies," and she shut the front door behind her.

———

Cal's on the Boulder Highway—Plugg's hangout, my hangout, small-time sports book, pool, snooker, those tall billiard-hall chairs you sat on and BS'd in, the kind that gave you a landowner's view of the tables. In one corner was a collection of photos highlighting my career, one of my belts on loan, a display which was both flattering and embarrassing. I avoided it. Never stood nearby. Still, there was pride. Plugg and I hauled Hector along to meet Tuttle. On the phone—he'd called—Tuttle was almost thee-and-thouing me. No way did he want Tommy Rooke telling Buzz about the shoddy roofing his crew had done. He lost one subdivision, and if word spread, it could cost him a business his father spent forty years putting together.

Hector in my arms, I said some hellos and caught the end of a Phillies-Braves game, then located Plugg, who was skunking some guy who believed he was expert at nine ball. All you had to look at was his stroke to know otherwise. Plugg didn't hustle you. He was always forthright. He said to your face in plain English so there was no misunderstanding or confusion, *I can do black magic with a cue ball and a stick—want to play for fifty? a hundred? two hundred?* A stack of twenty-dollar bills sat on the light over the table. Hector, arms flailing, cheered Plugg on. A railbird everyone called Almanac whispered to me that Plugg was five racks deep into a run that had commenced with the horse's ass missing a three-cushion bank. The sucker, Almanac hissed, didn't know jack. Plugg left the guy hooked shot after shot until the fool lost his equanimity and tried some five o'clock English that resulted in a wide open table for Plugg.

Ralph the barkeep passed along a message from Gus. *There is work to be done*, it said. *Asses to be fired. What am I paying middle-management for? Not to be up to date? Phone me. For example, Nevadans don't want urns. They want their ashes scattered to the winds. They want to return to the desert from whence they came. But they need containers for delivery. Strong yet inexpensive disposable cartons. They need airplanes to do the flying. Licensed pilots.*

"Word for word," Ralph told me. He said, "Gus made me read it back to him."

I had tried to reach Gus. From my place, from Jane's, from here, from his place. No answer.

Tuttle came in, and we took a booth. I handed Hector off to Almanac. First thing I said to Tuttle was, "You don't phone my ex-wife's looking for me. That never happens again." He had waltzed into the back room, all charm, too much spring in his step, hair moussed. His clothes looked like he was taking night classes at the local community college, not to get smart, but to meet women. He was in pants you see at dinner shows, pleated, cuffed. He wore bruised-looking loafers, and his gold socks matched his shirt. Second thing I said, after we sat down, was, "You were recommended, so when you do the kind of work you're doing, you toss both your good name and Buzz's out the window. Not to mention your own father's." I had ordered Tuttle a beer. I was on seltzer.

"I won't lie to you," Tuttle said. "I didn't do my job. I won't tell you it was a screw up, a misunderstanding. I wasn't on top of what it was my obligation to be on top of."

"You're saying the crew did this on their own?"

"They didn't do it because I said to."

"Your boy Neil didn't do his job."

"Fired," Tuttle said. "You can be sure, the whole lot of them. First thing tomorrow."

"I already talked to Buzz," I said. This, a bluff. I hadn't given Buzz details over the phone. Had only left that message.

Tuttle said, "Jesus, Tommy."

I said, "I'm holding this over your head. It's what I can do."

He sipped his drink. Eyes yellow. Piss in them.

I said, "I told Buzz to hire someone to check your work. I said if he wanted I'd drop by. No notice. I'm doing a favor for a friend. What a pal does for a pal." Tuttle understood I would be taking tile off. I would be counting felt. I would check flashing. I said, "You're okay with it, right?" I was stepping way over some line here. Tuttle didn't answer to me. I held my hands out front, making the scales of justice, and I said, "You tipped things in the wrong direction." I lowered my left hand, shrugged, and said, "But then who is without sin?"

Tuttle polished off his drink, got himself out of the booth. He said, "Yeah, well, Tommy, fuck you."

His way of thanking me. I said, "You're welcome."

Then, at the door, he turned and said, "The man Perry, you met him. He has a reputation for taking offense. You'll want to keep open the eyes in the back of your head."

"He working on Buzz's job?"

"He is."

"You're not firing him?"

"Not from that job."

"Then there's a chance we'll be coming to terms," I said. "But I don't think so. I didn't see it in him."

Jane located me and Plugg and Hector in the park a couple of blocks from her house. Plugg was close to a thousand dollars richer, had even talked the horse's ass into a game of how-would-you-play-this-shot, and, ball in hand, Plugg two-railed the nine from a messy cluster, leaving the cue ball a whisker from a scratch in the corner pocket. He imagined in his head and pulled off a combination he called an unholy alliance of luck and skill.

Jane said, right off, "There's a call from Gus."

I said, "He's creeping Ginger out."

"He's not making my day," Jane said. "He's talking dinner-party burials complete with live entertainment, including dancing and the music of your choice. You dress the corpse for its journey. Dracula is the number-one seller on the market. Gus says you use a fake stake through the heart, like those arrows that look like you've been shot in the head. The stake looks so real a priest couldn't tell the difference."

I said, "He's joking."

"He sounds serious," she said.

"I guess you give people what they want."

"Whatever happened to decorum? To class?"

Plugg excused himself, asking to borrow my truck, and Jane and I walked toward a playground. We could see up ahead monkey bars and the reds and yellows and blues of plastic slides and swings. Palm trees rattled in the breeze, and rainbirds chugged water in thirty-foot arcs. There was a baseball game going on, kids in Dodger blue at bat and in Yankee pinstripes in the field, the pitcher warming up between innings. Jane was wearing a cotton sundress so simple in its cut and fit you knew she could stand on a rock and argue convincingly that every life is of infinite worth. She was in flip-flops and had painted her toenails cherry red.

I fit myself sidesaddle into a rubber swing, my knees up around my chest, and Jane handed me Hector. I rocked in one spot, clumsy, me and Hector glued together, and I said to my ex, "In the movie of our life, me and you, we walk along the shore at Lake Mead. Barefoot. We're tan. Our teeth are white. We romp in the water until we fall down dog tired. Cut to evening, same day. We dress up and go to dinner, feed each other food."

"You know better," Jane said, and she crossed her fingers, made an X in the air between us. She said, "Nobody feeds me food. None of that. My mother taught me how to use a fork."

I did know better.

She said, "And when it gets to the sex scene, no one's tongue is in my mouth. Un-uh." She put up another X, and I squeezed Hector to me so I could let go with my hands, and I matched her X. I said, "Same here. None of that."

"In this movie, we retie the knot?" Jane said.

"We do," I said, "but we don't think of it as a knot."

She said, "Do we get a honeymoon this time around?"

"It's obligatory," I said. Night of our first wedding, I hopped a plane for a fight in L.A. My first pro bout. I came home to her after I had beaten the other kid into the hospital. Broke his ribs. He was spitting blood to the canvas.

Here in the park, she lifted Hector from my lap and said, "Tommy, you were always full of hope."

"Every morning," I said. "Like clockwork."

Next day, the fight came out of nowhere. If you could call it a fight. To say I was blindsided didn't quite cover it. Bushwhacked. Maybe. I was unloading cedar shingles from the bed of my truck and saw Tuttle and his crew pull in to the house next door. Three homes were going up side by side by side. He hadn't fired anyone. I had my back to the blow, but sensed it like a bad dream that hangs on and won't let you relax, and I turned enough to put a shoulder into Perry, the Coors man. His arm whapped stupidly against me, and I elbowed the wind out of him, and he held on so that we were doing this ugly two-step, like a couple of drunks dragging each other to one more bar. Give Perry credit. He came alone. The man came to repay me, not to show off for his cronies. Take away points for his being sneaky about it. I had brought Vic to the site and was going to run him by the vet's later. The dog didn't bother to get up, but was barking his dismay, more like a cough than his usual *harrf*. I box-stepped Perry in a bear hug until the whole thing got silly, him saying, "Goddamn," six or seven times, the two of us bumping my truck, then stumbling over the shingles and coming apart when we hit the ground. We sounded like timber. Perry got himself together quicker than I did. I was on my knees, sitting on my heels, leaning back, and he scooted over and headbutted me. Broke my nose and knocked himself to the dirt. He lay there moaning, and I yanked the tails of my shirt to my face. Third time I had had my nose broken. "Turn out the lights," I said, "the party's over." I looked up, and there was Tuttle.

"Jesus," he said.

Perry rolled over on to his back.

"What—," Tuttle said.

"Shit," Perry said, and he propped himself up.

I said, "You done?"

He hung his head, catching his breath. He said, "I am. You?"

I stood, gave him a hand to his feet, and said, "I deserved it. There's a better way to do business than how I did it."

"Damn straight," he said.

I said, "We even?"

"Even."

Vic moseyed over and was studying me hard. He sniffed, smelled the blood. He was worried and confused in his eyes.

"Tommy, Tommy." Gus was talking. Jane and I lay in her bed listening to him on her machine. We had made love, careful of my nose, and now, against the recommendations of Health Watch on the news, Hector was asleep on the bed, curled between me and Jane. "Words aren't enough," Gus was saying. "What I'm seeing your smartest genius couldn't have imagined. A coffin like that dress at the Oscar's, covered in credit cards. Television built into the lid. Stereo." Jane kissed Hector's forehead. His hands were tiny fists in his sleep, one more gift from his old man. From me. "There's a way to keep the music coming till doomsday," Gus said. "Electronics Einstein didn't imagine, or whoever it was invented electricity. Ben Franklin?"

I reached for Jane, and she said, "I want to fly to Las Vegas for the wedding."

On the machine, Gus said, "Tommy, Tommy, where are you? Jane? Life—" He was cut off.

I said to Jane, "Our wedding?"

"Our wedding."

I said, "We live in Las Vegas."

She said, "Where did you always want to be from?"

I didn't know.

"Think," she said. "Where?"

I said, "New Jersey."

"Be serious."

"What about you?"

"Bluebird, California."

"There is such a place?"

"There is." Jane sat up, and Hector opened his eyes, no focus to them. Our boy on his back asleep. She said, "We fly there, and then back to Las Vegas, where we rent a limo and we get married at one of those drive-up windows."

"Hector safely in a car seat."

"Exactly."

"Is it possible? I mean, can you fly to Bluebird, California?"

"You can fly close enough."

I said, "Who'll shoot the video?"

"Hector can," she said.

"From a baby's point of view?

"Who else's? Innocence. Purity. Freshness. All the good things God grants the new arrivals."

"And Plugg—he's coming?"

"We'll negotiate that."

The phone started ringing. Jane got into her bedside nightstand, handed me her wedding band and said, "I want a new ring."

I told her that it all made sense, and, the phone on its fourth ring, the machine about to answer, she reached to pick up Hector, one hand behind his head, and Hector chose that moment to give us his party grin and throw a few punches. Left, left, right, and gone, our boy's eyes flickering him toward the best moments of anyone's life. He was cradled in Jane's arms. Sound asleep.

How Would You Play This?

Carl T. Plugg's game was what he called the marriage of two beautiful women—*la boda de dos hembras*, a connection between shooting pool and living life that his Pluggonian logic wrenched from the old joke about the guy who has a choice between marrying a beautiful woman and a woman who sings beautifully. Groom wakes up the morning after the wedding, rolls over in bed and looks long and hard at his new bride. Sez, "Sing, woman. Sing."

Plugg set up a shot on the pool table, buttonholed the foolhardy, and said, "It's nine ball. How would you play this?" Or he laid out a side-rail kiss back, handed you a cue stick and said, "*La boda de dos hembras.*"

La boda de dos hembras.

Only to his Pluggonian way of making up the world. What he was saying was, Make a choice. Choose.

Like in bridge, when you see hands laid out in the newspaper, and you're being asked what you would lead with—spades? diamonds? hearts? clubs? Like those books on poker. Or reading a corner blitz and breaking off a route in football, not to mention baseball, where you're the runner on second, and there's one out with your team down two runs. It's the seventh inning, and the batter hits a slow roller toward third.

Matters of choice and the rules of the game.

There's an old Chinese saying, drive the spike or relinquish the sledge hammer, a thought which loses everything in the translation.

"Ball-in-hand," Plugg said to Tommy Rooke

The side-dish negotiation here was Plugg talking Tommy out of retirement. He had lined up a bout, a kid named Jarret who was hungry and on his way to a title fight. Jarret needed a quality match. All Plugg was jockeying for was the go-ahead from Tommy. You ever saw Tommy in the ring you understood there was no coming back from what he did to you. He changed you. Rearranged, as they say, your internal organs. Plugg was after him to take on Jarret. Big money for Tommy meant big money for Plugg.

We were in Cal's Billiards, me Tommy's sidekick because we were bidding roofs today. Plugg was baiting him. What was disturbing, like when you can't recall a word you know you learned in the third grade, was that there were wedding dresses hanging in Cal's, five of them here and there and looking like the ghosts families put in trees at Halloween. It was clear these were thrift store merchandise. Our pal Almanac told us Cal's daughter was getting married in the snooker room at 6:00 on the nose. No one was going to be wearing the dresses. They were decoration for the ceremony. There was also a couch and lamp and a coffee table, a throw rug, and end tables, ash trays, all of it storage from *The Donna Reed Show*, the idea being that the 1950s was a time in America when you made a promise and you stuck to it. You said *I do*, and you did. Cal had a buddy who was acquainted with some TV type who had juice, and three phone calls later the furniture was on a plane to Las Vegas. There was a grandfather clock set to chime during their vows. All of it Cal's girl's plan and you had to give her credit. Your everyday wedding this wasn't going to be.

The shot Plugg set up for Tommy was a mirage. It was a tempting combination on the one and the nine you didn't want to mess with. Yet the angle was there. Sort of. If you had a T-square and a yardstick. You missed and the other guy cleaned up the table, the balls being laid out like a gift. It was a matter of stringing shot to shot like freeway driving at four in the morning. Other side of the coin was, you made the shot, you ninety-nine times out of a hundred scratched. Game *fini* that way too. Turn out the lights, the party was over. Lock the doors behind you.

So, it was, as Plugg construed it, *La boda de dos hembras*. Sing, baby, sing.

Go figure.

Tommy said to him, "You're giving me ball-in-hand?"

"Ball-in-hand," Plugg said.

Tommy dipped into his jeans, dug out a couple bills, unfolded them, and laid flat two fifties side by side on the table. A pair of Ulysses Simpson Grants. Tommy said, "One, nine, corner pocket."

"Wise man's shot's a safety," Plugg said. "Finesse the cue into a cul-de-sac."

Tommy got into his wallet and put a hundred next to the fifties. He borrowed Plugg's cue.

"Five hundred says you miss and I run the table," Plugg said.

To my way of thinking this was not the way to be talking Tommy into fighting. You embarrassed a man you were hoping would do you a monumental favor? Not in my book.

But, as they say, who knew from Pluggonian logic.

Tommy picked up his two hundred, added three one hundred-dollar bills, and said, "Ball-in-hand?"

"Ball-in-hand," Plugg said. He cupped his own hand to his ear, asking if there was an echo in the room. Egging Tommy on.

Tommy said to Plugg, "Ball-in-hand." He showed Plugg the cue ball.

"Five hundred on top says you scratch," Plugg said. He opened his wallet and laid one thousand dollars next to Tommy's bills. He said, "A grand. It goes two ways for you. You make it, you win. You play safe, and I can't flush the table, you win."

Tommy matched Plugg's bet and said, "One, nine, corner."

"Corner?" Plugg said.

Tommy said, "Corner," and he used Plugg's stick to tap the one he meant.

Plugg said, "Not on my watch."

A grand was a sum of money to Plugg. It was chump change for Tommy. It was a tip he gave his caddie after Tommy shot a seventy-one on Summerlin's PGA course. Thing was, if Plugg talked Tommy into the fight, Plugg himself made six figures. Tommy took care of him. One of life's two-way streets. Tommy owed the man.

Tommy stroked the shot. Made the nine. It dropped half a heart-beat ahead of the cue ball. Scratched. Plugg said, "The play was a safety." He collected the money and said, "Sing, Tommy, sing." More Pluggonian logic. Confound a man and then razz him when he's down. Kick his stump when his foot's been amputated. To my way of walking about on the planet, this was not how you got Tommy back in the ring. Didn't matter that the two of them were as close as crossed fingers.

Tommy said, "Set it up again."

A request Plugg was all too willing to oblige.

———

Early afternoon, Tommy and me, we were assessing our last stop, mission-barrel tiles on a Spanish-looking place out in Paradise Valley. You didn't ask Tommy, given his fame and money, why he did roofs. Such a question was an insult. You kept it to yourself. He owned the company and he did a lot of the grunt work. The pair of us went all the way back to high school together.

They call me Spinoza, all because one day I was sitting on a roof—me and my crew laying shake shingles in 110 degrees—and, following a bite of a Wendy's burger, I said, "You solve all the shit going on in the world and in your own cesspool of a life and then what do you have to live for?" We were eating lunch, and I said it because of all the bitching and moaning and agony in the air. I told them you're fooling no one if you believe scientists want to pin down how the world jump-started itself. You think the doctors want to cure cancer? MS? Say they do, say they came up with a solution, and then they would be out of business like the fool who sells every shoe in the shoe store one afternoon. The result would be they got to move out of their think tanks and get real jobs.

Joker named Carl scratched the top of his head real obvious and said, "Deep."

Deep, my ass. But they ragged me. Wouldn't let go of it. Had *Department of Big Thoughts* lettered on the door of my truck. The crew passed the hat and paid a sign painter for professional work.

Thus, Spinoza. Tommy's contribution. Probably really his ex's—Jane, she would know such a name.

Aristotle.

Doc.

The Philosopher.

On it went.

They were like bulldogs about it. Randy, still in high school, he got a six-pack in him at parties and he climbed up on any roof in town, stripped down and did a Thinker pose right in my line of sight.

He did this in broad daylight a couple of times. One of us usually put a hand on his shoulder about the time he reached for his briefs.

Was funny, what he did.

I wasn't so proud I couldn't laugh at myself, and I wasn't so limited I couldn't see myself in a different light. I had to admit up front I liked what the truck said. It was a joke, only not really, me driving around town, *Department of Big Thoughts* right there on the door, under the elbow I rested out the window. We took my picture by it, Carl pointing at the lettering.

Thing about being with Tommy was he could get you and him both laid at three in the afternoon on a Wednesday no matter what the weather. Take the woman below us this day. You can see her shading her eyes and calling up to him. "Can it be fixed?" she was saying. The lady had an eye single to the glory of Tommy Rooke. She was not seeing me, and I stood closer to her, me at the edge of the roof, checking the bird stops at the eaves. We arrived, and she met us in her house robe, her hair under something pink and plastic. She pointed us around the side of the house. Now she was in a two-piece and was about to walk backwards into her swimming pool. She had taken a comb to her hair and was feeling good about being forty-plus and under the influence of a personal trainer.

The trouble was the roof needed to go, and she was wanting us to fix up some storm damage was all. Do spot repairs. Tile was dislodged, and there were areas where we would want to lay down plastic until we could get to the job.

I said to her, "You'll want to be watching out behind you."

Didn't register. Got me one flick of her eyes. I was the oddball on the sidewalk at a red light who was trying to keep her from walking into traffic.

"You're about to get wet," I said.

She turned around. Then back, eyes on Tommy.

––––––––

It was Tommy who went to the truck to write up a bid, and I wandered over to where this lady lay stretched out on a chaise lounge. I said, "Great pool." Quick as you can drop your keys I saw in my head her inviting me to take a swim, and me saying I wasn't prepared, and her undoing her top to show me how we could solve that minor detail if I'd follow the leader. Then she dives in the water, and she has the bottom of her suit waving in the air, and I am diving in and figuring out where I will come up under her. Reality being what it is and will forever be she didn't budge—no striptease, no swim. From where she lay she squinted hard at me. Put a lot of disdain in her one pair of eyes. Her pinkie finger knew more about life than I ever would. "You all finished?" she said.

I told her Tommy was figuring a bid.

She leaned forward, and her stomach puckered. Good, I thought. Justice at work. Mr. Personal Trainer missed that. She said, "If you could just do what has to be done."

"You need a new roof," I said.

We heard Tommy shut the side gate, and she stood, her doing so erasing those sad creases around her middle. She extended her hand to shake Tommy's. A tilt to her wrist.

He stopped short and said, "We can do the repairs, and then you'll be calling us in six months. You need a new roof."

I said, "He's quoting me."

"The whole thing?" she said.

Tommy said, "The house is fifty or sixty years old, and the roof, thirty, maybe forty."

She said, "We bought it last year."

"You want the repairs, I can recommend people who'll do them," Tommy said. "We won't. We'd be cheating you."

She said, "And they wouldn't be?"

"They don't mind," Tommy said.

Men of honor. That was us. Our slogan.

Tommy showed her the bid. She took it and walked a few steps away, one of those war widows in a Hollywood flick, getting the telegram telling her the husband had been killed in action. She looked at me, then Tommy, and she said, "Can I think about this?"

"We'd want you to," Tommy said.

Men of honor. There was them, then there was us. We should have had magnetic signs made and slapped them to our trucks at sunrise.

Tommy said, "I'm going to run over to Industrial and get some plastic for the base of your chimney."

Puzzled her.

"No cost and no obligation," Tommy said. "Sun's shining and it is supposed to be continuing to do so, but just in case something rolls in—some rain over night—you'll have a few days' peace of mind while you're thinking."

Summer, Las Vegas—rain? Right.

She thanked him. Her heart in it. And Tommy did, at that point, shake the hand she offered him.

"I'm leaving Spinoza here to keep an eye on things," Tommy said, and he clapped my back. "Won't be but half an hour."

He was pimping his buddy, plain and simple.

The lady looked me over, and I was thinking she was about to ask me to fix a leak in the pipes in her bathroom, and I was going to say, "Sure, my pleasure," and then go in there and study hard on the joint where it was dripping, and say, "Problem is your water's too thin. You'll have to call the city."

So here the two of us stood like a couple of pets watching our owner leave for the day. She glanced at me, and I was about to speak when she folded the bid in half and turned on a heel so hard you understood where that expression came from. She was inside her slider before I could say *boo*. The lock clicked into place.

She could have said, "Spinoza?" and I would have been obliged to explain how a man in my line of work gets such a sobriquet, me being a fellow of many words, a man of big thoughts who, had she given me the chance, could have talked her dizzy.

––––––––

I was sitting on the lady's front porch, loser written backwards on my forehead so you could read it from across the street when Tommy returned. He asked me if I would unload the plastic, and he went around back. Then he came out the front door and told me she was hoping he would go over the bid with her. He said, "Math isn't her talent." He wondered if I would get a head start on the chimney.

The plastic took me thirty minutes. Fifteen minutes later, I was shutting the tailgate, and Tommy walked out that front door again. Every step he took whistling while it did its job. This time his hair was wet so it was slicked down. Then we were on Tropicana, driving west, headed for Jane's. Tommy and Jane's baby boy, Hector, he had himself a smile you could have sold stock in. I said to Tommy, "I struck out." I was goading him. I was asking, *Did you?* as if it was a legitimate question. What I wanted was details.

He said, "It happens."

"To you, it does. *Not.*"

"Hey," he said, "to everyone."

I told him I chatted her up. I described a scene right out of every romantic comedy you've ever rented. I lied to Tommy about how I gave her my best song and dance, and she said, "I'm a married lady."

"It's an invitation," Tommy said.

I said, "How so?"

"She is inviting you as big as a valentine," Tommy said. "The lady was giving you one of those ten-dollar cards with a heart on a spring when you open it up. Cheap music playing."

I said, "She told me she loves her husband."

"She said that?"

"She said what I said."

"She probably does love her husband in her way."

"You think so?"

"Did she say no to you?" Tommy said.

I was knee-deep into what I was fabricating and wanted out, so I said, "She tells me she's a happily married woman is all."

"She said *happily*?"

"She said married."

"Married isn't no," Tommy said. "Like I said, it's an invitation. She's testing you. She's checking you out, and she's wondering, Can this gentleman express himself in interesting ways? She's telling you you talk long enough and hard enough and you make her laugh and you use the right words and the two of you are going to see what happens."

"I didn't pick up on that."

"You, Spinoza. You're a talker, man," he said. "The door was wide open."

I said, "You scored?"

"So crudely put."

"But you did?"

He said, "Once upon a time there was this roofer who once upon a time was a boxer."

"Shit, Tommy."

"You want to hear a story or not?"

I said, "You went for a swim."

He said, "You don't want to hear a story, a once upon a time?"

I said, "You did it in the pool?"

"The chlorine," he said, "it's good for you."

"You did," I said. "You did it in the pool?"

"Only in your head," he said.

Like I told you, three in the afternoon on a Wednesday no matter what the weather. Only I was and remain to this day a hopeless case. Piss-ass understanding here was she would have done me if he had asked her to. Charity work. If only I had dropped some big thoughts on her. Let her know my soul is like fire. Is shifty and moves in grace and love and free will. Should have done some quoting. *Tolle, lege.* Augustine. Should have winked. Cocked my head how Tommy did.

First thing Jane said once we got in the door and Tommy went to have a look at Hector was, "Mac"—which is my name. "Mac," she said, "what are we reading today?" She said it like it hadn't been months since I'd seen her, like we were building on a conversation we started yesterday or finished last night at 3:00 A.M., like we were sitting around that Department of Big Thoughts and drinking wine and hunting paradox. But it had been from before their break-up that I really talked to Jane. I had, back then, made a hard choice. Tommy? Jane? I took him and kept my mouth shut. Not sure I would do it the same way twice. She handed me a Coke she poured in a glass. Ice rolled in it.

I dug a paperback out of my back pocket, a book that compared Hebrew and Greek thought. Hard going, out of my league, but I was getting through it. Three pages a day. What sticks stuck. Like I should have said to the lady at the pool. *Tolle, lege.* Take, read.

Jane said, "You continue to amaze me, Mac," and I said, "Then I've done some good in the world." She riffled the pages and said, "Different ways to skin a cat, these Greeks and these Jews?"

"Sort of," I said.

She handed me the book and put a finger to her lips. She said, "You're not talking—is that it?"

This embarrassed me. I had insulted her, which I hated doing. Hadn't meant to. She was thinking I was thinking she couldn't hold her own on the subject. Jane probably read Greek. Latin. Hebrew. She was the lady who walked me through "Algebra and Infinity," a course taught by Mr. Ernesto Alverez himself, night class I took at UNLV. It was Jane who stopped us—me and her and Tommy—on a drive out to Lake Mead, Sunrise Mountain to our left, Frenchman's Mountain to our right, and she hooked our arms in hers and walked us into the desert far enough she could point out Horse Spring Foundation and introduce us to the mystery of 150 million years of geological activity not accounted for. Horse Spring shouldn't be sitting on Aztec sandstone. All of the evidence said there should have been erosion going on, not deposits. It was Jane who provoked me into separating hot-headedness from commitment and writing a dozen or so letters to congressmen and senators in support of the wolves returning to Yellowstone. Hell, we wrote to Mr. Bill Clinton himself. *Dear Bill,* our letter began. *All things are possible with you.* Took us all of one day to compose that sucker.

Tommy returned, carrying Hector. Proud daddy. *Offspring* was what he stood here for. *Fatherhood,* capital F. Jane said to him, "You tell Mac our news?"

He shook her off, said, "It didn't come up."

"It wouldn't," she said. Happy, though. Good times in her voice.

"What?" I said.

Tommy said, "We're getting married."

"Second time around," Jane said.

"Twice," I said, and I thought of Cal's, the wedding dresses, the couch and lamp. Cal's daughter. The last roof me and Tommy bid on. The lady. The swimming pool. I checked to see if Tommy's hair had dried. Sure. Of course. We lived in a desert. I said, "Soon?" Cuff me up the side of the head. This was not my shining moment. Where was that soul that moved like fire and with love and grace and free will? Where was my congratulatory handshake? My hug? The gifts one gave to those you truly loved.

"January first, stroke of midnight," Jane said. "The day the world turns brand-new."

I hugged Jane, shook Tommy's hand, only it all got awkward, me with a drink, Tommy holding Hector. I raised my Coke to them, a toast, wishing them happiness beyond what comes in boxes. Jane took the baby from Proud Daddy, and she handed Tommy a medicine bottle. It had an eye dropper in it, which she squeezed full, and Jane rolled the boy so Tommy had a clear shot at Hector's ear, left first, then right. They'd done this before. I said to Jane, "You coming to Cal's tonight?"

"I'm staying with Hector," she said.

I said, "You're worried about what he's got?"

"Your everyday infection, but both ears," she said. She was holding the boy so he was facing away from me. "You going to go?" she said.

Tommy stepped in and said, "Me and Spinoza."

I hadn't known this.

Jane said to me, "You and Tommy Rooke in tuxedos. Look out world. Lock up your daughters."

———————

An hour later, we had grabbed burgers and were at Tommy's place. There was a for sale sign out front. Tommy got me in one of his monkey suits, and he was tying me a bowtie. My collar was up. He tried doing the tie on me, but that wasn't working. He yanked it free and said, "Next we'll be doing a sleepover." Now the bowtie was around his neck, and he was talking and looping the long end through the knot he made. He said, "Plugg ever tell you about Pinya the Deep Thinker?"

"Plugg and I don't talk," I said.

Tommy adjusted the tie. Tweaked the ends. He said, "We'll rectify that. He's full of wisdom."

No way was Tommy going to be able to get the tie off and over his head. He loosened it. It wouldn't come. We decided he would tie his, and I would follow what he did. We tried this side by side in front of the mirror, and Tommy crossed one end over the other, then looped it through at the neck. I couldn't keep up. He said, "Pinya the Deep Thinker will, at high noon, argue that day is night. He'll persuade you that a circle has corners."

"Like Einstein," I said. "Time is different for everybody."

"Exactly."

I said, "There are people like that."

Trying to follow Tommy in the mirror was vaudeville. I stepped aside where I could see him straight on. We looped the long end down and toward our chests. Tommy said, "Pinya the Deep Thinker is a Helmite." We pulled our ties tight, and they looked great. Batwings, no wider than our collars. "To a Helmite only a Helmite is rational," Tommy said. He stepped over and poured us Scotch.

I said, "Tommy, say what you got to say."

He slugged home his drink. "I'm telling you what Plugg would tell you, is all."

"Is there a subject?"

"Pinya the Deep Thinker."

"Pinya the Deep Thinker and me," I said.

"You're advertised as the deep thinker."

"Only on a rooftop."

"It's a funny story, is all," Tommy said. He located his keys and we headed for the door. In three minutes we would be two men in tuxedoes riding east toward Cal's in a pickup that belonged in a junkyard. "Pinya the Deep Thinker," Tommy said, once we were in the cab, doors shut, windows down. He said, "The story, it's a hoot." Helm, Tommy explained, was a city of fools. He told me I would want to read about it. There were books. Tommy assured me a story was a story. That was all it was. He liked this one. It would fill the drive over. He wasn't trying to make a point. He had no agenda, he said. He said, "It ends with a great line. Pigs is pigs, dogs is dogs."

"I've heard that one," I said.

"From Plugg?"

"From life."

"Oy," Tommy said, which was what Plugg would have said.

I said, "You know what the Talmud says, Tommy?"

He was on Tropicana, and we were passing over I-15, its traffic headed south to L.A., north to heart of the city or to Utah. Up ahead like a joke side by side was New York, New York and the Excalibur. We wanted to find a city of fools all we had to do was park. Las Vegas, a Helmite's paradise. Diaspora for Helmites.

You could see Tommy didn't want to ask. Talmud schalmud.

I said, "I bring it up thinking it's what Plugg might do."

Tommy was a killer in his tuxedo. The man had stepped right out of Oscar night. Hollywood. He would be at home on a red carpet.

I said, "The Talmud says, silence is consent."

"Right," he said. "Pigs is pigs. Dogs is dogs."

Okay. Sure, to each his nature. No need to spell it out for me. We do what we do because we can. Fact of life.

You roll the dice. You make your choices. I had made mine. Months ago, I chose my man Tommy. I wasn't about to renege.

―――――

You came sporty to the wedding you were given a tie at the door. It didn't match, that was fine. There were six or seven of us in tuxedoes. Cal was one. The *Donna Reed* furniture was perfect. Talk about your ambiance. Me and Tommy had our picture taken with Cal and his daughter, the groom off toasting his good fortune. Tommy stepped around and took Cal's daughter in his arms, then kissed her, there, to the lips. I couldn't have done that. Not on your life.

She read her vows, and the grandfather clock took its cue. Chimed six times. Cal chanted along. Said: To good health. To happiness. To tranquility. To kindness. To wit. To understanding. To love.

I didn't see much of Tommy. Noticed him a few times huddled with Plugg. Saw him glad-handing pals, kissing the ladies. Then, 1:00 A.M., he asked me to take a walk. Outside, in the parking lot, he lit a cigarette. He said, "Spinoza, you think I should take the fight?"

We strolled along the Boulder Highway. What traffic there was was going to Henderson, not into the city. Dealers, cocktail waitresses, shift bosses—they were getting off work. These everyday people owned two hundred thousand-dollar homes and bought their cars on their tips.

I saw Tommy street fight once in high school. He was capable, at seventeen, physically and philosophically, of killing the other kid.

We reached a car lot close by Cal's, a place where they would sell Christmas trees come November. Now it was yard art. Clay planters and toads. There were concrete donkeys, woven baskets as satchels on their sides. You grew flowers in them.

Tommy wouldn't push me to answer him. We could walk two miles, and he wouldn't ask again. He lit a Kool off his first one.

I said, "I think you're making a mistake."

"To fight?" He blew smoke.

I said, "It's an error in judgment on Plugg's part."

Tommy said, "It's a true pleasure to hit people, Spinoza. To take them over completely."

I said, "All the more reason not to."

He flashed his Tommyness at me. Charm to the nth. He said, "Deep, my friend. Deep."

I said, "Is it about money?"

"Not for me," he said.

"For Plugg."

"For Plugg," he said. "For him."

I said, "Have Gus give him a mortuary."

Behind us a car pulled off the highway and slowed to the curb. It was a limo I had seen outside Cal's, white, tinted windows, six doors. One of the back ones opened, and a woman stepped out.

So many beautiful women in this world—what's the point to all of them?

Can you tell me?

Here was one more and I let the chance to ask get away.

I had seen her talking to Tommy in Cal's. Right now, all promise and expectation, she said to him, "You need a ride?" The lady was not looking my way. Tommy flicked his cigarette to the street, got into his pocket, and underhanded me the keys to his truck. He said, "You want to define error for me sometime tomorrow after you've had a chance to think on it?"

God but you had to appreciate that smile he passed on to his boy Hector. The one he gave me just now.

I said, "When you've got a century or two to listen."

––––––––

Yes. I had made my choice.

Me and Tommy, him a d/b, me at safety—our high school football years, and we were hell in a hat box. God, but we could stick you out of nowhere. Decleat you on the spot.

The two of us swift and fatalists. Like you had run into a cyclone fence if we jammed you at the line. Backpedaling, we were eloquent as piano can be. Tommy, between the lines on a Friday night, was skinny hearted and hideous as a big knife. He hit you the way chunks of pavement could if hurled through the thin fall air. We had us a blitz we disguised like bandits. You recognized it on your way to the darkness that came with being driven three feet into the turf.

––––––––

Six A.M., and I was sitting in the one chair there was in the living room of my bungalow. The front yard was desert landscaped. I got home somewhere between two and three. My lady's car was in the drive way, her home from a three-week trip to San Francisco. She drove to and from because she liked highways and motel rooms. Outside the front window the sun was softening the night into a purple you see so often on lilacs. My Love was asleep. I didn't wake her when I came in. We had been together three years. Had been friends in high school. Aced French together. We met up later, after her divorce, and here we were. One day—a week from now, a year, maybe even five—she would be gone. One of life's events you and I will eventually have to swallow. Along with our meds.

I built the bungalow paycheck to paycheck. It took me ten years. My love and I had three pieces of furniture in this room if you didn't count the built-in bookcases on two walls. They were half full. Nothing was shelved until I read it. Like the Greek and Hebrew book which I would be at for another few weeks. Then it was a trip to the bookstore, three, four hours. I drank coffee, and I talked to the regulars. The chess and checker players. I would pet the cat. Someone would say to me, "You got to read this." So I would give it a try. Read a few pages. Finally, I bought.

The chair I sat in here in my bungalow, soft and wing-backed, cost four thousand dollars. It was Mediterranean blue. The floor was hardwood. I laid it myself. Tile in all other rooms. In front of me, to the left of a Navajo rug, was a coffee table my lady and I sat through an auction for and almost lost to a dealer. We owned one painting, called *Frank's Live Bait*. If I could describe it to you it wouldn't be worth the fortune we paid for it. It was done on a section of blackboard taken from a school, and there was something to the paint itself so it looked like chalk but wasn't. The frame was the original wood, including the lip where extra chalk rested. The painting itself gathered together a sequence of lowlife characters you might have coffee with but not invite to your home. In a crowd they would pick your pocket for the fun of it. In your house they would swipe small objects they could squirrel away only to toss in the trash bin down the street.

The third piece of furniture was a standing ashtray we stole from the Dunes Hotel before it was imploded and made the national news. You see that? End of one more thing that counted in America. Fucking country might as well elect George Bush's boy president.

Couple years after high school I saw Tommy fight for the first time in the ring. There was a pop to his blows like two blocks of wood smacked together. This kid who grew up in all his dad's money had the penitentiary in him waiting to come out. Tommy dropped the guy with a body shot. You don't see that anymore in the ring. Most fighters are too stupid to understand that the body is where you do the damage. They're head hunters. Glory guys. Tommy's opponent crumbled. Sat on the canvas like he had been given unbearable news, and he wept. Right there in the ring, sitting up, his gloves between his legs, his back against the ropes, on national TV. He cried like a baby.

———

I sat in our blue chair, and I could see Tommy's truck where I parked it on the street.

My Love woke. The portable TV came on in the bedroom, CNN, most likely. Her name was Robyn. She passed through the hall to the kitchen and didn't realize I was in here.

I said, "Good morning," and she appeared in the doorway. Delight on her like the bird she was named for. She planted one sweet kiss high on my forehead, and we glanced up and saw Tommy standing by his front bumper. He was in his tuxedo. Light and windows being what they are early in a morning he couldn't see us.

He had come to talk about the ramifications of error or pick up his truck. Which are you betting on?

Robyn said, "Your pal's one pretty man."

I sat in our blue chair, and I raised my arms, needy as any two-year-old. Hell, I was still in a tux.

"Not as pretty as you," she said.

Ah, mercy.

"Two men dressed to kill," she said. "What are you up to?"

I said, "You know, and I'm quoting, 'pigs is pigs.'"

"Too early in the morning for such thoughts," she said. "Let me get some coffee in me."

I would explain later that we were coming not going. I would tell her about the wedding, about the lady and the roof, about the lady and the limo, about Jane and Tommy getting remarried. I would mention Hector because you can't leave him out of the equation. Silence is consent. What you take from one side you must give to the other.

Tommy walked around the truck, leaned in and honked the horn. The sound was nothing like the sound cars make today. It could have gathered a throng. Tommy stepped around to the front. He peered in at us. Cocked his head some. All of what Tommy did out there on the street, every move, the choreography of him, made Tommy Rooke look better.

It was no wonder women saw only him.

Robyn hunkered down next to me, and she said, "That man belongs in prison he's so sexy."

Again, I gave her me, the big empty sink sitting here, and she said, "For his own protection."

No One Is
Going to Ask
You to Sing

A snowball's chance in hell. In a pig's eye.

You're hearing Gus on UNLV football winning even one game this year. The news was out that the school had hired a new coach. UNLV was paying big money for a guy out of California. Me and Gus, we were sitting on his patio.

Buffoon.

Chump.

Putz.

Schmuck.

Add *Sap*.

There you had Gus on me that I was damn fool enough to bet with him that that same football team and its big money Pac-Ten coach made a bowl game. The school was grandstanding was all.

"Piss from honey," Gus said to me. "Color, texture, flow, taste and touch. Not to mention smell. And you, Tommy, you're mistaking the piss for the honey."

I raised our bet.

Gus collected the cash and matched it. He stuck it in a drawer in the liquor cabinet behind him. Came back, sat, and he said, "Fat chance, Tommy. Fat chance." He poured himself some Jack.

The slider wonked open and out stepped Ginger and Snyder. She pulled in close a plastic chair, settled on the edge of it, and crossed her arms. Something was up. Snyder kept to his feet. He was acting funny, like we caught him with his dick out a window. Ginger said, "Look," which sounded like *Wook*, and she showed us her tongue.

"God almighty," Gus said, and he was on his cell phone dialing his internist pal. Used the man's private number. Ginger's tongue was bloated and the color of a bruise. Her high school graduation gift to herself had been a tongue piercing. The day after she got it, first thing to go wrong was the ball that screwed to one end of the post and held it in place came off and she swallowed the damn thing. That night she couldn't feel her tongue. Next day she was sure the rocket scientist who did the piercing hit a nerve. *Relax*, they said when she called. *Initial swelling*, she was told.

Now, the four of us in the car on the way to the doctor's, stopped at a light, Gus described what could go wrong. He had watched a TV show about piercings. He told her there was a good chance she would infect her brain. He said, "If not your brain, then your ability to have children. Who'd want you then?"

Ginger was riding shotgun. He turned to her and said, "Your old man speaks, you close your ears. So life goes. We expect what we get. You know what I mean?" He hit the gas, sped up, talking. "Burying your head in the sand don't alter what is true," he said. "What I'm presenting to you—it's fact you can't turn away from or flush down a toilet. If the trouble don't go here"—he touched the crown of his head, took his hands completely off the steering wheel—"it finds its way to your private parts, and you won't be bringing any little Guses into the world."

"Is that comedy or tragedy?" she said. Ginger and her mouth. She could take your head off with a comment. Was like our mother, Edna, in that way.

Gus said, "How old are you so you talk like this to me?" He changed lanes, said, "The young, the old, different planets, different orbits."

"Jeeez," Ginger said.

"Anger don't change a thing. Not an iota," Gus said. "What happens physiologically happens. The body does what it does." He went on to say that what he saw on the TV wasn't schlock. The show wasn't *Entertainment Tonight*. It was Dan Rather. CBS. It was a documentary. "They can't afford to make up what isn't true on those programs," he said. "You see every night how they're getting awards for broadcast excellence."

To all this, me and Snyder were eyewitnesses from the back seat. I had the newspaper on my lap, open to the *Sports*, section C, page one, and a full-color, three-column-wide photo of me. Some reporter dipped into the archives. The picture felt like ancient history, your classic boxer pose, me in my corner, my arms raised. I had defended my light heavyweight title. Left a Cuban kid on the canvas.

The paper was reporting that I might box again.

Say I do go back to fighting, it will be because I miss hitting and outsmarting people. Your opponent, you spin him and spin him and spin him. You like to fly in the face of all the odds and go against all the king's wisdom and hook with a hooker. You keep yours short and maintain the angles. I like getting in your face, boxing circles around some guy calls himself The Barbarian or Spider. Fighting again, if I did, it would be because I wanted it.

Ginger wagged her tongue at Gus, and he turned so he could see me and said, "Your sister, the high-school graduate, the adult."

I said, "Eyes on the road, Gus."

Ginger said to him, "Don't talk like I'm not here."

Gus, in the rearview, looked to the heavens.

"I do what I like," Ginger said.

"Set your hair on fire and jump up and down," Gus said, and he turned left and pulled into the doctor's. He said, "You see me stopping you?"

She said, "Like you could." Snyder got her door open, and she bolted.

We were supposed to be let right in, but Gus's intern buddy ran into a snag. In the waiting room, across from us, cutting glares at Gus and his cell phone, a woman sat next to an old lady in a wheelchair, the two of them rehashing their morning. How it screwed itself to the floor and refused to go right. How the grandkids slept over. One boy they called Me Not. It didn't take a genius to figure that name out. Me Not refused to do what Me Not said no to. Ginger squirmed at her end of a leather couch. Snyder worked at disappearing, and Gus yakked into his cell phone. The old lady, I picked up, was the woman's mother. She couldn't hear a word her daughter was saying, and it was clear the daughter didn't have enough of what it took to repeat the details.

Ginger had hold of her tongue like she was trying to dislodge it from her mouth, and she was saying to Snyder, "It's like some jerk's yanked it and won't let go." She sounded retarded. She made noises like she was chewing muscle.

Gus looked past his phone. "For God's sake," Gus said to Ginger. "No one is going to ask you to sing. You're not auditioning."

Ginger narrowed her eyes at him, and he went back to the cell phone he was talking into. The waiting room was crowded, and Gus was loud, was wheeling and dealing with a crony about a sailboat Gus was buying from the guy. Gus needed to tone it down, so I asked him to.

He said, "What? It's not company we're sitting with. It's strangers," and went back to his call. My second try, he said, "You know these people?" He waved at the other patients. He said, "What, you made friends? I'm offending your new buddies?"

I said, "You're not in your car."

"Also," he said, "it ain't 1950. We have the technology. We use it."

I gave up.

You saw in the old lady what she had been at twenty, twenty-five, thirty, forty. Beautiful. Refined. Your artist's picture of grace. She had knocked men's *and* women's socks off. Such elegance. Dignity.

A nurse came out and stooped so she was real close to the old gal's ear, where she said, "They tell me you're going to be a three-century woman." Close as she was to her, she talked loud. Even Gus glanced up from his call. The nurse fiddled loose the wheelchair's brake and rolled the lady forward a couple of inches. Then back and forth. "Come the new year, I'm told," the nurse said.

The old lady said, "You would bring that up." Not out of malice. More matter of fact.

"It's worthy of celebration," the nurse said. "How many people can say they've accomplished that?"

The lady said, "You say so."

The nurse said, "Well, fingers crossed."

The lady said, "I have a name too."

"You're Mrs. Cabott."

"Lucille," the lady said. "Lucy."

The nurse wheeled this angel toward the examining rooms, the daughter at her side, watching out for her mother's feet and the way they sat sideways on the wheelchair foot rests.

———

Ginger fought the internist about the barbell until he gave up. Her argument was the swelling was a fluke. She could count on her one hand three dozen pierced friends. Tongues, but also eyebrows, navels, foreskins, lips, cheeks, nipples, dicks themselves. Some of these fools got infections in the worst places but *they* didn't remove the hardware. Doctors treated the problem. "You behind in your journal reading?" she said to Gus's pal.

His argument was he wasn't going to waste his time arguing with her. He cleaned up the tongue and wrote a prescription.

She kept the piercing.

On our way out, the internist handed Gus the name of another doctor. Best Ginger go there if she needed more treatment. He had done what he could.

––––––––

That evening, back at Gus's, my dad poured Scotch for him and juice for me, and we hauled our drinks down to the pool where Ginger lay on a towel. Drinks, snacks, Ginger, me and him—Gus's idea of a family dinner. We sat, and she got up and walked toward the house, bad-mouthing us, saying, "It's a big yard, we don't need to cluster."

"Someone pays the fiddler," Gus said to her back. "Chew on reality for five minutes."

I told him he sounded stupid, and he agreed. "Still," he said, "you show me a seventeen-year-old who's an actual human person, who has feelings that extend beyond one foot of their own body."

"She's almost eighteen and she's a smart kid," I said.

Gus said, "Sure, she's on the cusp of adulthood."

She was. She and Snyder were moving to Salt Lake City in a couple of months. Supposedly there was something complicated so they weren't getting married at this point. Real or imagined, we didn't know. The decision was Ginger's, not Snyder's. Gus learned quickly to shut up about this particular issue. Snyder was ready for a ceremony, the cake, buying himself a tuxedo. It was Ginger who decided they would live together. You pushed her at all, and her explanation stunk when you put it under the gun. It had to do with everything from freedom and babies to the right and wrong way to open an umbrella. Snyder had a full-ride scholarship to the University of Utah. Basketball—the kid had the tools. Ginger's room was already half empty. There were boxes stacked in Gus's garage and lining his hallway.

Gus raised his Scotch so the setting sun backlit it, and he said to me, "I drink to old men saying stupid things." From where we sat we could see the heart of Las Vegas, the Strip, even Fremont Street. A soft violet haze lay on the city.

I raised my drink and said, "To good mental health, Gus."

"By the by," Gus said.

———————

I was up on a roof, trimming a shingle I was about to fit to a pipe flange, and I heard a car stop out front. A quiet neighborhood, a buddy's house, a pal I was doing a favor for. He had some bad shingling done, and the crook who did the job was now a phone number that was no longer in service. The car pulling to the curb had to be Snyder. Gus had sent him to talk to me. From below, on the driveway, Snyder called to me, and I walked to the edge of the roof and told him there was a ladder out back.

"Gus told me I'd find you here," he said.

I suggested he climb up. We could talk on the roof.

From where he stood, he said, "I was thinking lunch. I buy."

"Where's that, McDonald's?"

"Denny's? Around the corner."

I asked him to give me five minutes and went back and trimmed the shingle snug to the collar, then cemented it. Tough job here was going to be getting under the air conditioner. I told my buddy he ought to get the unit off the roof. I would have to use a hand-pumped jack and planking. Then, when I was done, reset the braces.

I found Snyder sitting sideways in his car, door open, thump thump music on. He stood and shook my hand. "I appreciate this," he said. "You got work to do, I know."

It had cost Gus juice but he got Snyder summer work on the Strip, nights because Snyder spent his afternoons playing basketball at UNLV, pick-up games with university players and some pros who drifted into town. Something went wrong on the job. A week ago, Gus got a phone call from a shift boss. The man gave no details. He didn't want to be specific on the record. He said, "Have a conversation with him."

"About?" Gus said.

The man said, "You'll come to understand."

Gus sent Snyder to me. "He'll lie if I talk to him," Gus said.

Not true. I couldn't see Snyder lying and told Gus so. It wasn't in the kid not to be square with you. Snyder grew up in Cleveland, Ohio, mostly on the streets, in gyms, on ball fields. He could throw a baseball through a brick wall and played scratch golf. His father's brother and the guy's wife raised him in Las Vegas. We hadn't heard the story behind that. Why they brought him here. Where the parents were. Dead? Alive? Ginger didn't even know. What I had come to understand was that Snyder was solid and looked you in the eye.

Headed for lunch, we talked basketball, Snyder's range, his left hand next to his right hand, the way he posted himself. I had been okay myself, starting junior and senior years in high school. Could have gone on, I was told, but lost my love for the game and quit—turned to boxing. Put my quick hands and nifty footwork to a different purpose. Mastered a new dance step. The rumble, as they say. You learn, under the basket, taking the ball to the hoop, not to blink, not to close your eyes. Such knowledge serves a boxer well. You've probably heard tape of Ali himself on that particular subject.

––––––––––

We took a booth, and Snyder said, "So, you going to fight?" I had directed him to an Italian place off Paradise Road. *Forget Denny's* was my message. You don't want to be cruised by hookers in broad daylight on your walk through the parking lot. Snyder ordered pizza.

I said, "Pizza?"

He shrugged.

Truly a waste of cuisine. Eighteen years old is eighteen years old. Taste, I supposed, if it comes, comes later.

I told him my fighting or not fighting was up in the air.

"You want to?" Snyder said.

Caught me off guard. No one else was asking that question. All the talk had been about money. About potential draw. Everything was a matter for negotiation. There was a Las Vegas kid who needed a quality match-up before a title fight. The hype was it was the boxer, him, versus the puncher, me, which showed how short memories can be. Sure, I hit like a car wreck, could go toe to toe, but could also dance like ballet if that was how you wanted to go about it. *Would I take the kid on?*, was all anyone cared to know.

I said, "Best question I've heard."

He said, "It's the only one needs answering, isn't it?"

I told him he was wise beyond his years.

"Snot-nosed is what I'm hearing," he said. "Everybody is telling me I'm one more dumb kid on the block."

My cue. Our pizza had arrived, and I said to Snyder, "You're good company, but I'm wondering, why did Gus send you to me?"

"I owe him gratitude for the job," he said.

"I'm eating pizza so you can tell me that?"

"Sort of. To show respect."

I said, "Gus doesn't keep accounts."

Snyder wasn't touching the food, so I took a slice of pizza and he followed suit. The kid was thinking, the wheels spinning. "They say that about Gus," Snyder said. "I'm told there are no strings attached with him."

"It's how he does business."

He used a fork to eat his pizza. I said, "Now a grudge, that's a fish of a different color. Those he holds onto like counterfeit coin."

Snyder said, "Do you know what he's been told about me?"

I said, "Someone called Gus. Someone said to have a talk with you."

Snyder shucked his head.

I said, "Gus asked me to do the honors."

All Snyder could do was study his food.

"Help me out here," I said. "What's going on?"

Turned out he got greedy, was supposed to pool his tokes at work, but another kid—a punk who called himself Smoke—showed Snyder how easy it was to pocket a percentage. Smoke convinced him it was assumed. Everybody did it. In fact, you didn't, you were a chump. You became suspect. Word spread you could be a stoolie or you could be too much the greenhorn. Smoke, Snyder said, was a thief too. Stole wallets, purses. He had a band of accomplices. Their m.o. was distract the slot machine players and swipe. He pimped a couple of teenage girls who hadn't yet learned that the girls don't need a manager in Las Vegas. Snyder swore to me he was clear of the outright stealing and the pimping. Smoke tried to recruit him, and Snyder flat out turned him down.

There had to be more. A hand in the toke pool would be taken care of by the men Snyder worked with. No one would call Gus about it. The men he worked with didn't care if Snyder was tall and could shoot a basketball. He was going to college. Big Fucking Deal. He might end up on television, maybe sign with the Lakers some day. BFD. He could shoot the three. BFD. The marvel of it meant nothing to them. He was a teenager taking money out of their pockets. They would handle it.

Gus would not be called about petty theft, about a kid getting himself in a jam.

"There's more," I said.

Snyder, forking his pizza, admitted drugs.

"Selling?" I said.

He said, "A little is all."

"For Smoke?"

"Yeah."

"You take a percentage?"

"Delivery money is all."

"You doing drugs?"

"Some."

"You're an athlete."

He had nothing to say.

"Walk away," I said. "From the job. From Smoke. From the money." It wasn't a suggestion I was making, and I was telling him to turn his back on fifteen, twenty thousand dollars legit, which was the paycheck and tips he earned straight up from the job Gus had gotten him, money he would need for school. Who knows how much was involved in the drug dealing. My guess was it was penny-ante, which could seem like big bucks to an eighteen-year-old.

"Can I?" he said, and I said, "You already have."

"Walk?" he said. "Just like that?"

"Just like that," I said. "Walk away."

"You'll tell Gus?"

"It will be taken care of."

———

Plugg was quoted in Sunday's *Sports*, and there was another photo of me. This one of me in street clothes. I was in a ring, a prefight parade of the celebrities. *WE'LL BE THERE*, this Sunday's caption said.

Ginger wandered down to where I was sitting by Gus's pool. Earlier, when I arrived, she let me in the house, was sitting on the front porch, like the potted cactus at her side was her best friend, and I asked her about her tongue. Her answer was to wag it at me, that barbell flying. She told me Snyder told her what I asked him to do.

I said, "Asked?" and got, in return, the finger from her.

Now, here by the pool, she knocked off her flip-flops and said, "Any ideas what we'll do for money?"

Like what happened was my fault.

"You taking your antibiotics?" I said.

Eye for an eye, she ignored me, so I went back to the paper. She laid out her towel and set lotions on a patio table. "You mind if I take off my top?" she said.

I told her to grow up.

"So you don't, is that what you're admitting?" she said.

I said, "Save your tits for someone who wants to see them."

She sat on her towel and said, "I might do that. I'm thinking about dancing on the Strip. You know, like *Enter the Night*. Topless." She screwed the lid off a bottle and said, "We'll be needing the money."

"You can dance?" I said. She didn't unless you counted whatever it was kids did for their sock hops here at the end of the twentieth century.

"I can learn," she said. "We got muscles and coordination, jocks all the way through the family." She rubbed lotion up and down her arms. "You'd think I'd have some abilities."

I said, "It doesn't work that way."

"Meaning?"

"You go in a dancer. They don't teach you."

"Plugg taught you."

"Different world."

She lay on her stomach. Reached back and undid her top. She said, "I'll call myself Nell."

"Nell the topless dancer?"

"Why not?"

"Sounds like a donkey's name."

"All the better."

A man Ginger didn't know had been sending her gifts and

flowers at Gus's funeral home where she worked part-time. Snyder had told me about it. So I asked her what was going on, and she said, "Maybe I'll call it off with Snyder."

"Because you think he clued me in?"

"The boy's a tattletale."

Tattletale or not, it seemed to me that you didn't mess around with gifts from strangers. I said, "What do you know about this guy?"

"It's not what you think," she said.

"Tell me about it."

The gift-sender was from L.A. She met him when he came to Las Vegas to bury his sister. He grew up here, moved to L.A. to attend UCLA, and stayed in California. Gus knew the family. He had buried the man's parents ten years ago. The Millers. They crashed in a piper cub on a flight from Las Vegas to Reno. The gift man himself was Albert Jay Miller. Ginger called him Jay, Albert being the father's name. Ginger did Jay's paperwork, and a week later flowers came. Then an antique, a tin horse. She had mentioned she liked to ride. Next, a phone call. Could he take her to lunch? He was coming to town, had to iron out his sister's estate. What did she think? Sure. She didn't tell Snyder about the lunch. She told him only about the gifts and the flowers. She convinced Snyder she was irked by all of it. Miffed. Annoyed. Two weeks later Jay took her to dinner, the Renoir bistro at the Mirage. They caught Wayne Newton at the Sands. Jay wanted to fly Ginger to L.A., Marina del Rey. He described for her Venice Beach and its lunatics. "More than worth the trip," he said. There was Santa Monica Pier and its Ferris wheel way out over the ocean. He offered a sail on his boat and mailed her a picture of it. He sent her a postcard of the beach front. *My Place*, he wrote, an arrow pointing to the third floor of what looked like a condo. He sent a second post card—a pier shaped like a banjo extending into the Pacific, the circular end farthest out, the photo shot from the air. Another arrow pointed to the outer rim. One word, *Me!*

You had to like the guy. He had stepped out of a Bob Hope film.

I said, "So you're seventeen and he's what?"

"I'll be eighteen before you know it."

"Whatever."

"Not to worry, Tommy," she said. "I carry pepper spray."

———

What happened the day after Ginger took off to spend a week with Jay Miller was an incident I wanted to tell her and Snyder about. Thought I would invite them to lunch when she got home. Ask them to sit across from me. It would be like telling them an Uncle Stuck story. Here's one for you. Uncle Stuck grew up in southern Utah, so he worked as an extra in westerns. He met John Wayne. He shook Duke's hand. You may have seen Uncle Stuck playing an Indian. He and fifty other extras, they're in some make-up person's idea of war paint, and, bareback, they ride pintos and buckskins out to the edge of a ridge. This is black-and-white late-fifties filming. They come charging toward the camera, rein their horses to a halt, fit arrows to bows they've been issued by the prop people, and let the arrows fly. Of course, there's nothing out there where they're aiming. No cavalry. No settlers. Nothing. Except desert, rocks, creosote bush. The arrows fall to the ground. You see the movie, and those arrows are lethal. You watch soldiers bite the dust. You see a close-up, and you see fear in their eyes.

Uncle Stuck—rest his soul—he sat you down and he told you that story. And others.

Trust me, a human voice, a story—they can help.

I would be their Uncle Stuck. Snyder and Ginger, I would invite them to lunch. I would pay for the meal and say, "You didn't know Uncle Stuck, but let me tell you what happened."

———

Gus had given Ginger his blessing for the trip. "Like it makes a difference," she said to him. "Like you can stop me." Jay Miller hadn't come in through a window or parked around the block and asked Ginger to hop the back fence. He phoned Gus. He asked him to meet for a drink. He said, "I'm a nice guy." From L.A., he mailed Ginger a grain of rice with her name on it. It came in a box big enough for a small TV, included was a magnifying glass, not some cheap-ass hand-held thing, but a beauty you set up, one you bolted to a table—a solid base, a neck you bent, big lens. Hefty. Belonged in a lab. You looked through it, and there was her name inscribed on a grain of rice. Neat printing. *Ginger*.

Albert Jay Miller had a sixth sense for what constituted a gift.

What happened at the house—the story I wanted to tell Ginger and Snyder over lunch—was that I was, late one afternoon, working my own roof and waiting on Snyder again. Me, and roofs, and Snyder—getting to be a habit. I was fixing up my own house so I could feel good about selling it. The plan was I was moving back in with Jane and our baby boy Hector. Snyder asked to lay some tile for me, see if he could earn money working roofs. Just mornings. His request, but I didn't think it was smart. All the climbing and squatting robbed you of your legs, and if you don't have legs, you don't have a jumper. Roofing exhausted you, which is why I did it. You had to think a little, but mostly it was physical. It was under the sun. It was off the ground, and there was air all around you.

So here's the story. I was in the garage, checking clay tiles, and an air conditioner guy I had called pulled into the driveway. Took him ten minutes to settle his business in his van and climb out. A real Sluggo. Bald and fat like a landslide. Football player's neck, and he walked on the sides of his feet. I shook his hand, and he said, "You *the* Tommy Rooke?" He was reading from his work order. Pen out, clicked to write.

I told him I thought I was.

"Yeah," he said. He shook his head.

I had to give him credit. He didn't set himself and act like he was going to box. He said, "I saw you once. You killed the other guy." He gave me his hand. "Kennedy," he said, "like the president, only it's my first name."

We shook. "Jiggs," he said. "Kennedy Jiggs."

I walked him around the side of the house and was unlocking the gate when he said, "You don't see morning glories open this time of day."

To my left, there were five flowers looking like ballerinas, white, yellow centers exactly like tiny buttons, on a vine that climbed the fence where it met the gate. The leaves were perfect hearts, green Valentines. Jane—before she was my ex—she planted them. For hours, she sat at the kitchen table one morning and filed a notch in each seed. Then she put all of them in the ground.

Sluggo reached for a bloom, then stopped. He said, "This late in the day they're rolled up tighter than a cigarette. You got a rare thing happening here."

I looked at this guy and wanted to hug him. You're hunting, always, for one solid reason to listen to all the talking going on. Here he was. I ushered him through the gate.

God—I mean, think about it—within five feet of me was one hell of a human being. Next he would be speaking Russian. I would end up in over my head, him wanting to discuss the woody plants of Ohio and asking me to name the parts of the inner ear. He would lay out one of those story problems for me—suppose an airplane leaves Washington, D.C., at 3:00 A.M. and there is a headwind of fifty miles an hour—or he would ask me an essay question. What did I think was of greater significance, truth or error? What if Robert E. Lee had not surrendered, how would that have affected the growing of corn in Iowa or our daily vocabulary? Kennedy Jiggs, he would give me advice. If you are ever bitten by a snake, kill it and take it to the hospital with you. He would forecast the weather for the next week and test me on unusual cloud formations. Did I, he would want to know, believe in luck? He would ask me to explain folly's place in our daily lives.

I stood by, and he removed the side panel of the air conditioner. He looked at the roof and said, "This where you hang your hat?"

"For a while yet," I said. "I'm selling."

He was looking at my knee pads, my roofer's hatchet. We skirted two ladders getting to where we were. He said, "You do your own work?"

I told him I did.

"You're rich, right?" he said. "All those fights? You got to be rolling in it."

I said, "You want a Coke?"

He didn't. "I get it," he said. "I'm the help."

I said, "So am I."

"Keep your secrets," he said.

I didn't need his permission.

———

Out front Snyder was stepping from a gray Lincoln, and a guy who, haircut to zippered shoes, could only be Smoke came free-wheeling around the front end.

"Smoke here gave me a ride," Snyder said.

I waited on them.

Snyder, ushering Smoke up the driveway, said, "He wants to shake your hand. He's telling me not even Foreman had your power."

Smoke did what a man who called himself Smoke would do. He flashed a grin you could have used to help you see in a dark hallway, and he crouched, shadowboxed. This joker hadn't seen me fight. Not once. You got to hate the police for their profiling, but here was a man who made you understand the basic principles behind such bias and appreciate its value to civilized society.

Me, I can be agreeable. I took Smoke's hand and held on. I said, "Smoke? You give that nom de plume to yourself?"

"I roll my own," he said.

I turned to Snyder and said, "What part of walk away did you not understand?"

Produced in Smoke more of what you would have expected. Mock puzzlement. You can imagine the gestures. The tilt of the head. His wink. His smirk. He said, "Man—"

And, because I still held the fool's handshake, I said, "Don't talk, Mr. Smoke." I gave him my own wink and a squeeze. Then let go and said to Snyder, "You came to put down some tile, did you?"

Snyder dropped his own mooncalf's grin, and Smoke said, "Man, you got—"

"Mr. Smoke," I said. "Don't talk. Silence is golden."

I walked over to the driver's side of the Lincoln, opened the door, and—he had tagged along—said, "Go."

He climbed in, buzzed his window, said, "You humiliate a—"

I said, "Don't talk, Mr. Smoke."

I recommend a roof if you need to sit and rewrap your thinking. Your own roof, or, even better, a stranger's. First, somehow—say it's 110 degrees, it don't matter—there is always a breeze. Second, is perspective. You can see two, three streets over. Third, if you jumped or fell, what damage would you do? Break an ankle? Get a few bruises? Not enough people get to a place where they can take a look around. Unscramble. A roof would be a good spot to hold a barbecue, if you could keep the drinkers from toppling off.

Find a roof. Take a seat. Count your blessings.

I had already stripped the tile from mine, and I repaired the deck and installed the flashing at the eaves, but I walked Snyder through the basics. Showed him what to do. Hands-on is the only way to go about life. He wanted work, he would need to work. I was using thirty-pound felt, two layers. We started at the corner rake and eaves and began rolling and stapling. I taught him to eyeball the seventeen inches of overlap course after course. We nailed down the lathing. This job also required battens. There was one pitch at the south end where we had to use roof jacks, and Snyder's long legs kept cramping. We were using roofer's hatchets to drive the nails, and he nicked his hands, once bad enough I had to put tape on the cut. But the kid didn't quit.

Few hours passed, and me and Snyder were sitting next to the chimney. We had finished capping and putting in rake tiles. I showed him how to work a ridge at the same time you lay the deck. You don't, and you're going to crack tile walking on it, which is a bitch circumstance to be avoided.

Snyder made a dinner run for us, and we were chasing double cheeseburgers with Gatorade. You couldn't see us from the street. I figured Ginger had something to do with his being here. Roofing could pay some bills, but Snyder wasn't going to be needing a job. He would put in his time at Utah and go early in the NBA draft. First round if he got some real coaching. The kid was that good.

Next up would be me showing him how to counterflash a valley.

We—Gus, actually—had gotten a postcard from Ginger. She was staying in L.A. a second week. Maybe longer.

I didn't know if Snyder knew that, and I didn't want to bring it up.

"Met an old lady," I said, "who, when the year 2000 rolls around, will have lived in three centuries."

He said, "My aunt was like that."

"Your aunt was born in the 1800s?"

"No, but, you know, smart. Like she'd been on the earth for a longer time than most people and had survived war and other crap," he said. "A lady who cut through the bullshit."

"I get it," I said.

"You could believe she knew those geniuses you learn about in history books. Not the ones who ran the country, but like the guy who invented the cotton gin or how to make a train go. You know, the steam engine. Or even farther back, the people who figured out what plants you can eat and not die from. She'd have been the lady who discovered you can cook an egg over a fire."

Made me think about the air conditioner guy and the morning glories, so I told Snyder about the man. We had heard him drive off earlier. "Sure, like that," Snyder said. "She knew what you needed to know to keep yourself alive."

"Your aunt would have filed the seeds before she put them in the ground," I said.

"And she'd know how deep to plant them."

A plane, low on the horizon, was approaching McCarran. Wind from the north.

Snyder asked about me and Jane. He wondered why we had split up. "Not something I talk about," I said. "My fault all the way. I'm a careless man."

He said, "But you're getting married again."

"We're planning to."

"Your boy Hector part of the reason."

"It's a package deal."

"Sure."

I said, "You and Ginger, what's up?"

He said, "You tell me?"

Her postcard to Gus said she mailed sand home. She collected it from Muscle Beach. *Don't lose it,* she wrote to Gus.

I said to Snyder, "She's being seventeen."

He said, "Yeah. Me too, only I got almost a year on her."

I said, "Snyder, you want more advice?"

"Like before?" he said.

I said, "Exactly like before. Only you don't have to listen this time. I'm butting in." He turned to look at me, and he had to squint, the sun was that low. The breeze cooled us. "Walk away again," I said. "Pack your bags and get yourself to Salt Lake. Find a gym and work on your left hand."

"Like with Smoke," he said, and I said, "Like with Smoke. Go."

"Leave Ginger here?"

I said, "She's not here." Saw that register. Said, "Go. If she follows, she follows."

She wouldn't. Not on her life.

Snyder studied the roof between his legs. He reboxed his burger and set it next to his Gatorade like he was going to get to his feet right this second and take off.

I said, "Walk."

He said, "You telling me this for my sake or for Ginger's sake?"

I said, "Does it matter?"

"Probably not," he said.

It was then I thought about showing him the postcard she sent Gus. We could drive over to my dad's, and Snyder could see her words with his own eyes. She wrote, *Having the time of my life. Sun. Ocean. Mr. Jay Miller.* On the front was the ocean, swimmers, surfers, sunbathers. Then one of those arrows and the word *us.*

Snyder said, "It's what my aunt would tell me, isn't it?"

"Her and that three-century lady," I said. "And throw in the air conditioner guy. It would be a choir. Plus me. A quartet, I guess. The four of us singing, *walk away. Walk away.*"

It was then I saw the kid smile. He had a jumper and he had his smarts. He would do all right. So I let him have it. Added Uncle Stuck to our singers, and I told him an Uncle Stuck story, the one that had to do with a bar in Mississippi and a drummer and a pair of pants, the story that, if you listened closely, was really about swallowing the prayers you wish you had the balls to speak out loud in a church. Its theme was redemption. Uncle Stuck finished a story, and he lit a Kool, and he made you pay attention. You were instantly wiser.

———

At the rakes, west side of the house, Snyder gone—to pack, I hoped. Maybe just to shoot hoops at Gus's, out back by the pool, and wait for Ginger. I pictured him putting up shot after shot, day after day, long after dark, under the outdoor lights, until Ginger got home from L.A. Then they talk for a simple and straightforward five minutes, and next he is gone. He becomes a star. Ginger, she moves on from Mr. Jay Miller. Hell, you can buy a man for a goat in some countries. I was working the fascia, using nails to secure an overlap and then repositioning the tiles themselves. There was one trouble spot where roof intruded on roof, where I needed to redo the flashing. Then I would feel good about putting the place on the market.

I was sizing tile with a hatchet, and the phone kept ringing. No patience at all. Ten rings, then a five-minute break. Fourth time, I climbed down and grabbed the cordless. Got there too late, but took the phone with me. I was about out the door, and it rang, Gus on the other end. "Tommy, Tommy," he said, "I'm calling to tell you that I'm eating crow."

I said, "How's that, Gus?"

He said, "Put your sunglasses on."

I told him I was wearing a pair.

He said, "Get the video camera ready."

I told him it was loaded and I already checked the battery.

"I'm on the Boulder Highway," he said. "I'm the old guy in the Cadillac. Top down. The wind is blowing what hair I've got left."

I said, "The camera's rolling, Gus."

"Yeah," he said, "get an angle and shoot this."

I heard traffic the way you can when the person on the other end of the line is in a car on a cell phone. I knew how wide and solid and blue the sky was because I had stepped out on my patio, and Gus and me, we were both living under the same one.

A coil of fire, a coil of snow, and the Holy One created both the heaven and the earth, so Carl T. Plugg once told me.

Gus said, "This old guy you're talking to is at the wheel of his mile-long red Cadillac—one like those the Hollywood moguls drive—and your dad's pulling a boat twice that size. Car's red and white. It's swoopy. You've seen what I'm talking about with those fins on the back. This car would give you a hard-on. It's got those 1950s white walls for tires. The boat is white. You can see from five miles away it's a sail boat. All the rigging and whatever they call it."

"Fore and aft."

"Sure," he said.

"Portside."

Through the phone, I heard a horn honk, and Gus said, "I'm getting hustled by gorgeous blondes."

"Gus," I said, "I don't think you're eating crow is the way to put it. I think you're in the catbird seat."

He said, "That's what it is. I'm eating the canary."

I could tell he had stopped, and I asked him where he was. He said he was headed for Lake Mead. He was meeting some people who could show him his fore from his aft.

I said, "Gus, you might want to stop by sometime."

Do you remember what I said about going against all the best advice and hooking with a hooker? About spin and spin and spin? About beating your opponent's left with your right? Don't just counterpunch. React. React.

I said to my dad, "Back here in the city, your house is burning down."

"What are you telling me, Tommy?"

"Gus, I don't have to spell it out for you."

Got back silence. He might have shut down his cell phone, but I thought I was still hearing traffic. Then he said, "Your mother never wanted a boat, Tommy."

My first thought was, *grow up, Gus*. Then, *schmuck*, which I didn't say. I didn't express what I was thinking.

He said, "You live forty minutes from the largest manmade lake in the whole frigging world, and you don't own a boat? How is that a way to live a life?"

I said, "I can't imagine she stopped you, Gus."

"You explain it then," Gus said.

"It's not the point."

"You ever see the ocean, Tommy?" Gus said. "Where Ginger is this minute you and I are talking in. I don't recall if we took you. Edna and I, did we? Drive you to California? Show you the Pacific? You'd remember if we did."

I said, "I'm talking about Ginger, Gus."

"I know about Ginger."

I thought I heard him guzzle something. Smack his lips. Then he said, "Ginger is at the beach while we're talking here. She's staring at the ocean. She is, and I'm quoting here, having the time of her life."

"She's going to dance topless."

"So she says."

"She told you?"

"It's a ploy. It's a seventeen-year-old talking." He hollered to someone from his car. Grinned, I knew, like a floodlight. He said to me, "We padlock her in her room, and we drill two big holes in the door shoulder high, and from the other side we tell her to reach through. We make another hole so she can see us. We convince her a surprise is coming her way. We give her something big and expensive. Say diamonds the size of baseballs. Soccer balls. Basketballs. One for each hand. So big she can't pull them through the holes. So there she is. Sitting in her room, hands through the door, and she's holding her diamonds. This is what you want?"

I said, "That's stupid. What you're saying doesn't make sense."

"It makes as much sense as she makes."

"You're willing to bet on that?"

"Ginger says a lot of things. Your sister is seventeen going on twelve. You want her to marry the basketball boy, ruin both of their lives—is that the future you see?"

I said, "That's not the issue." I heard Gus honk. Whoop. I pictured the wave he was giving someone. "Gus," I said, "You still have a daughter to raise."

"You don't have to tell me my business."

"It's family business," I said.

Which was when he told me I sounded like my mother, and I said, "Your wife, is that who you mean?"

He said, "My wife, your mother."

I imagined him flip-flopping his hand. Wife. Mother. I got out, *Edna*, and he said, "Yeah, well, you kids, both of you, you got her mouth. Ginger, she's the spitting image of your mother, right down to the way she butters her rolls."

The phone went dead.

Only I swear I could still hear him, Gus at the wheel of the Cadillac, him and the boat gliding through the turn in the road where you first see the lake, Gus big as life saying, "Having a good time ain't a felony, Tommy."

Five Times
for Disorderly
Conduct

Dinner, but not a dinner party. Tommy
Rooke's father, Gus, won't grant it that status. Twelve guests is all.
Interested folk is how Gus describes them. The get-together is at
Gus's place near Red Rock. Tommy invited and accounted for—sum-
moned, requested, dragooned, eventually, he figures, to be ambushed
in this box canyon. He's the focus of a certain kind of calculated attention. Tommy is attired, tuxedoed, a red carnation in his lapel, in
honor—no one, as far as he can tell, has caught on—of Dino, of Dean
Martin. Three A.M. this morning, Tommy watched *Oceans 11* on TV,
a big screen at Jane's, Dino's cool cooler than the others all put together. There's half a joke going around town, one that begins, *What
do you call a rat pack if all the rats are dead?* and there's a radio contest for the punch line, $1000 cash to the winner. Sinatra's gone.
Sammy Davis Jr. is gone. Who's left? Joey Bishop? He got by on his
dry wit, but was marginal, was always the last call made.

Gus is hosting tonight, and these are Gus's friends, men and, on
their arms, third, fourth, and fifth wives, not as young as the number
twos were. The men are an enterprising lot, and this evening they
have one goal. They've come to talk Tommy back into the ring. They
want him to fight Eddie Jarret. They've got truckloads of money and
they've heard that fighters need backers. There was that Louisville
consortium behind Ali. The mob took care of Liston. Boxing's a different world today, only they don't know it. They're baby boomers in
Jaguars who want to know what it's like to live in a trailer park.
Their wives, women in their forties, are taut and fit. Their cheerful

dresses show off their workouts. These are women who lift free weights, who do yoga and Tae Bo and stair-step. They swim. Their hair is short or up. It's dark and highlighted. The dinner help, hired, is uppity and indifferent, is nipped and tucked and corseted. The food—Gus had the night catered—is humble chic and healthy. You want—he was told—stingy. Ascetic. Basic. There is a bean salad, cannellini beans, capers and pine nuts, and there is the watercress with blue cheese and pralines. There are mahimahi skewers and a pineapple mandarin sauce. There's a tomato soup. There is bass, Korean style, or salmon. There's a tuna-and-chickpea pasta. The wine, Ott Rosé, House of Burgundy, New York, New York. There is a red zinfandel. The talk is of Hollywood, who had what celebs for dinner when they were in town. There is talk of the city's aquifers—where's the water coming from when the taps run dry, when only dust flows through them? Is Las Vegas going to desalinate the ocean and pump it across the desert? Is the city going to buy up and divert the Colorado River? There is talk of the Rembrandts, Picassos, Van Goghs at Steve Wynn's Bellagio.

Tommy is one glass of wine the near side of surly. Drink handcuffs his soul, and has since he was thirteen. It queers his thinking. A minute ago, he heard from clear across the room, "Talk to Tommy, and he'll tell you." Gus at it. "He'll tell you how it works," Gus said. He is talking to a man in a chalk-white suit. The man's wife is looking over her shoulder. She's taller than her husband is. She could arm wrestle him to his knees. Gus says, "Tommy tells me you take away where your opponent wants to be. The ring is square, so you work it. You figure the angles and move and stick."

Boxing.

"The ring," Gus says, "is not a complicated puzzle."

Old timer, Tommy thinks, *can it.* The other side of every coin is a brawl. He polishes off his wine.

"Your prizefighter can be thought of as a mathematician," Gus says. He waves Tommy over. Tommy, sitting in the wingbacked chair he's asked to be buried in, recognizes in himself that heart of stone they say soldiers feel in foxholes. Darkness at noon—is that the phrase? Tommy's not drinking. His other self is. The one who recedes. He raises his empty glass to Gus, is saying, *Give me a minute. I need a refill.* He's filibustering.

Tommy's worse than a bad drunk. On that scale of one to ten he is, as the joke goes, an eleven. So he's quit, for the most part. Five times in his life he has been arrested, but not booked, for disorderly conduct. He was guilty. Had blood on his hands. Gus made phone calls, and his father's pals stepped in. Always he was loaded, was engaged in celebratory boozing, and he did some coke. This was years ago. He was a kid. Eighteen. Nineteen. The night would begin pleasant enough. A party. Tommy was funny. Clever. Witty. He was Cary Grant. He was Clark Gable. Out of the blue he used big words. He quoted people you wouldn't have believed he had read. Each time he had just won bouts. Tommy Rooke was establishing himself. There was his first amateur fight. Stopped by the referee. So Tommy drank to that. Got in a brawl. Then he won the Golden Gloves for the state of Nevada. What could he do but drink to that? The brawl followed. On to the pros, one of his knockouts, sixth round. He wore out some guy's midsection. Tommy hadn't yet hurt anyone beyond repair, so he did a string of coke followed by the brawl, the arrest, the phone calls. The argument was Tommy was a kid who would one day make the city proud to call him a hometown boy. Would it hurt to look the other way? To think of the big picture?

"Pleasantries is all I ask," Gus says. He has tracked Tommy down. They're in the bathroom off Gus's bedroom. It's big enough you could play catch in here.

Tommy swirls new wine in his glass.

"They talk, you listen," Gus says. "It's like Red Rover, Red Rover, send Tommy right over. You're playing a game, and you're under no obligation. Only you, on the other hand, can give your heart to it if you want."

"Gus," Tommy says. He's trying to put an end to the conversation, which he's not quite following. His brain's like a slot machine that won't stop.

"It's sport, is all," Gus says.

Gus seems to be talking boxing, but not really. What Tommy is sure of is tonight's question, which is, will Tommy unretire himself? He still works out. He spars. He trains like a demon. Not, though, like he's getting in the ring for real. That's another dimension. That's hell itself. It's ten notches up from what he's doing these days. There was talk months back of his fighting Auggie Sanchez, another Las

Vegas product. Hometown bombers throwing grenades at each other. Pronto bucks. Big money. Tommy nixed it.

"I didn't trick you into coming tonight," Gus says.

Tommy says, "No. You didn't. You can be trusted. You can go to your grave knowing you were up front with your boy."

Carl T. Plugg is here, but like he's undercover in the bushes. He did the behind-the-scenes work. The finagling. Plugg arranged lunch with Gus behind Tommy's back. You see, Gus never saw his boy fight, not even on film. Tommy's mother, Edna, didn't want to see her boy in the ring. An old story, sure. So Gus has no idea what it takes to earn a shot at the two titles Tommy never lost. Gus doesn't understand how the odds of Tommy getting to where he got you couldn't even calculate. He wants to see Tommy in the ring. Before, during the Sanchez fiasco, Plugg met with people who could make the fight happen. He wrote some checks and signed his name to his line on the agreements, saying he could guarantee Tommy's signature. In the end he lost money. Big chunks, he's hinted. So now, for Tommy, there is the guilt thrown in. There is Plugg's loss—money, prestige, his standing in his particular community. There is Gus, who never saw his boy fight. Edna has passed on. There's no wish left for Gus to honor. He can sit ringside and give and take important handshakes.

He says, "You can't say you didn't come here with your eyes wide open."

"Eyes wide open, it's how you throw a punch, Gus," Tommy says. Tommy places his glass of wine on the counter next to the sink and, because Gus likes to see it, he sets his hands like a fighter and says, "You're measuring him, and you watch your opponent's eyes, Gus." He stares holes through Gus, says, "Look at my eyes."

Gus glares back.

"The eyes," Tommy says, "they're a dead giveaway. They're telling you he's going to let one go."

"You're preaching to the choir," Gus says.

Tommy says, "They say Ali didn't blink like a normal person, the way we all do. So many times a minute, or is it a second? How many blinks is it?" Tommy knows how many, but can't get his brain to tee up the answer. He drops his hands and says, "Ali didn't blink at all."

"Talk never killed anyone," Gus says. "Negotiating is too strong a word for why these men are here. Tonight is chitchat. Tonight is friends and acquaintances getting together to see about possibilities."

"I know what you're saying," Tommy says. "You're dead wrong, though. You're on the wrong boat. Talk can be a killer."

"Sure." Gus shrugs. "It is. Can be. So is breathing."

Tommy says, "Bring them to me. I'm taking on all comers."

———

A woman, one of the servers, is sitting in one of Gus's guest rooms. Other than the bed there's only one spot to sit, an old desk chair, and she's taken it.

"I'm not stealing," she says to Tommy who, passing by, stalls in the doorway. "Just a short sit down." He noticed her out of the corner of his eye. Gus has gone for the interested parties, is collecting the men who have come to talk to Tommy. The woman is empty-handed except for a cigarette she hasn't lit. Her purse is on the bed nearby. It's one of those that clicks shut at the top. She's in black mostly, though there's a white crocheted collar and apron to her uniform. Her hair is twisted tight to her scalp so it looks like it's been hoed. The room she's sitting in is less inviting than a motel. There is nothing to steal. Gus lives like the mortician he is. No loose ends. Life is, for him, a package deal, especially since Edna died. Gus stripped the house, left it mostly bare. On one wall, behind the woman, there is an oil painting. It's an American primitive. Gus invites you to look at it and then quizzes you. "What's off about it?" he says. The boat on the river is what he's after you to see. It's obvious. It's too obvious. Everyone hunts for something not so clearly out of whack. Everyone wants to be smarter than earlier guesses. "The bridge," or "the field," they say. "They're big where they should be small." They say, "The perspective is ass-backwards." Gus says, "Okay. Okay. But look at the boat." He gets excited about the boat. His cheeks fill with air. He turns a little red. There is no way this boat, the way it's painted, could float.

Tommy finds a book of matches in a chest of drawers Gus must have bought at a yard sale. The wood is cheap. The drawers, wobbly, pull out and drop down. He lights the woman's cigarette.

She says, "I'm just waiting on the bathroom."

There are sounds from in there. Water running. A flush.

Tommy says, "I overheard one of the wives say the words *delimiting bourgeois heterosexuality,* and I ran for cover."

"Don't hit on me," the woman says. "These old white men, every one of them married—shits to beat the band, they are. Wherever I work, they think the help is easy pickings. You're black, you're working for minimum wage, you're easy."

Her accusations, as Tommy calculates them, are that Tommy is old. That Tommy is married. He will be again, to Jane, but isn't right this minute. This is a distinction, only now is not the time to argue it. This woman has more or less called Tommy a shit. Worse, she's declared herself the help.

"You know the advice about targets, don't you?" Tommy says.

The toilet flushes again. They hear a man say, "Towel?" There won't be one. Gus is in charge of the house, and the niceties have gone out the window.

"You're hitting on me," she says.

"Not here. Not now," Tommy says. "I'm not a stupid man. Your hint wasn't lost on me."

"Ha," she says. She looks around for an ashtray, and Tommy goes back into Gus's bathroom, fetches his wine glass, and hands it to her. "I'm tired is all," she says. She flicks ash, and it sticks to the inside of the glass." She says, "So tell me about targets."

"The story's lost its joke," Tommy says.

She says, "I bet it has a lesson to it." She makes an *O* for the smoke to escape her mouth. Her lips are crimson. She says, "They should print lessons on small pieces of paper and roll them up in tiny tubes you can buy in grocery stores there by the checkout stand. You know what I'm saying? Like your horoscope. You know, neither a borrower or a lender be. They could be categorized."

A young man comes out of the bathroom. His hair is freshly spiked. He is realigning his cummerbund. "All yours," he says to the woman. She taps ash, says to Tommy, "So tell me about targets. I'm all ears."

The young man slips by. Says to her, "You still need that ride?" Wink, wink in his voice. Like, *looks like you're taken care of for the evening.*

"Lame," she says to him. Tommy starts to follow the man out, and she says to him, "So you think I'm a target?"

"Hadn't occurred to me," Tommy says. "It was me making conversation, was all. Me holding up my end of the social structure. Being civilized."

"What's the punch line?"

"There isn't one."

"What's the point?"

"I was hitting on you."

"You were. Of course. The big question is, how hard?"

"The joke is they say you shoot first and paint the target on afterwards," Tommy says.

"I get it. You paint around where you've already hit."

"That's the idea."

"Ha," she says. "Bull's eye."

"Leave 'em laughing," Tommy says, and he starts to go.

She says, "You're who they're all talking about. You're the fighter."

"Once upon a time."

She gives him a hard look and stubs out the cigarette in the wine glass.

He says, "It's one of those to be or not to be questions."

"So you're the target tonight."

"I'm the target."

"Shoe's on the other foot," she says. She stands, gets into her purse, and hands him a card, saying, "You don't look married." Her name is Elise Winters. The card says she's a CPA.

He says, "You're an accountant?" His tone adds, *What are you doing serving dinners?*

She studies the wine glass, the cigarette butt, the mess she has made, and says, "Not quite. I've got one more semester of school." She clicks her purse shut, says, "Anyone can print up a card" and hands the glass to Tommy.

He says, "My ex-wife and I are talking. Thinking remarriage."

"You're one of the misunderstood."

"I am, by a mile."

"At least," she says. She stops at the bathroom door and says, "I'm a big fight fan."

———

Outside, on Gus's patio, dusk, Tommy can see the lights of the Las Vegas Strip. They're strung like a necklace. The afterglow of the sun intensifies the neon. Night is ten minutes away. A passenger plane is circling McCarran. Tommy hears his mother plain as day. Dead almost a year now Edna asks him to give Gus a break.

No problem, he tells her. Gus is in there hobnobbing. Tommy's out here. Tommy grabbed a bottle of Scotch and a coffee cup and sneaked out a side door. Avoided Gus and his posse. Vic is in the yard. Tommy has no treats and can offer only friendship, a pat on the head, a chuck under the chin, which is fine with the dog. Vic isn't greedy. They're pals. Tommy spins the cap off the Scotch and pours himself a drink. He sets the bottle at his feet and relaxes in a lounge chair. Sips from his cup.

Your father is proud of you, Edna says. Your father takes his hat off to you.

Tommy surveys his duds. He's not spilled anything on his clothes. His carnation flares. He raises his Scotch to Gus's being proud of him. He salutes pride. He toasts sloth. Envy. Gluttony. Spite. He would like to take his own hat off to himself. Tommy has always wanted to live when men wore hats. Not caps with those stupid bills on them. He means hats. Fedoras. Panamas. Hats made out of felt and beaver. He wants to wear three-piece suits and an overcoat, even in Las Vegas.

Edna tells Tommy she used to say to Gus, "Go. Go. Your boy is fighting. You go. What's stopping you?" Gus would say, "Plugg will phone. He'll tell us what round and what kind of a shot Tommy threw." She would say, "Go. Sit ringside with the men. Drink. Go." "Enough," he would say. "Plugg will let us know." It was how Gus honored her. He walked the streets. He smoked his cigars. He ran to the phone when it rang. KO, eighth round, Plugg would say. Gus stayed on the line, listened to Plugg's blow-by-blow account. Edna explains to Tommy she couldn't watch him hit other young boys. She says, "You hit like concrete. It was like having a chunk of it tossed at you." How does she know? "A mother knows," she says. "You hit like a train at a crossing." She says now Gus would like to see his boy fight. Would it cost Tommy so much? To please his father? To please her? "Everyone," she says, "they called me a fighter. I had gumption. Live up to my reputation."

"Are we toasting something?" one of the wives says. Tommy knows her name is Philadelphia. You can tell she has retiled herself in her early forties. She clunks the slider closed and steps onto the patio. Her longish skirt is crinkled and reaches her ankles. It's called a broomstick. You can roll them into the smallest ball for traveling. Tommy's bought one for Jane. Hers is blue-gray, plum. This woman's is exactly the color of the wine Tommy was drinking earlier. Vic barks. Once. *Harrf.*

Tommy says to the woman, "Do people really call you Philadelphia?"

She says, "My husband and people who aren't friends."

That equation doesn't quite equate. She's made a poem out of thin air and handed it to Tommy. She says, "They're arguing about whether you'll fight again or not. Your father's brokering."

Tommy says, "What about the celebs? The aquifers? The bourgeois heterosexuality?"

"Gus, my husband, and the man named Arthur," she says. "Your friend Plugg is involved." She extracts a cigarette from a pocket-sized handbag that's beaded and sparkles.

He raises his cup to her and says, "Scotch?"

"The trick," she says, and she hesitates so she can light her cigarette, then says, "when you're in New York, and you're alone on the street is to act crazy. To jabber and get that look in your eye. Or go so quiet you're scary."

The goddess of wisdom, she's giving Tommy a tip? To what end? She's advising him. On what? Tommy's not sure. She's appeared bearing this message.

He can give tit for tat. He says, "'A lady's nice. She has a heart. A lady don't blow on some other guy's dice.'"

He's sort of singing. Mixing Dino and Frank and Sammy.

Philadelphia sits at a glass-top table. She is spooled here in Gus's backyard, and Tommy is six feet away in his lounge chair, a bottle of Scotch within reach. She taps ash to the patio. The shrub lights wink on. "I haven't been to New York ever," she says. "I wouldn't know if crazy actually works."

"You're from Utah?" Tommy says.

"Salt Lake City."

"Not Mormon?" He nods at her smoke.

"Way back we are."

The slider opens, and out come Gus, Plugg, Philadelphia's husband, and Arthur, a schmuck who, if he were to get a nickname, would have to give it to himself. No one else would bother. It's a fact he buys jewelry and claims women gave it to him. The Saint Christopher's he wears is an example. There is his pinkie ring. Plugg hangs back, acts like he has only recently been released from the attic. His posture this evening has been that he's present and accounted for, but he's spending his time in corners and behind curtains where he can hear but not be noticed. As always, though, he is dapper. His thin mustache looks sharp. Philadelphia's husband is not like the men you see in Las Vegas newspapers. He lacks the sagebrush hair. The tan. The teeth.

Tommy stands, and Vic *harrfs*. There's trouble afoot and the dog's got it spotted. Then is not so sure. Vic surrenders and moseys past the pool, the water lighted from underneath, turquoise in the sunset.

The sun, about to exit, is a perfect red circle.

Everyone but Gus takes a seat at the table. Plugg sits and scoots his chair back. Philadelphia's husband and Arthur end up flanking Philadelphia. She is a corker. Her husband takes her cigarette and drops it to the cement.

"We're not here to bug you with fancy footwork," Gus says, and he dances some in front of Tommy.

"Sit," Tommy says. "Please."

Arthur slides in close, and Gus takes a seat next to him.

"The women having cigars in the parlor?" Tommy says.

Gus says, "There's some magic show on the TV everyone wants to see. The guy's going to make the United States disappear."

Vic stops halfway up the steps. A starling has caught the dog's eye. Now you see it, now you don't. Like a name there on the tip of your tongue you can't spit out, Vic's chasing days are over. His bags are packed. The dog's just outside the frame everyone else is in. Hour after hour he stands on the patio and *harrfs* for no good reason, except he's enjoying himself, like he's at a ball game.

"I'd like to talk footwork," Philadelphia's husband says to Tommy. He offers one of those three hundred-watt smiles. Tommy would like to tell him what a stupid line that is. That it wouldn't hold up in a 1950s B-movie. The man's name is Fogelsong. Everyone calls him R. K. He is a doctor, oncology at the University of Utah up in Salt Lake City. Fogelsong was the first person Gus called after Edna's diagnosis, and he confirmed the bad news. He walked her into and through her dying. R. K. was Edna's pal for years before she married Gus. "I saw you fight," Fogelsong says to Tommy.

Tommy says, "Box," because he wants to be annoying, to be a pain. To feel a little disorderly in his conduct. Tommy Rooke, Tommy Gun Rooke has been told he had an unusual run of bad luck. You hit like concrete, you hurt people. All the king's men can't do anything to help the injured. He left another fighter blind. He collapsed a guy's lung. He put a seventeen-year-old kid in the hospital, swelling of the brain. Today the kid walks and talks, but not the quite the way he used to. He's slower than he was. He drags one leg, moves like he's attached to strings. All of this Tommy did in front of thousands of people, the rich and the poor, in a twenty-by-twenty-foot square. National TV, millions watching. Only thing he didn't do was kill anybody. Not so far. Tommy was told it was unprecedented the damage he caused. Flukes. What he understands is that if he had done on the street what he did in the ring he would be in prison, and they would throw away the key.

"Your mother," Fogelsong says to Tommy, "she could talk the way you box."

So she's told Tommy.

"She could talk her way *out of a box*," Arthur says, his two bits not worth the breath.

It's all family lore. Tommy says, "She spoke her mind."

Gus says to Fogelsong, "She didn't see Tommy fight. She didn't go. I didn't go." He flip-flops his hands, says, "Didn't. Didn't." Morse code. Tappity-tap-tap. He says, "It was like a duet. Only different, if you get what I'm saying."

Tommy sits so he is directly across from Philadelphia. She won't look at him. He says to her, "So if they don't call you Philadelphia, what do they call you?"

She hunts for and finds a cigarette in her purse, and Fogelsong says, "Who doesn't call you Philadelphia?"

She says, "I don't want to have this conversation."

"You can talk your way out of it," Tommy says.

"You got yours from your mother," Fogelsong says to him.

"His footwork?" Gus says.

Arthur says, "His talking."

"Fighting's up here," Fogelsong says. He puts a finger to his temple. "It's mathematics my ass."

"You know these things as facts, do you?" Tommy says, and he gets out of his seat. This guy wants *noir*, Tommy can give him *noir*.

He circles behind the table and locates a deck of cards in a cabinet Gus keeps outside. "Shuffle. Riffle and cut," Tommy says to Gus. His father does. Tommy sits and says to Fogelsong, "We go two out of three. We go high card first. Then low card. Then high card." He stops Gus's shuffling, touches his wrist, and says, "You'll wear them out."

"They're offering only an undercard," Fogelsong says. "You and Jarret before he can fight Roy Jones Jr."

"He loses and he won't be getting that fight."

"That's a given."

"He sees me as a walkover?"

"You're a fight is all he knows."

Tommy says, "Sure."

"You have a reputation."

"But maybe I'm rusty, he's thinking?"

"You take to the bank one quarter what he takes."

"One half."

"Done," Fogelsong says.

Arthur says, "You fight at the MGM."

"Plugg's in," Tommy says. Plugg has been part of all this since day one. Tommy says, "That's not negotiable."

"Another given."

Tommy and Fogelsong shake. "You do the cutting," Tommy says to Gus. Then he says to Fogelsong, "Let's make it personal. You win, I fight. I win, what do you lose? What's the trade off?"

"It's business," Fogelsong says.

Tommy says, "No it's not. One faces facts."

"Pure and simple business. Like buying the inventory."

"I'm the inventory?"

"You're the inventory."

"One faces facts," Tommy says. He sips from his cup of Scotch, then says, "Off the record, then? What would you see as comparable? An arm? A leg?"

Arthur says, "You're exaggerating."

"Am I?" Tommy says.

"I have nothing in mind," Fogelsong says. "Top of that I'm not inspired to think of anything."

"You won't have to do it," Tommy says. "I won't hold you to it, whatever it is."

Fogelsong shakes his head.

"Imagine is all," Tommy says. "Imagine what your side of the bet would be. You have an imagination, right?"

"High card?" Gus says. "Who am I cutting for?"

Tommy defers to Fogelsong, and Gus cuts, one-handed, the cards stacked on the table. Shows the five of diamonds. "The downhill side of no luck at all," Fogelsong says.

Gus says, "Reshuffle?"

"Same shuffle," Tommy says. "Agreed?" Agreed. Gus cuts. Seven of clubs. Tommy's one up. Gus reshuffles, saying, "Low card this time—we're on the same page?"

Fogelsong and Tommy nod yes. Gus cuts for Fogelsong. Four of clubs. "Sweet as it can be," Fogelsong says. Through it all Philadelphia sits like she's frozen in a different time zone. No one has offered to light her cigarette. Gus shows the king of clubs for Tommy. It's one to one. Gus reshuffles and makes sure who is first is confirmed. It's Fogelsong. "High card this round?" Gus asks.

Agreed.

Tommy says to Fogelsong, "What if it cost you Philadelphia here, say?" He strikes a match for the lady and says to R. K., "I don't mean forever, but in some way."

"Insult me," Fogelsong says to Tommy. To his wife, he says, "Please." She withdraws her cigarette, and Tommy shakes the match out and says, "I'm curious is all. No insult intended."

"Your thinking is antiquated," Fogelsong says. "It's almost a new century, and you're talking like it's 1940. I don't own this woman. There's no trade off. I said, it's business is all."

Gus says, "Tom—"

"The last time I'm in the ring," Tommy says. He puts his hand on Gus's to stop his interrupting. He says, "I cut a nineteen-year-old kid above his eye, and all I have to do is work it. There's enough blood we could collect it in buckets and donate to the Red Cross. So, then, it's the start of the third round, and his corner's got the bleeding stopped, and it's my job to get it going again. Left, left, left. Easy as picking lint off a suit. He can't see—the blood is pouring out of him, there is no way he can see—and he keeps coming at me."

Fogelsong is bored. The oncologist is peeved. Give the man a break. There isn't a life-and-death story he hasn't heard already.

Tommy faces Philadelphia, and he says, "Luck, be a lady tonight." He can't help himself. Left, left, left. He is picking lint. He releases Gus's hand, signals for him to go ahead. Gus cuts, low in the deck. First card for Fogelsong is the king of clubs.

"Call the newspapers," Fogelsong says. "We got a fight on our hands."

Gus shows the five of spades for Tommy.

"We'll talk tomorrow," the oncologist says.

Tommy nods toward Plugg and says, "Everything starts with Plugg. See him."

———

It's dark. Vic is asleep on the lawn near the pool. Philadelphia is standing next to Tommy, who says, "The red carnation, who does it make you think of?"

She huffs smoke. "No one," she says.

"The bow tie?"

She has no idea.

He borrows her cigarette, holds it just right and cocks an eyebrow. He's being cool here on the patio, and she's clueless. Tommy is floored. He says, "Dean Martin?"

"I saw him," she says. "When he was in his prime." She takes back the cigarette. "He was completely different."

Tommy says, "When he died, the day they put him in the ground, that night, the casinos on the Strip, they blinked their lights for a second." He tells her he was standing right here when it happened. Philadelphia inhales, and Tommy says, "They didn't do that for either Kennedy."

"You can't do it for everyone," she says. "Like putting the flag at half mast. You have to have rules."

Tommy says, "Dean Martin died at 3:15 Christmas morning, exact same time, same day his mother died, only years later for Dino. Fifteen, twenty years after she did."

———

Tommy bums a cigarette from the guard at the front gate to the community where Gus lives. The man's name is Roy. From where they stand they can take in all of Las Vegas. The night's wine flows through Tommy. The Scotch steadies his feet. He walked the three blocks here from Gus's place. Tomorrow, first thing in the morning, he starts training. Plugg probably already has the ball rolling. He's made phone calls.

"You ever see *Ocean's 11?*" Tommy says to Roy.

Roy says, "Loved it."

Tommy drags smoke deep into his lungs, then lets it float free, like the way the genie curls out of the bottle, and he says, "You think I look like Dean Martin?"

"The truth?" Roy says.

Tommy says, "Lie to me."

"Give us a tune," Roy says.

"Croon one?"

"You got it."

So Tommy does. He sucks on the cigarette, blows smoke, cocks his head like Dino, swaggers, croons.

> *Luck, be a lady tonight.*
> *Luck, be a lady tonight.*
> *Luck, if you ever been a lady to begin with,*
> *Luck, be a lady tonight.*
> *Luck, let a gentleman see*
> *How nice a dame you can be.*
> *I know the way you've treated other guys you've been*
> *   with.*
> *Luck, be a lady with me.*

Roy says, "So, you want me to lie?"

"I can take it."

Roy hitches up his thinking, scratches behind his ear, and finally says, "You don't look anything like Dean Martin."

"I didn't think so."

"You sound even less so."

"Sad but true."

Roy says, "The radio's doing that joke contest."

"What do you call a rat pack if all the rats are dead?" Tommy says.

Roy says, "You got an answer?"

Tommy says, "Not me. You?"

"I think so," Roy says.

"Don't keep me in suspense."

"You'll have to wait. I'm refining it," Roy says. "Keeping it close to the vest until I'm rolling in the dough they're offering. Don't want anyone stealing from me."

"You'll tell me when you win?"

"I'll be famous when I win."

Roy lets Tommy out through a small side gate, and Tommy has a choice to make. He has left his car parked at Gus's. He is in no condition to be driving and screw that designated driver shit. If he goes south, he is on his way home. It's a mile. There will be a message on his machine from Plugg. Carl T. will have a gym lined up. The ball is rolling. If Tommy goes north, he's headed toward Jane's. It's five miles. He can run it easily. Get started on his roadwork. Hector will be asleep. Jane will lead Tommy in to show him their baby, and Jane and Tommy will end up in bed where they'll express their love for each other.

Tommy loosens his bow tie. His black shoes stiffen and shine in the street lights. They scrape the gravel. He knows what it's like to run in a tuxedo and five-hundred-dollar shoes. In a bowtie. In a starched shirt. You feel like a monk. Like you're right and the world's wrong. Like there is such a thing as right and wrong.

Five strides, and he will be loping.

He hears a horn behind him and turns to see the wide gate swinging open for Elise the CPA. There's nobody with her. She's got her own ride. A convertible. In the time it takes to throw a punch, Tommy will be in the car by her side. He'll be sitting next to this boxing fan. Sure he's a fighter, but even a fighter needs to be looked after. To be taken care of. Needs his R&R. The myths must be maintained. A fighter needs someone to lick his wounds. Who better than a woman who is almost a CPA?

Love is grand. Jane is grand. Hector is grand. Sure. Sing it.

But.

But tonight is tonight.

Tomorrow he begins training.

Tomorrow the sports section's headline will say, BOMBS AWAY. They'll call him Tommy Gun. Somewhere in the article will be the words rat-a-tat-tat. There will be a file picture of Tommy, his arms raised, Plugg at his side, some contender on the canvas, the guy's handlers on their knees, surrounding him. They have cupped a hand behind his head and raised it even though they know better. If you could move the people in the photo you would see the kid lying in the middle of the ring is not even old enough to vote, and there is blood trickling from one ear. Tommy has ruptured the eardrum for him. The fight doctor is leaning in. The kid will be okay, but if you could get his chest open, if you separated the ribs and cut through the pericardium, if you could get past the heart wall, you'd see Tommy has bruised that organ. All we're talking about, after all, is muscle.

Until Liquor Is
Made Legal

"It's a wuss game," Tommy's buddy Pete
Hitchcock said to him. Subject was the softball on the field below
them.

Tommy toasted Pete and the softballers—Jack Daniel's, and he
said, "To wusses and their offspring."

Plugg rejoined Tommy and Pete. He had survived a journey to
the public john under the stands. Plugg had asked Tommy and Pete
to escort him, and they declined, saying they would come running if
he wasn't back in ten minutes. Right under his nose, just to rag him,
they synchronized their watches. The young needling the old. Roasting Carl T. Plugg on the spot. "Holler at the first sign of trouble,"
Tommy said, and Pete said, "You know how to holler, don't you?"
Plugg was dressed like he was about to give testimony in front of
Congress. He was begging to be mugged. The man was looking like a
moneybags here in the bad side of Las Vegas. Plugg impeccable right
out of the shower. Talced. Scented. Tidy. Avuncular. Today's attire
was a light-weight, silk-and-wool summertime leave-the-jacket-open
suit, cocoa-brown, three-button, a pattern to it, if you looked close,
if you put your nose to the cloth. Woven necktie. Argyle socks. Hat
and shoes like he was auditioning, that hat in hand, for a forties detective movie. Plugg had bought himself a ballpark hot dog. He stood
behind Tommy and Pete, one row up. Fewer calories if you ate on
your feet.

Pete snapped a photo of two boys roughhousing near the visitors'
dugout. Their hair was braided so scalp showed, was herringboned,

tire-tracked, and the boys were strutting, cocks-of-the-walk, styling in their shades, frames like wraparound bumpers. One snatched a pair from the other one's face. Then it was a wrestling match.

Tommy, Pete, and Plugg, loose in the city, wandered into this sports complex, four baseball diamonds in a circle, backstop to backstop and backstop to backstop, across Las Vegas Boulevard from Cashman Field where the Las Vegas Stars played hardball. The wusses Pete was bad-mouthing—they were city league, and it was not real softball, but slow-pitch softball, men and women on the same teams, one side wearing black T-shirts and matching knee socks, cab-yellow shorts. Red shirts on the other team and red shoes, not spikes, but high-top fashion statements. Their laces and shorts were blue. So were their socks. No one was going to be sliding headfirst or otherwise on the hardpan infield. Anyone tagged anybody out it was done standing up and politely. You okay? I'm fine. You sure? I'm sure.

Do-si-do. Grab your partner and promenade.

Wusses.

A guy drove a ball through the gap in right and was racing around second when the third baseman stopped him. There were no fences, which meant he was held to a ground-rule double.

"Christ on a pogo stick," Pete said. "Fucking pussy game." Loud enough the two boys and the other ten or so people sitting on these cement bleachers cut him looks. Pete displayed, for them to see, the carton of Jack Daniel's he and Tommy were drinking. It explained so much. For the world to hear, Pete said, "It's the booze talking." They brought along pocket-sized bottles in a cardboard carrier the size of a handbag, leftovers from Jane's refrigerator. Their drinks were Country Cocktails, Lynchburg Lemonade. "Pussy drink," Pete said to Tommy. He twisted the cap off another bottle, glanced over his shoulder at Plugg, and said to Tommy, "Guess it will do until liquor is made legal."

Tommy's pal singing the blues, the ones he was born to. First thing you noticed in his baby pictures was the gloom, the sorrowful ride infant Pete was about to take. Down his road waited turmoil. Violence. Sweet-talk and stray cats. Merriment followed by recriminations. Tommy's friend Pete Hitchcock arrived on planet earth smart and cursed and wretched. About to be wronged or do some wronging. Pete was, now and then, fooled, and he did his share of fooling. Was mistreated and thumbscrewed, and not understood was a given. His song claimed Pete had been run over by a train. Spent time shoeless and bottomed out. Pete one moonless night sat down to dinner with the devil and the next morning walked and talked with angels. Pete himself a wreaker of this and the savior of that.

So went his melodrama, which was hokey and sung solo, guitar accompaniment, classic twelve-bar blues, Pete's howl at the moon.

Reality was that five years ago Pete Hitchcock—the man a CPA and a lawyer—hauled his act to Utah. Hand-over-fist money followed, computers, real estate and a housing boom, franchises. Then he did what he wanted to do and started taking photographs. Became an *artiste*. Tommy and Pete friends since third grade, John S. Park Elementary. Now Tommy saw him maybe twice a year. They caught a UNLV game, played eighteen holes at Spanish Trails. Pete returned to Las Vegas to see his family, mother and father both alive and awash in Pete's assets, and he had his own ex here and a boy who was growing up to be hell on wheels. Pete took his photographs and was earning himself the beginnings of a big-time, national reputation. He was here to document Tommy's comeback. Freelance. *Sports Illustrated* had money on the table. As did *ESPN Magazine*. Even *Time*. *USA Today* wanted Tommy to include a weekly five-hundred-word diary.

"Pussy liquor," Pete said. He stink-eyed his Country Cocktail. "You're a thinker," he said to Tommy, who clinked his bottle to Pete's and said, "Ditto again."

"To the wuss in all of us," Pete said.

Tommy said, "To our inner wuss."

Pete said, "So it is written," and Tommy said, "In the book."

Any fool with a camera, Pete was arguing, could photograph the physicality of boxing, the blood, a freeze-framed shot of knees buckling, of a face hammered into a shape a face shouldn't find itself in. Pete claimed he was after what was in Tommy's head. He hoped to stumble upon one shot of the killer in there. "*So and so has heart —* fucking cliché," Pete said. "The fuck who doesn't." He sipped, said, "You don't, they chew you up no matter what your business is. Boxing or selling flowers." Pete studied Tommy hard and said, "You were always a thinker. A boxer, a thinker—for you the two go hand in hand."

Tommy said, "It's good to hear you say so."

Plugg said, "The public should hold such a high opinion of the sweet science. Citizens should not continue to view the sport with such public disfavor."

"Hear, hear," Pete said, and then he did what everyone did. He faked slipping a punch from where he sat. He said to Tommy, "You took French."

Damn straight. Tommy did. Madame Pivornick, junior and senior years, Las Vegas High School. College required a foreign language, and Tommy was considering attending. But then along came Mr. Carl T. Plugg. Followed by the boxing and Plugg, who taught Tommy his stick and tag from his thunder. "Tommy, Tommy," Madame Pivornick said. She kept him after class, after they recited dialogues. She said, "Tommy, join the French club. We go to Paris in the spring." Twirl and perfume in her words. The lady was the real McCoy. "Come with us to France," she said. "Tommy, you can't *not* see the City of Lights." She promised him the Paris tourists missed. All he wanted out of French class was Pam Upson, straight over, two seats to his left. Lovely in her comportment, how a seventeen-year-old could be, a temptation to the blind and their mysterious way of knowing things.

Tommy said to Pete, "Spanish too," and Pete said, "Doesn't count."

They drank to the truth he spoke. Both knew Tommy never went to class. Not one. Their baseball coach taught Spanish and gave Tommy As. Tommy had range at third, an arm, and a quick bat.

————

One of the players on the red team popped up, offered the spectators a loopy fly ball lopsided in its flight toward second base. The ball coming off the bat was pathetic, sounded like glass breaking. The scoreboard behind third base was blank. Only the players knew who was winning. If anyone was. Probably they didn't keep score. Didn't want to promote competition. It *was* a wuss game all of them were busy at.

"The world," Pete said, "used to be round and we knew what to write on tests."

Plugg said, "Here we go. Piss and moan."

"We knew who to root for," Pete said.

Tommy said to him, "I could make a list as long as my arm."

"No one lets us piss and moan," Pete said. "We try it, and we get dismissed. They make laws against it. There are cities where you can't smoke on the street. What the fuck is that?" He raised his bottle toward Plugg and said, "Your generation perfected the piss and moan. You gave birth to it. Like Adam bringing sin into the world. You pissed, and you moaned. Loud. You still do it."

Plugg had his handkerchief out and was dabbing at his lips.

"Our dads had the green light," Pete said.

"Piss and moan is all Gus does," Tommy said. Gus stored complaints in every pocket, like the guy selling watches out of his overcoat. You gave him a minute and he dressed you in sackcloth and ashes.

Plugg said, "So you spend your days pissing and moaning about pissing and moaning."

"My point exactly," Pete said. He finished his cocktail and opened the last bottle. The two boys he had photographed sauntered over stroking their hairdos. The pair had the world by its tail. One said to Pete, "Dude, you take our picture?" Pete slugged half his drink and offered the boys what was left. "We on probation," they said. They looked thirteen. Not old enough to drive. Pete handed the bottle to Tommy and said to them, "You want your picture taken?"

"You did already. More than us saw you. Other folks did," the taller of the two said. He was wearing a Philadephia 76ers jersey over a T-shirt and acting like he was a gangster. Probably was a made man in the two-block-square neighborhood he roamed.

Tommy polished off the Country Cocktail.

"I'm photographing Mr. Tommy Rooke here," Pete said.

"He so significant?" the tall kid said.

"Significant?" Pete said.

The tall one said, "We ain't dumb. Not how you think. We seen him from where we was sitting." The kid's partner danced like he was boxing, arms fluttering like a big bird's, the kid not guarding his face. He made fists. The kid had no idea the fist arrived with the blow itself. He said, "Float like a butterfly. Sting like a bee." He and the tall boy exchanged open-handed punches, slapping. They couldn't fight, didn't understand the first thing about it. Sparred like two fools putting a potato between their foreheads and trying to keep it wedged there and jitterbug at the same time. Pete snapped a shot of them. He asked Tommy to mug with the boys, and Tommy obliged.

Pete was doing his documenting with Polaroids you used one time and then sent the whole unit in for developing. He had a bag full of cameras. He offered one to the boys and said, "Here. Knock yourselves out." They retreated a row, suspicious. "Why not?" Pete said to them. "Against your probation to take pictures?"

The tall one reached for the camera and Pete, handing it over, said, "Easy as pie. Wind and click." He showed the kid how the camera worked and had him take a picture of Tommy and him and Plugg. Pete said to the kid, "You got a photograph going to be worth a million bucks some day. When they write up Mr. Tommy Rooke's life."

Tommy trashed their empties, and in ten minutes Tommy and Pete and Plugg were walking up the backside of Las Vegas Boulevard toward Fremont Street. Risking their lives here. The riffraff out and on the prowl, and Plugg looking as if he was headed for a fashion shoot. Life where the three of them walked was a crap game. Turnabout was not fair play. Thugs were thugs. They stepped up and took. Pete said, "Our question tonight, our topic of discussion, that issue that haunts the best minds—can God do what he doesn't do?"

Plugg said, "Your generation—too much thinking going on."

Pete said, "Nah. No, no—not a generation thing." Earlier tonight, dinner at the Golden Gate, and Pete's talk covered the serendipity of sorrow.

Now Plugg said to Pete, "Two and two is what? You can add on your fingers." And Plugg did. He sprouted one, two, three, four fingers. He said, "Not for you, Hitchcock. Always with you it's difficult. You make drinking a glass of water a question of good and evil. Of God and what God does and doesn't do. What's two plus two?" Plugg showed Tommy and Pete two fingers on his left hand and two fingers on his right hand. He said, "You own, like I say, fingers. Your private property, and all you got to do is add." Plugg counted his fingers. "One, two, three, four." He said, "But no. Not you. Not Pete Hitchcock. First you cut off your fingers." Plugg tucked his fingers under. He said, "No. I correct myself. You chew off your fingers. You hold up your bloody stubs like you're Marlon Brando in a downpour. In your eyes is the glory and the pain of what you've done in order to holler at the heavens. You rewrite the book of Lamentations every single goddamn day."

"You're wrong," Pete said. "On this one, you're wrong."

Plugg said, "Spilled milk."

Pete said, "You got me wrong."

"I call them as I see them," Plugg said. "The balls and the strikes."

"Not the question—spilled milk. Spilled milk is not at stake," Pete said. "Can't be."

"Wrong. Am I wrong?" Plugg gave the question to Tommy, who produced the hands of a third wheel. He was the railbird on this one.

"You're talking spilled milk," Plugg said. He pretended to nibble at his fingers. He was taking them all the way down to the knuckles.

"There is the hurt," Pete said. "There is guilt like an anchor."

"Unspecified angst," Plugg said. "God save us from unspecified angst."

"I can specify. Take my boy," Pete said. "My son. For an example. Say my boy gets a girl pregnant."

Plugg looked to Tommy. Pete's boy was seven years old. Plugg said, "Your boy?"

"You know what I'm arguing," Pete said. "You got to look ahead. See what's down the road. Anticipate around the bend to the time my son learns that there's more than one reason to take it out of his pants."

"Oy oy oy," Plugg said. He acted like he was nibbling harder with each word, more vigor at his fingers. "It's a time of celebration. It's small potatoes."

"Okay, my girls," Pete said, "I can't tell them apart."

Plugg said, "Oy."

Pete said, "I'm not sure if I saw them in a different place from where they should be that I would recognize them. You know what I mean?"

His daughters came from marriage number two. That ex had carried them off to Nebraska where they lived smack-dab in the center of a cornfield. "Why's the house so tall?" Pete asked, his first visit. "So you can find it," some stepchild said. The ex's new husband walked and talked like he thought he was Sam Shepard. Pete called his girls Curly One and Curly Two. Twins, three years old.

Plugg said, "A mountain you make out of every mole hill."

Pete said, "There are implications."

"Oy," Plugg said.

"You can't appreciate the issue," Pete said.

"Can't? You, Tommy—the two of you, you're babes in the woods. You're not yet old enough to cry for real, either one of you."

"Times have redoubled in complexity," Pete said. "The issue—"

"Issue? Small potatoes," Plugg said. "War is an issue. Poverty is an issue. Starvation is an issue."

Pete said, "Small can be big."

"You can't tell your kids apart. Find the simple answer," Plugg said. "No, not for Pete Hitchcock. You eat your fingers instead."

Pete got out "It's—" and Plugg said, "Tattoo their ear lobes. Dots. One red, one blue. They'll love it. Will be the only ones their age. Tie ribbons to their fingers. Add wristbands—pretty ones they'll like. Use tape, different colors."

"They're their mother all over again," Pete said. "That's what I'm saying. There's the harm I'm talking about. The harm I'm doing. I'm out of the picture, and they're growing up to be her. You got a ribbon for that? I don't think so."

It was late summer, Saturday, and Tommy, Plugg, and Pete were living in that gap between night and day. Downtown was crawling. It was a carnival. The big top. You paid your money and you saw whatever you craved. There was music on boom boxes and banging its way out of cars. Trash filled the gutters. Pockets of men gathered in clots and were sideways lookers like they had your car up on jacks and were about to strip it. A geezer in sweats asked for a buck, and Tommy gave it to him in quarters. Pete skipped around a man who had tied himself into a knot and was sitting in the middle of the sidewalk, a tin cup in his lap. A woman coming the other way said to the guy, "Hey, Speedbump." Pete whirled Tommy and Plugg together under a neon Keno sign and took a picture. In front of the Horseshoe Club Pete buttonholed a couple and asked the husband to shake Tommy's hand. He and his wife were from Gallipolis, Ohio. The guy said to Tommy, "Who are you?" To get some distance on the photo, Pete waded through the crowd, saying, "Risking my life here, folks. Don't try this at home." He said to the man, "You'll be famous. Trust me." Half a block from the Golden Gate, behind them someone called out. Said, "Hey, Tommy."

An old sparring partner, a hard-hitter fighter called Flipside. He fought with equal audacity lefty or righty. Here on the street, he and Tommy were drawn together like old school chums. They hugged, and Pete aimed his camera. Plugg greeted Flipside knuckles to knuckles. Pete dug out his Leica. Click click click. Traveling with Flipside was a six-foot-six skinny dude. Made you think of a drinking straw in its paper wrapping. He was dressed completely in white linen. Like those kids, he had plaited hair, a beaded skirt of it at the back of his neck. He was narrow enough he could have slipped a watch over his head and worn it around his waist. Used it as a belt. He wore cotton gloves like it was not eighty-five degrees. Pete took a photo.

"Whoa," Flipside, raising hands against the flash, said. "What's this shit?"

The skinny man said, "Don't be doing that."

"My pal Pete," Tommy said, and the four of them put together more handshakes. Skinny was called Joshua. Tommy explained he was fighting again and Pete was photographing the experience. Tonight was *Tommy Rooke Does the City*.

"Tomorrow," Pete said, "is *Tommy Rooke, the Family Man*."

"We caught you in the paper," Flipside said to Tommy. "I wrote myself a note in my head to phone you my luck, but you know how that goes. Out of sight out of mind."

Tommy asked him if he needed work, if he was still sparring.

"Too much hurt," Flipside said. He put his hands to his ribs like he was testing their give and take. Turned out he and Joshua owned together a floor tile business they were thriving on. Carpet was passé in the city. Tile, in. They started out laying it for a company and now ran a dozen trucks of their own.

"You change your mind, call," Tommy said. "All of us need to get hit upside the head now and then."

Flipside said, "I won't be doing that."

Plugg handed him a phone number and said, "We're going first class, if you have second thoughts. We're already rolling. Top money. We could use your speed."

More handshakes and hugs in parting, Flipside saying, "Don't hurt anyone, Tommy."

A boxer's joke. Hurting people being the whole point. Like actors, and break a leg.

Pete's rental was parked at the Golden Gate's garage.

————

What Tommy realized after the fact of the gunshot that killed Pete Hitchcock was that it happened a few feet short of an alley, up a side street, half a block from the car. There was a retaining wall, which was painted white, and there were palm trees, and the wind softly rattling them. There were oleanders. *Pop* was all the noise the gun made. The shooter saying, "Didn't—" Then, "Ah, fuck." Then, "Shit." Then, gone.

It was like a big boxy crate dropped on all of them, open on the bottom so it could collect the group, and the gun came up an inch away. Tommy and Pete and Plugg moving along and talking, Pete checking his pockets, hunting his parking stub. He held his Leica and the bag of one-time-use cameras in one hand. Then movement, a jagged shadow flickered and there was a sound like a two-by-four hit the pavement, tossed from high up, to the side, near where Plugg was. Somebody hustled around a dumpster. Then, *pop.* Then the "Didn't—"

"It's not like it's dark here," a detective said to Tommy, the two of them sitting in a cruiser. His name, Tommy learned days later, was Bernard Bantz. You didn't call him Bernie. "Black? White?" he asked. Tommy couldn't say. Tommy also learned later that Plugg, who was in a different car, an unmarked one, talking to a regular cop, said the man was Hispanic. No question about it for Plugg. Bantz said to Tommy, "Male?" Tommy said *sure,* and he wasn't guessing, but he didn't really recall. He assumed. He was thinking, *Would a woman step out of nowhere and shoot a man in the chest, one she didn't know?*

"Clothes?" Bantz said.

Tommy said, "Clothes?"

Bantz said. "Describe them. A jacket? Light? Dark?"

Tommy couldn't say.

"Hat?" Bantz said.

"Of some kind."

"Meaning?"

"The ones you pull down," Tommy said. "You cover your face, like when you ski."

"A stocking cap?" Bantz said. He was writing.

What Tommy knew was it happened and you couldn't undo it. You told the story later and it wasn't convincing. The telling didn't accommodate the event. You boiled it down and the cruelty of it evaporated. What were words in the face of a gun?

There was the stuttering movement, a shuffling like the sound of cards, which seemed out of sync, the smack of wood, then *pop*, then *"Didn't,"* and Pete was on the ground, his sack split open, cameras scattered, and blood Tommy couldn't stop or slow, Plugg shoving his coat at Tommy. "Use it, use it," he was saying. Tommy couldn't find exactly where Pete was hit. The blood gushed from near his heart. Tommy pressed hard. It was the only thing he knew to do, the whole time thinking, *Tourniquet. Pressure points. Where? Neck? Arm? Where?* Pete's Leica had hit the sidewalk, and it was banged up, dented. It was putting out a sound, a whirring, a buzzing, like a timer on an oven. The lens was cracked.

Hours later, Tommy phoned her and Jane was coming to pick them up. Pete had been taken away, the ambulance in no hurry. Plugg and Tommy sat on the low wall. Blood pooled a few feet from where they were, still enough life in it that it reflected the yellow street lights. Tommy had Pete's Leica. The police took the film and the one-time-use cameras. The palm trees at Tommy's and Plugg's backs stirred—grass skirts, hula dancing—in a hot breeze. Impeccable Plugg was blood head to foot. It had dried on his suit and looked more like paint than anything human. There was enough blood for the three of them to have died here.

"The Yetzer," Plugg said. "Evil Yetzer." He tapped his chest where his heart kept house.

Across the street, people gathered, stared, elbowed each other like the tourists they were. They looked stupid in their clothes.

Plugg said, "So it is written, God asks, as if he speaks from a cloud, *'What damage have I done?'"* Plugg held his hands in front of himself like he was about to sop up the blood from the pavement. *As if you didn't know, didn't see it coming* was what Plugg's whole body was shrugging, was what he was saying to God. As if it wasn't obvious to every half-wit on the planet. It *was* what He hadn't done. It was what *He* could have done but didn't bother to get off his butt to do. Plugg said, "Old Man, take the blinders off." He stood and said, "I curse God in public." A woman across the street was gawking. You would have thought she was hinged in agony. Plugg said, "I stand on one leg and I curse God." He stood on one leg. He said, "I spit in God's face," and Plugg spat. He said to God, "I stand on one leg until You make it right."

And Plugg sustained his protest—he was here on his one leg—until Jane arrived, and she and Tommy walked him to her car.

———

Jane didn't ask Tommy what it was like, so he told her. He said, "It was like this huge wooden box dropped on us, like on a loading dock where big ships are, and the gun was there." He explained how it was like a magic show, one of those extravaganzas you saw on TV, where the magician combed his hair like a Viking warrior and called himself one of those names that always sounded as if they should be written by a sword, the kind of performance where Armondo the Magnificent made a small town and the lake that fed it disappear. *Shazaam*, and the box was on top of Tommy and Plugg and Pete. It corralled them. Lassoed them, a word which seemed to confuse the picture but was true. Later, after he thought more on what happened, Tommy said to Jane, "Imagine you're in your closet, and the door shuts on you on its own, so you pull the string on the light. Right in your face there is a gun, and it goes off."

"Was it loud?" she said.

"No, and not the point," Tommy said. "The proximity is the point," Tommy said. "How close it can be and how quick it was."

"Close enough to touch?"

"It seemed closer and farther at the same time."

Plugg would say a couple of weeks later, "He tripped. The kid tripped and the gun went off. He tripped on his own foot." This at a hearing, and Tommy thinking, *You were looking at his feet?* Police arrested a fifteen-year-old named Fletcher Chicago—his real name, printed right there on a driver's license. The kid had a mother and a father, grandparents, brothers and sisters, aunts, uncles. Tommy and Plugg had been called in for some kind of testimony, and Tommy was a problem. He was present at the shooting. He was walking close enough to Pete he could have hooked his arm through his buddy's. They could have square-danced, but Tommy could not identify Fletcher Chicago. He couldn't say to the police or the judge or Jane if the shooter was black or white, which seemed simple enough, you would have thought. Plugg was able to, and you didn't have to be racist to make such a distinction. Fletcher Chicago was Hispanic. Plugg nailed it. Tommy was a second eyewitness who wasn't sure, who stood not five feet from the shooter and was hesitating to finger him, ID him, pick him out of a lineup if there actually was going to be one.

Question: Was the shooter wearing a mask? No, Plugg said. A hat? Tommy stuck with the stocking cap idea. No—Plugg said. It was a baseball cap. He showed the cops how low the kid wore it and how its beak was curled so it hid Fletcher Chicago's face the best he could manage. Plugg described Fletcher Chicago's clothes. He identified the tattoo on Fletcher Chicago's neck. Told an investigator what it was before he ever saw Fletcher Chicago. It was a monkey climbing a rope.

What Tommy did was a boxer's instinct. The other guy started to put his combinations together, and you covered up, making sure you moved your feet and your head. So there was the shadow, the flickering, the shuffling, the wood sound on the pavement, and Tommy weathered it. It was what fighters did. Cats, dogs, animals—they rolled into a ball. Say a lion, a bull, a bear chased after you, you didn't race it to safety. You got to the ground and you tucked your knees up and interlocked your arms around your face. You did the smart thing.

Or suppose a different kind of trouble. Say your opponent had reach on you. The man had fire hoses for arms. Your spot was in the pocket. You got in the pocket and dictated from there. You sat inside. You took the tickets and ran the show. You were in the kitchen cooking up a storm. The pots and pans flying.

———

Three A.M., the morning after the night Pete was killed, and Jane and Tommy climbed out of their sleep and made love, which Tommy tried to complicate, and she said, "Quit watching HBO," and that was true, Tommy getting ideas from the television, so they had sex the old-fashioned way and afterwards ate ice cream in bed.

Then at four, Tommy was up with baby Hector, outside on the patio, and there in the sky was a crescent moon, waning, spilling its water, predicting a storm. Nature in sympathy.

Pete met the end his song had predicted.

Tommy was the first awake and on his feet at 7:00 A.M. Stuck to Jane's kitchen cabinets, taped to her refrigerator, and laid row by row on the counter were Polaroid pictures. Pete's. His first day here he and Tommy stopped at an AM/PM, and Pete bought ten Polaroid Instant Popshots cameras. Four bags full. They looked like weapons Buck Rogers would have aimed at Captain Zarcon or some other intergalactic lunatic. $19.99 each. Tommy razzed Pete, told him he could buy him a fancy camera if Pete wanted, if Pete had fallen on hard times, if, that is, he knew how to use one—Tommy would gladly pay, and Pete said, "Joy to the world." To which Tommy said, "So the hooker said to the john."

Pete had said, "Surprises in these babies" and patted his sack of cheapo cameras.

Jane and Tommy left the Polaroid photographs where Pete had arranged them, the pictures grouped. Popshots of Hector. Popshots of Jane. Plugg. Tommy. Heartless and unforgiving pictures. Primitive. The kind of photos dogs would take of each other. It wasn't in Pete to set up pretty shots. In the ones of Hector Tommy saw the old man his boy would become, long after Tommy was gone. In the ones of Jane he saw the woman he divorced. He saw the woman he was remarrying. Tommy ignored the pictures Pete took of him. Who, when the opportunity truly came, really wanted the truth, the whole truth, and nothing but the truth?

What we're all pleading all day long, day in and day out, is, *Don't tell me. Don't tell me.*

You know what I'm saying.

———

A month passed, and Tommy was not training. Couldn't. No desire to throw even one punch. He screwed up Plugg's schedule. The meter was running, and the backers, reading what the newspapers were saying, were e-mailing, sending faxes, stopping by. Plugg was not complaining to Tommy. Yet. He handled it all—shuffling phone calls, rerouting the news people, babying Tommy.

Plugg and Tommy flew to L.A. a week ago. Publicity. *The Jay Leno Show*. Interviews. Tommy fifteen pounds over what he should have been. His clothes didn't fit. In the airport, coming home, waiting on a red-eye, Tommy sat there watching this kid moving deftly up and down the rows of seats, in and out of the passengers. It was like one of those special effects you saw in commercials where somehow they stopped everyone except for one guy who moved freely and easily among all the frozen-in-time-and-place people. The kid laid cards on empty seats. One next to Tommy. *PARDON ME, I AM DEAF* it said. Pardon me? Tommy thought. For what—for being deaf? There were stickers on the cards. Pooh Bear, Tigger, and Piglet. Tigger hauling a pot of honey. Pooh Bear ice-skating, complete with scarf flying out behind. *Donation $2. Made in Taiwan. Ages three and up.* The kid cruised back around to collect the cards and Tommy gave him twenty bucks. The kid went to his pocket for change, and Tommy shook him off and said, "Keep it." The kid squared himself up directly in front of Tommy, cupped his hands about chest high like he was trying to hold water, set his feet together army-style, and nodded toward Tommy. He was mirroring exactly the gesture Tommy made at the start of the only three final rounds Tommy had ever fought, the respect he gave to the fighters who went the distance with him.

Plugg, pretty much asleep in the seat next to Tommy, said, "Jesus, Tommy, it's a scam. Grow up."

Tommy promised Plugg he would. Tomorrow. Or the next day. First chance he got.

Or, how about when Pete got back? When Pete rose from the dead?

Directly across from Tommy and Plugg, a teenager sat on the edge of his seat and held a red rose. The kid a dead ringer for Kobe Bryant. Not as tall, but close enough to put the likeness to use. His girl was flying in, and you could hear his heart under his shirt. Thump. Thump. Thump.

———

Plugg called and asked Tommy to meet him for a drink. Three in the afternoon. Today was going to be the tomorrow Tommy had promised Carl T. Plugg. It was time to grow up. On the phone, Plugg said, "Did Tommy Rooke want God to destroy the universe in Pete's name? Did Tommy want the sun to stand still?"

Where they met, dancing for them was Natavia Ice. Her music hip hop. Plugg and Tommy at the Palomino Club, waiting on a woman Plugg was dating. She called herself Magadelina Peach, like a name could change your luck. Natavia Ice. Magadelina Peach. Fletcher Chicago. Pete Hitchcock. Tommy was drinking seltzer Plugg ordered for him. Flipside had come with Plugg, who was on his second Coors. Flipside was willing to go some rounds with Tommy. Get him off the snide. Against his better judgment was clear. Tommy guessed Flipside was getting a ton of money, for the sparring, for being here today. He came to aid and abet Plugg in talking sense into Tommy. Flipside's pal, Joshua, Skin-and-Bones, sat next to Flipside and was looking like a linen napkin folded for a fancy dinner. His drink had an umbrella in it.

"Me and you, like before," Flipside said. He raised his hands, offset them high and near his chin, loose fingers. A fighter. The fist arrives with the blow. He bobbed where he was sitting.

They touched knuckles.

Flipside had watched film of the boy Tommy was fighting. He said he could do the kid down to the way he laced his gloves and peed in the men's room. "The youngster jabs like a kitten," he said. He showed Tommy, and he was dead-on. Tommy had seen footage, had seen Eddie Jarret in the ring. "Your right can beat his left hook," Flipside said. "He throws, you throw."

Plugg said, "It's time, Tommy. Tote that bag. Lift that bale."

Tommy knew the song.

Flipside said, "Don't let Jarret set up. Make him move his right foot. Turn him. Spin him. Keep his right foot moving."

Plugg said, "Tommy, let the dead attend to the dead. The living, to the living."

Tommy pictured Plugg standing on one leg the night Pete was killed. He saw Plugg spit in God's face.

Behind the Plugg who was sitting here with Tommy and sipping at a Coors, Magadelina appeared in a hallway. She was wearing glittery orange—blouse, pants, shoes, and her hair looked like gift wrapping.

"I understand what you're saying," Tommy said to Plugg.

Plugg said, "You see my point. You're chagrined. I'm chagrined. It's only logical. It's only human. But there is always a but." Tommy got it. He saw Plugg's point. Pete. Their pal. Dead. Move on. There was a fight on the table. Contracts.

Magadelina Peach was coming their way, and Plugg said, "Rabbi Tarfon."

131

Tommy said, "Oy."

Flipside said, "Oy."

Tommy said, "Sunrise, sunset." Put sadness in each word.

"A wise man, Rabbi Tarfon," Plugg said. "I'll make it short. Get to the bottom dollar. Rabbi Tarfon, he says you purchase your clay jugs from the best who can make them, from the genius of such things, and you fill them with your hot water. They crack. You invest, you lose. You lose your water, and you lose all the way around. You fill your jugs with icy cold water, and they crack. Same result."

Flipside said, "You lose both ways."

Tommy said, "There's no winning."

Plugg touched his own brain pan and said, "You mix the hot with the cold and fill your jugs." He raised his hands, saying *and?* Left a blank hanging in the air, which Tommy didn't bother to fill in. Plugg said, "So it is with mercy and justice."

Magadelina stroked Plugg's shoulder, and she leaned in to plant one big smooch on his cheek, all the time talking to Tommy, saying, "My, but I bet the heavens shook when God pulled you out of the oven."

Tommy said, "Magadelina, once again you leave me speechless."

She slid into a chair, and Tommy got up to go.

Flipside said, "The gym, Friday?"

Plugg said to Tommy, "Good and evil. Justice and mercy. It's all peas in the same pod."

Nothing helped.

So much for the theater of standing on one leg.

Outside was the Las Vegas sun, which lacked even an ounce of common sense.

Pete Hitchcock was dead.

Two days before Pete got shot, Tommy's Jane hugged him into her house. She was clutching Hector in her other arm. Pete had the one boy himself, the two girls, and the two bad marriages. His third one was teetering. Pete had a way of wearing women out. Tommy reached for Hector, and Jane said, "I got him. He's okay."

At the door, Pete held onto Jane and slumped. He was on safe ground here. Out there anything could happen.

"Roger called," Jane said to Tommy.

Another pal, Pete's and Tommy's. His message was he had comped Pete a room at the Mirage if he wanted it and finagled for

Tommy and Plugg and Pete a tee time at Summerlin where they could walk the greens and fairways the celebrities strode when they came to town.

"I'm telling the whole wide world how the world works," Pete said to Jane.

Jane, on her way out of the room, Hector ready to go down for the night, said, "Eat something. You'll cheer up."

"Plugg's advice was I should sit on a stove," Pete said.

She said, "One or the other."

Pete slumped more profoundly, and Tommy phoned Roger, got his machine, his tough-guy message: *if you must, leave your name.* He had his reasons. Tommy told him Pete would be staying at Jane's. He was selling his own house, so it was out. Pete jacked open the refrigerator, unscrewed the cap from a bottle of beer.

Tommy's life was simpler than Pete's. Sappier. It was Hector. It was Jane. Tommy and his ex ready to remarry. Had a date set. A place. A time. Cake ordered. He was fighting again, one match, for a truckload of money. Not that Tommy needed it. Not every fighter turned the money he made into shit. Later he would see about more bouts. If he won. If he lost. Tommy's life was like Plugg's, whose philosophy said, *You win. You lose. It's all rack 'em. Next game.* Which made good sense to Tommy. He wrapped his mind around that analogy and mailed you the details if you liked. Sent you a pamphlet. There was the game you were participating in. Maybe it was simple rotation or even straight pool. Maybe it was eight ball. Or there was nine ball. There was one pocket. There was the cue ball and the object ball. There was this angle and that angle and English and backspin, the kick shot and the bank, the masse, path A and path B and the hole. It was onesy, twosy. It was all *rack 'em. Next game.*

There were even trick shots you could learn for the fun of it.

Unless you were Pete.

Okay, for him, too, life was simple. We got cheated. We got short-changed. We got gypped. For Tommy, life was too short. For Pete, way too long. Tommy being a thinker, that was a joke Pete and Tommy tossed back and forth like two kids playing catch, Pete talking about Tommy studying French, taking Spanish, Pete pointing out the one didn't count. It was what they hollered across canyons to each other. Pete read Augustine. Plato. Levinas. Fucking Leibniz.

Fucking Spinoza. Fucking E. O. Wilson. On top of Pete's camera equipment waiting on one of his kids to realize that one day they would be needing their father was a leather-bound copy of *The Summa Theologica of St. Thomas Aquinas*. Pete had used his boarding ticket as a bookmark. On one page was a passage he had underlined, in ink, Pete showing no respect for the fine paper. The book was dedicated to *The Blessed Virgin Mary, Immaculate Seat of Wisdom*.

Pete suffered from the intelligentsia's curiosity about Sonny Liston. Honky-assed rubbernecking, Tommy heard it called. Profound it was to Pete that the first time Liston fought in prison they couldn't find gloves big enough for him. Or was it shoes? Shorts? Books were coming out, and movies being made. Pete couldn't wait. Plugg borrowed old film for him, Liston against Patterson—two fights that didn't total five minutes, Patterson down and counted out before the wealthy took their ringside seats, and Pete said, "Liston's like your id coming at you. Your goddamn id."

He said, "What part of no doesn't he understand. All of it. Not the *n*, not the *o*."

He said, "He's taking no prisoners."

He said, "A ton of bricks."

He said, "The man's a conflagration."

Tommy and Plugg and Pete sat in Jane's house and toasted Sonny Liston. Champagne. You bet. "Is you," Pete said, and Tommy said, "Or ain't you," and Plugg joined in, the three of them chanting, "feeling rowdy?"

"Here's to pillage," Pete said.

Tommy said, "To showbiz."

Pete said, "To writing bad checks."

"To the rabble on the move," Plugg said.

Pete wanted to shoot some photos of Tommy standing by Liston's grave, out at Paradise Memorial Gardens here in Las Vegas. He saw an article in the Sunday *Review Journal*. Tommy vetoed the plan. "Embarrassing," Tommy said. "It'll be a contrast," Pete said. "Brute vs. Thinker. You took French," Pete said. "You're a multilingual man," Pete said. He said, "Liston was bad taste itself. Could the man speak English? Tommy Rooke—you're a thinker."

Tommy said, "And Spanish," and Pete's reply was supposed to be, "Doesn't count," only he passed on it.

A small dose of flattery to get his way.

———————

So here Tommy was at Sonny Liston's grave. Flights landing at McCarran passed directly overhead. Low, but not so you heard them. Every day he could Tommy came here. His first visit had been hunt-and-peck, Tommy making his way up and down and north and south and east and west, and he couldn't find the marker. There was a mausoleum at the end of a row of trees cut to look like popsicles. Wasn't Liston's grave. Tommy asked a man and a woman who arrived in a pink Cadillac convertible. The man was reaching into the back seat, and Tommy said, "I was wondering if you know where Sonny Liston's buried."

The man came up with a bundle of irises, and the woman took them. "I'll show you," he said. Pleasant gent. Fifty, fifty-five. White hair, long and tangled. Baggy butter-yellow pants and a shirt that said Eddie's Diner on it. Something of the beachcomber about him. "Fight fan?" he said.

"I am," Tommy said.

"You see that Tyson debacle?" the man said.

Tommy said, "Which one?"

The man nodded and said, "You got that right."

They walked across the grass, row after row of flat-to-the-ground plaques. No real tombstones here. The woman went off in her own direction. On the other side of a low hedgerow a family had gathered at a new grave, lots of kids. Spanish floated in on what there was of a breeze. Out here, the heat wrapped around you. You had to love the sky for being the blue it was.

Tommy said to his guide, "You're talking about him and Holyfield's ear?"

The man was studying Tommy, looking him up and down like he might know this character from somewhere. But recognition was a few hours away. Probably would come in the middle of the night when the guy got up to pee. Maybe Tommy was the salesman who sold him that outrageous car. He said, "Here we are."

And there was the grave. Charles "Sonny" Liston.

Tommy shook the man's hand, and the man said to Tommy, "I know you. Don't I?" Tommy assured him he didn't.

Now, when Tommy came, he pulled in off Eastern Avenue. Maybe there was a plane, so he lifted a hand against the sun. A 747, tail blue and a red swirl on it. First you saw the plane in the distance. The sun glinted off it. One spot of light on the horizon. Still in your car you swung through a curve, past one marker that sat upright under an olive tree. GARDEN OF PEACE. Then the lane straightened out, and you parked on the road. Tommy counted the rows from the curb. Seven. All the flowers he walked by were fake. What chance would the real thing have had in this kind of heat? Liston was at the end of his row.

The markers were a dull weathered gray, placard size, and flat. Liston's said, CHARLES "SONNY" LISTON 1932–1970. Then "A Man." Quotes around the words. The year, 1932, was somebody's guess. Who really knew how old Liston was? His mama didn't know. Liston only confused the question when asked.

Every time Tommy came, dead Pete and living Tommy had the same conversation. Did Liston throw the fights with Muhammad Ali? Tommy claimed Liston outright admitted he flopped the second time around. Ali's phantom punch was just that, a phantom punch. Step-and-Fetch-It taught that short blow to Ali? Yeah, right.

Dead Pete said, There's no proof.

The whistle blowers are talking, living Tommy said.

Pete said, Liars for money. For their fifteen minutes. For spite. Revenge. It was all after the fact. A court of law would see them for the lowlife self-aggrandizers they were and toss out their testimony. Bunch of admitted felons. They had nothing better to do than get down on their knees and hunt for clay feet. Too much debunking going on. It wasn't healthy.

Sonny confessed all of it, Tommy said.

BS, Pete said. BS, from day one.

Tommy said, There's a theory the cops killed him. Made it look like an overdose. They can make it look real.

Pete said, Not with his survival instincts. Not when you live on the earth so bluntly.

Not, Pete said, when you're that big.

That first visit, Tommy knelt by the grave, and he was not sure he was ever going to stand again. Had Sonny Liston been Pete's pal, Liston would have stepped up the night Pete was shot. Liston would have sensed Fletcher Chicago before the kid appeared out of the darkness, and he would have coldcocked him. Somehow he would have stopped the whole thing before it got underway. Sonny Liston wouldn't have let it happen no matter how it played itself out.

Liston would not have done the smart thing. He would not have covered up. He would not have weathered the storm. It was a side street, not a ring. There was no canvas. There were no ropes. There was definitely no referee ready to step in and save somebody's ass.

Sonny Liston would have uprooted a palm tree and tossed it at Fletcher Chicago. He would have fought a fucking tornado if he had to.

Tommy got to his old banger of a truck, dialed Jane on his cell phone, and she talked him through the drive to her house.

The night Tommy carried Hector out to the patio at 4:00 A.M., after Jane and Tommy had sex, the morning after the night Pete died, Tommy told his son he had covered up, like a fighter learns to do. Tommy told his boy how smart Tommy Rooke had been to get in the pocket. Body punches, Tommy told Hector. They'll break you down.

Tommy showed Hector that crescent moon and said, "It's about to spill its water," which the boy took, Tommy thought, as well as a child could take such news. So, encouraged, Tommy said, *Die Welt weltet.* Words from one of Pete's heavy thinkers.

The world worlds.

"Sing it," Tommy said to Hector.

And the boy did. So help us God.

You Missed
Something Good
with Hats

Three A.M., and Tommy Rooke and Jane were up and waiting on the police. Rare, but now and then, serious rain hit Las Vegas, summer gullywashers, and if you didn't unplug Jane's cordless, the phone dialed 911 on its own. They woke half an hour ago to a flash of lightning, followed by thunder, and seconds later, a dispatcher called, a woman this time. Tommy was the one who answered, said, "Delivery or pickup," and Jane grabbed the phone from him.

"It's the weather," Jane said to the woman. "We've been through this before."

Sounded to Tommy like they would be going through it again.

"You'll have reports on your records," Jane said. "Check them."

Not going to happen. You could hear the lady saying *ma'am* from Tommy's side of the bed.

Jane said, "Okay?"

It wasn't okay.

Jane said, "All's well. There's no trouble. You don't have to send anybody."

Did her no good, as you can guess. The law required the cops to step into their hats, holster their guns, and come. No one wants to be sued or be the subject of bad press for not doing their job. The only fact they had other than the 911 call itself was that some smart aleck answered the phone. It wasn't likely, but it was possible Tommy was one of your A.M. crazies holding a pistol to Jane's head, making her lie, telling her to talk nice or else.

"You didn't help," Jane said to him. She had hung up. She said, "You don't joke with these people. Their sense of humor is the size of peanut." She collected a file and nail polish from her dresser and said to him, "What are you, a little boy?" She settled on the end of the bed.

From Jane's bedroom, they could see through her slider the lightning take potshots at the Las Vegas Strip. There was a great view of the MGM Grand, the Tropicana, Luxor, and New York, New York, the hotels' colors the primary reds and blues and greens you see in cartoons, only vibrant, jazzed by the atmosphere. Hector lay between Tommy and Jane. Oblivious. No fear in the kid. The TV was on. Jane had her back to it. Sitting against the headboard, Tommy could see the screen over her shoulder. She was painting her nails.

The problem was cordlessness itself, AT&T told Jane. Their suggestion was unplug the unit if she left the house. One time she forgot, heavy rain surprised the city, the phone did its thing, and the police, getting no answer at the front door or around back, came in through the slider. Jane was at the doctor with Hector. Cops, defending their breaking and entering, would later ask her, what if she had a heart attack, was lying on the tile in the bathroom, alive, but not able to speak up? What if a kidnapper had her by the throat? She was, after all, Tommy Rooke's ex-wife, the mother of the big-time fighter's boy, of Hector Rooke. So there was fame and a lot of money involved. Wouldn't she want them coming on in? To protect and to serve. They had lifted the slider from its track, set it aside, and walked right through. Afterwards, one of the them came back and showed her how to drill through the metal at the top of the slider and what size bolt to buy to fit to that hole so nobody else could do what the cops themselves had done. A slim piece of wood laid in the tracks wouldn't stop anybody who was serious about getting in.

Tonight's thunder and lightning hadn't bothered to check in with Tommy or Jane, and they hadn't been awake when it rolled across the valley. Weird things happen when electricity is involved, AT&T claimed. Disconnect the phone when you go to bed, they said. Their records showed that she owned a wall phone. Rely on it was their suggestion. Jane went through three different cordless models, AT&T more than happy to send her new ones to try, free of additional charges. All the lines, coming and going, the company tested and retested. No problems there. She didn't want to give up the cordless and be stuck in one spot in the kitchen, unable to busy her-self when people called, and she didn't want a cell phone because of the cancer that would crawl into her head the first time she put such a device to her ear, Jane's logic being the same logic the Greeks called tempting fate.

"Would you not move?" Jane said to Tommy. "You're jiggling the bed. Stop it."

"God," Tommy said, "you got to see this."

"Seen lightning before."

Wasn't what he meant. On TV three GIs were dancing. Turner Classic Movies. The fifties, Tommy was thinking. Maybe the forties. Each man had a trash-can lid on one foot, the metal kind you don't see anymore, one lid to a soldier, the right foot. Looked like they had jammed the toes of their dress shoes under the handles. "No, no," Tommy said. "The TV."

"I can't," she said. She stroked polish on a nail. "Sit still, will you?"

"Look for yourself."

You got to wonder. Who, dancing like gangbusters, stops and thinks, *What we're doing, it's okay*, but then they spot trash-can lids lying on the floor, fit them to a foot, and off they go into another di-mension?

The soldiers were wearing their dress uniforms. Probably on leave in the movie. Must have been around World War II. God, what a time that was to live in. So lyrical, so fierce. Full of causes and crossroads and grand possibilities. Ups and downs that counted. What these GIs were doing, it made you want to put the blues in your back pocket forever. There couldn't be one thing on this earth worth being sad about. Not hunger. Not death. Not cruelty to ani-mals. Not when soldiers who had trash cans on their feet could hoof it the way they were.

Jane capped her polish. "Done," she said. She blew on her nails, then showed Tommy. Metallic blue. "You missed something good with hats the other night," she said.

"What do you mean?"

"On TV," she said, and she turned to get a look at the soldiers. Too late. They had quit dancing and had turned into regular joes speaking lines and talking about a place to eat. She said, "That's that dancing-in-the-rain guy."

It was. The men had shed their garbage-can lids and replaced them where they belonged. Neatnicks, these GIs, responsible lads. Clean-cut fellows. Apple pie eaters. They went into a cafe.

Tommy said, "What do you mean *with hats*?"

"On the television," she said. "Tap dancing with hats."

"They were wearing hats?"

"They juggled hats and tossed them back and forth. They twirled hats on canes."

"While they danced?"

"You'll have to see it for yourself," she said. "It was a movie. I can't describe it."

Tommy told her it couldn't have been as good as the GIs. There on the portable in her bedroom had been the best reason Tommy had seen in ten years to get up and breathe in and out all day long. Consider the possibilities. Given time and some room to move around in you could learn to tap dance with a garbage-can lid stuck to your foot. You would need days, months, even a year, and you would need to be able to walk and chew gum at the same time. That was all it would take. Tommy said to Jane, "Tricks with hats is nothing. You see tricks with hats all the time. There isn't anything you could do with hats like what they did with garbage-can lids on their feet."

"It took practice," she said.

"And the garbage-can lids didn't?"

"You should have seen it."

"Zora Folley," Officer Carl Six said. Tommy was escorting him through the French doors into Jane's kitchen. His partner, a woman, walked Jane down the hall. Two pros doing their job. Separating Tommy and Jane. Only way to get to the truth. Carl Six was a fight fan. He had seen Tommy box. "*The* Tommy Rooke," he had said at the front door, right off. Turned out he knew Tommy's father, Gus. Carl Six was cognizant of the fact that Tommy retired never having lost or relinquished the two titles he held. Officer Six mentioned fights he went to.

Tommy's thinking was Officer Betty Schiller and Jane would end up in the back bedroom talking nail polish or Hector. Crucify Tommy that he was stereotyping, but he knew Jane and how she handled particular situations. She sized you up and pinned you to the wall, and she was seldom wrong. Name your subject. Jane held her own. Wyoming, the Crow and Shoshones, their epic battles and blood shed over hunting ground? Money market funds versus certificates of deposit? Rembrandt's brushwork? The waltz they claim is mathematics? Nail polish, its ins and outs. Babies. Don't accuse Tommy of disrespect. You didn't marry her. Tommy married her, and she divorced him—irreconcilable reasons, which was her joke—and now she was remarrying him in a couple of weeks. Together, they produced Hector, who, should you ever meet the child, you would understand for yourself was a miracle kid. Officer Schiller, half an hour from now, when she came down the hall, Jane at her elbow, and when the five of them—Hector in Jane's arms—met in the foyer under its bright chandelier, she would be holding a gift, a knickknack, a bauble Jane gave her, Jane calling her by her first name, saying *Betty* like they grew up together. Maybe it would be earrings or a brooch, a doodad, turquoise inlay.

Carl Six said to Tommy, "Zora Folley never really got his chance. Not until he was too old. Everybody—the champs, they ran from him. You can look it up." He had turned down coffee and was pacing between Jane's kitchen and where her breakfast nook was. Tile to carpet, carpet to tile, on his rubbery shoes. He kept sniffing. He was cut from your hero mold toes to hairline. "Patterson ducked Folley," Carl Six said. He looked closely at a photo of Tommy and Jane.

"Didn't he fight Liston?" Tommy said.

Carl Six said, "The exception that proves the rule."

"A knockout?"

"In three. One of a handful of fights the man lost."

Tommy said, "He fought Ali."

"Another exception that proves another rule." Carl Six brushed against a counter. "You mind," he said, and he gestured toward a stool.

Tommy told him to take a load off.

"Liston was a Cossack," Six said. "A one-man pogrom. No way did he lose those fights to the butterfly-and-bee man." Six tested the give and take of the stool. He said, "You know what they say about photography. If you want to improve your photographs 100 percent, get closer, fill your frame with your subject."

Quarter to four in the morning, lightning cracking Las Vegas open. Thunder like a Civil War battle. And from Officer Carl Six, craftsmanship and wisdom.

He said, "I'm still talking Folley. Photography and Folley, there's a connection. Choreography and his footwork—it got him closer to his opponent. His subject, you could say. Folley kept you inside his shoulders. You filled up his frame." Carl Six made a frame in the air. He said, "He got you inside his frame, kept himself low, and beat the snot out of your internal organs." Carl Six stood, walked a few steps away. He waved Tommy off, like they were in a skit and said, "Who am I telling tales to? I seen you fight. You don't need me explaining to you about not getting tall in the pocket."

"Folley's only a name out of the past to me," Tommy said.

Carl Six said, "I'm only talking is all. Flapping my gums uselessly." Tommy nodded, and Six asked if he had a Coke. Tommy found one in Jane's refrigerator. Six took it and said, "You know we haven't come far enough from being monkeys to be feeling good about ourselves."

Four A.M., lightning, thunder, craftsmanship and wisdom. Now, the science report. Evolution revisited.

Tommy said, "Officer Six, am I missing something? What is it you're telling me? Folley. Boxing. Monkeys."

"I got to ask," he said. He opened his Coke. Sat.

"Yeah."

"O. J. Simpson," Six said. "You recall him talking about getting physical with the wife?"

"Me and Jane?"

Six shrugged.

"Doesn't apply." Tommy said. "Isn't an option. Never happened."

Carl Six was on his feet and pacing again, hesitating only to sip his Coke. "You guys divorced, right?" he said, his face and his hands and his shoulders saying, *Doing my job is all.* "It was what information we was given on our way over. There was a 911 call, and a hang up. Then you being here creates some questions. The information we get is she lives alone, divorced and a kid."

"You guys know that kind of thing about people?"

"If we have to."

Tommy explained the cordless, the weather. He said, "Me and Jane, we're remarrying."

Carl Six tipped his Coke in congratulations. "Here's to you and yours and long life," he said.

"I sold my place."

"Yeah."

"It's logical, my being here."

Officer Betty Schiller, coming down the hallway, was talking, saying, "I'll phone you with the title," and she and Jane stepped into the kitchen, Schiller saying to Carl Six, "We out of here?"

So it was the five of them saying their good-byes, and there was Officer Schiller, under foyer light, holding a brooch, a sterling silver pink flamingo, its eye turquoise. Carl Six said to Tommy, "I have film of Folley. I'll bring it by."

———

"Phone you the title of what?" Tommy said to Jane. Close to 5:00 A.M. by now, and they were tucking Hector in, their boy limp in Tommy's arms, so deeply asleep Tommy could have wept. Tommy would be skipping the morning's roadwork. Maybe even the gym this afternoon. He didn't have the heart for it. He had a fight coming up, Tommy Rooke getting back into the ring. Three years out of boxing, and Tommy was unretiring, was supposed to be training.

Jane said, "A book on dreams she told me about."

Turned out, Jane, talking to Officer Schiller, described the dream Tommy told Jane he was having when the dispatcher phoned. "Betty says what you're doing is called lucid dreaming," Jane said. "You dream you're dreaming."

First names. *Betty.* Had Jane spent her time with Officer Carl Six, it would have been *Carl* when they left. Tommy said to Jane, "I do it all the time lately."

"You need psychiatric help," she said. "If you dream you're dreaming, you need professional help. There's hidden stuff that has to be brought to the surface."

"Brought to the surface is the scientific term?"

"So Betty says."

"Betty the cop is advising me on dreams?"

"Officer Betty Schiller. It's her avocation."

"She moonlights as what, a dream analyzer?"

"She knows what she's talking about."

Before they got back into bed, Jane offered a prayer for Tommy and her and Hector. She read from her little book *The Night Watches*. Tommy stood by the slider and watched lightning splinter the skyline. Behind him, Jane addressed God in his ubiquity. God's eyes, she read, were everywhere. She said *pillar of cloud, fire by night*. Jane said, *Jesus!* She said, *Blessed Savior! Abide with me.*

––––––––

Put.

Three days later, dinner over, and Jane said, "Put." She was reading from Officer Schiller's dream book, and Tommy was taking notes. The book, which Betty dropped off, had a quarter moon on the front. "Put *riding it*," Jane said. Tommy rode a bicycle in last night's dream. He dreamed he was dreaming that he found a bicycle and hopped on it, let it coast down a long, slowly curving driveway.

Tommy said, "Is riding the same as letting it roll along on its own?"

She said, "Put *downhill*."

"That means something?" Tommy said.

She said, "We'll find out." She flipped pages.

Tommy said, "Should I write that I wasn't actually pedaling?"

"Put *downhill*," she said. "Just write *downhill* and add *driveway*." Tommy did. She said, "What was the condition of the bike?"

Tommy described it. Thick tires. You could see the treads. Chrome fenders. A big seat. Tommy said, "An old-fashioned sturdy bicycle."

She said, "Put it down. Put it all down." She asked if he pushed the bike before he got on. He didn't think so. She said, "What color was it?"

"Green," Tommy said. "Except for the fenders."

She said she would look up *bicycle*.

They had read the preface, and they had checked the index for *lucid dreams*. Nothing told them what it meant when you dreamed you were dreaming. The book didn't back up Schiller's telling Jane that Tommy needed professional psychiatric help.

Jane said, "Put *green light*. "

"Light?"

"Write it down." She spelled the word, l-i-g-h-t.

She took his list and said, "Let's split it right down the middle. Put *Positive* on one side. *Negative* on the other side."

Tommy drew a line down the middle and labeled each half.

She said, "Positive is *growth, healing.*"

"Like plants," Tommy said. "Makes sense."

"Related to heaven," she said.

Tommy said, "Is that positive or negative?" Which earned him a dirty look. "Negative as in dying, not as in heaven," Tommy said. "Heaven would be a positive. I was only thinking of dying being not a good thing." Got him a second dirty look. You only joke with the religious on their own terms.

"Dark green is negative," she said. "It relates to sickness and envy."

Tommy wrote green under *Negative.*

"Like a fish which hides its arms," Plugg said. He was talking about Tommy's opponent in the upcoming fight, Carl Jarret, kid who believed he was one step from a title bout. Jarret's people saw Tommy as a big name and walkover.

"Smoke and mirrors," Plugg said. "Mirrors and smoke."

Tommy didn't know what was up with Plugg. He wasn't normally a mouth. Not Carl T. Plugg. His nature was he shut up and put up. In a pool hall, taking down some joker, Plugg dressed like a barrister and didn't waste one word. You watched and understood how silence could get under your skin. No yakkity-yak from Plugg. You sat there and it was clear you were watching a professional stickup. If he got pissed, he prolonged the other guy's misery, crackerboxed him shot after shot. He played himself out of position five or six strokes in a row, then potted a dozen impossible makes to remind you that you might as well retreat to a corner and cut your toes off one by one with a dull knife. It wasn't your day. That was Plugg's way of talking when business was at hand.

Today Plugg couldn't shut up. All the time Tommy was getting his hands wrapped Plugg paced back and forth inside his ear. Tommy needed to pay attention to what was being done, but Plugg kept at him. "Body shots," he said. "The body. The body. The body." Tommy brought Hector to the gym, and Plugg was holding the boy. He sailed Tommy's handsome son through the air, playing the pilot game, and saying, "Who don't we hook with, young man?" Hector rewarded him, gave up that grin of his. Tweaked your heart, it did. "Young man," Plugg said, "we don't hook with a hooker." Hector was flying. Plugg was wearing a satin jacket, THE KING OF TUCSON R.V. PARK on the back. Most likely he won it off a tourist. It wasn't the way Plugg dressed. He was a clothes horse. Always crisp, snazzy and with class.

You're coming up a young fighter, you do your boxing in those sideways back street gyms for a monthly paycheck and for fight tickets you can't give—forget sell—to the homeless on a subzero night. Back then, Tommy worked for Plugg. Now Plugg worked for Tommy.

"He's a fighter doesn't know where he wants to be or where he doesn't want to be in the ring. You can move him. You're the crossing guard," Plugg said. "SOB's got a wild hair up his ass." He winked at Hector and said, "The kid's erratic and a lefty. He throws hard from down under and to the body."

Tommy moved to the heavy bag and worked combinations and angles. Stepped around, and then jab, jab, right. His footwork was still the A B C D stuff of Dick and Jane. It hadn't come back to him like he thought it would. Surprised Tommy. His DNA forgetting like that.

Plugg said, "He fights in spots. Explodes." Plugg drifted away, to one side, which felt good to Tommy, like when a line cleared from behind you. Plugg had been crowding him. Plugg said, "His feet give him away." For weeks he had been preaching one message: Don't let Jarret set up. Had been saying the kid had one gear, forward. The kid couldn't go left, right, or back. "We don't hook with a hooker," Plugg said to Hector. Jarret was a one-way street and a cul-de-sac, but had a lethal hook, short and tight. "If we do," Plugg said, and he looked at Tommy and said, "Sing it, Tommy. If we hook with—"

Tommy wasn't about to be the entertainment.

It was clear to Tommy that Plugg loved Hector but was pissed at Tommy's bringing the boy to the gym. Squaring that pissed was his anger at Tommy for refusing to change the day Jane and Tommy were remarrying. She wanted January 1, which meant she was getting January 1. Fight was set for February 9, seven weeks down the road. So that was pissed squared, only then add that Tommy had refused to walk away from Jane and set up a camp. Plugg wanted Tommy to bring in Max Wilcox out of Tennessee, a big name trainer, and Plugg had arranged for facilities outside of Palm Springs. He was dreaming of doing things the way Ali and Frazer had done them. Tommy passed. Slept at Jane's. Stayed with her and his boy Hector.

More pissed: Tommy was missing workouts.

This minute, to shut Plugg up, Tommy said, "Give me a count."

"One-multifarious," Plugg said. "Two-multifarious," and Tommy tattooed the bag, thirty seconds, everything Tommy had. Somewhere around sixteen-, seventeen-multifarious, he thought he would black out.

Plugg tossed Tommy a towel, and Tommy wiped down. Got his gloves off. The tape and gauze. He reached for Hector, and Plugg handed him over, settled him in Tommy's hands. "Soft and softer," Plugg said. "It's how the famous lady pool shark tells you to hit a cue ball. It's how you hold a baby."

Tommy asked him if he had ever seen Zora Folley fight. Lit up Plugg's eyes. He gave Tommy one of those tip-of-the-fingers kisses you saw from chefs.

"What?" Tommy said.

"Folley, a fucking work of art," Plugg said. "Not pretty but simple and to the point. Like torture."

Plugg was all drama today. In a corner of the gym, sitting on his hands, was a shifty character everyone called Moss because of the way he hung around. His name was Freddie Griffen, and his story was he came to Las Vegas in the early nineties to play basketball at UNLV. He was being counted on to continue the dynasty. The man got caught taking booster money and a car. Dumbfuck thought he could, at six-eleven, age seventeen, three days out of high school, drive around the city in a Mercedes and no one in the wrong kind of suit would notice. He never walked onto the floor at the Thomas and Mack, not even to show his stuff. The story broke, he dropped out of sight, but you heard he stayed in town. Now what he did was anybody's guess. He put some moves on Jane when she and Tommy were divorced, so that when he saw Tommy now he had a way of disappearing. There would be none of that today. Not now. He left, he would lose more face than he could afford. Tommy pulled on sweats and wandered over, talking, saying, "Looks to me like you're making a living, Moss."

"Time to stick a fork in the fool," Moss said. He meant the featherweight in the ring at Tommy's back. The youngster's sparring partner was out to hurt the kid. Moss said to Tommy, "You can call me Freddie, first names being so much nicer."

Tommy heard Plugg behind him. The man had wandered over to the ring and was yelling at the fighters. "What is this, junior prom?" Plugg was saying. "Can I have the next dance?"

Moss got into his jacket pocket and extracted a small box of kitchen matches. He said, gesturing toward the door, "I'm thinking I'll get me a smoke." He stuck a cigar in his face. The cigar, which was a stubby fat sucker, and the kitchen matches—Moss's trademarks.

"How you going to stop Plugg?" Plugg said behind Tommy, who turned in time to see Plugg throw some punches, shadow boxing. Plugg said, "How you going to do this? You can't stop Plugg?"

Moss said to Tommy, "You never saw me dance, did you?"

Tommy said, "Are we talking about actual dancing?"

"We are."

"I heard you played ball."

"Not ball. Dance."

"What are you telling me?"

"You'd have admired me, is all," he said. "A fighter with your kind of feet, you'd have appreciated what I can do."

Behind Tommy, Plugg said, "Smoke and mirrors."

"Ballroom dancing," Moss said. "I was outstanding."

Tommy said, "Ain't you too tall? You'd stick out like a sore thumb."

Moss said, "All the more to dazzle with." He stood—the man seven, eight inches taller than Tommy—and he said, "A boxer like you, you would have applauded me." He looked at Hector in Tommy's arms and said, "I need that smoke."

"We'll walk out with you," Tommy said.

Moss said, "You done?"

"Workout's fucked," Tommy said. "Something in the air."

Moss detoured over to Plugg where he collected some money. Outside, there were Christmas trees in a lot next to Cal's. A sign had been rolled in. TED PARKER'S BACK WITH THE BEST TREES IN TOWN. Yellow bulbs blinked in sequence around the edges of the sign. The sun knocked their impact. An arrow curled across the top and pointed toward the lot. Tommy held Hector up high, sailed him through the air. He said to his boy, "Welcome to the world, little pilot." God, it was a day to behold. Seventy degrees, if that. The air thin and clean.

Moss came out, magnificent grin on his mug. A short ponytail poked out at the back of his neck.

Tommy said, "Freddie, so I'll know, what happened with you and Jane?"

Moss lost that grin.

Tommy said, "I'm thinking of clean slates."

Moss said, "Tommy, I got all the respect for you in the world, but my business is my business. I hear you and Jane getting married again, and that news come to me as the kind of thing a body, man or woman, got to appreciate, there being so little actual happiness running around these days." Moss touched his heart and said, "It warms me."

Tommy walked over, still flying Hector.

"I won't be answering your question," Moss said. "I'm not under arrest here." He fired up his cigar to make his point.

Tommy looked at the Christmas trees, at Ted Parker's sign, at Cal's, at the miracle of Hector, and Tommy said, "Ballroom dancing?"

Moss, like Plugg earlier over Folley, lit up. He did several steps here in the parking lot. Hand at his waist—you've seen dancers do that. Mesmerized Tommy and Hector. Hector clapped, the way babies put their hands together. You could see in Moss's and Hector's eyes what it meant to be fresh to this planet.

"I got to admire that," Tommy said.

Moss said, "You got to."

Tommy said, "Freddie, you have yourself a Merry Christmas."

"True," he said. "And you and Jane."

———

Carl Six caught up with Tommy at Gus's house. Some of the furniture from Tommy's place, which he was selling piece by piece through the want ads, was stored in the garage. Tommy and Jane, they planned to sell her house too and create for them and for Hector a new environment. Tommy was shooting hoops on the cement court near Gus's pool. Earlier, Tommy drove Gus to McCarran, a flight to L.A. His kid sister Ginger was at the house, feeding Vegas Vic.

"I hear you played the game at a high level," Carl Six said. He made a shooting motion. A set shot. Ginger stood behind him. Gus's backyard dropped three tiers to the pool, and Carl Six was up above, on the patio, wearing Levi's and a T-shirt. He had to speak up for Tommy to hear him. Six started down the steps, and Tommy let fly a three, which rattled out.

"Not my game," Six said.

"Football?" Tommy said. Flattery, taking Six's size and all-American good looks into account and giving him credit for both. Tommy's real guess was Six sat in the stands and chugged beer. The man was a car jockey, not a gym rat. His game involved sitting around watching NASCAR. Carl Six probably drag raced in high school. Probably had himself a juvenile record, was likely one of the kids the cops chased after.

Carl Six said, "Hockey."

Tommy looked toward the expanse of desert he could see from Gus's and said, "You didn't grow up here."

"Born and raised in St. Paul, Minnesota," Six said. He had reached Tommy and was holding out a video. "I brought this by," he said. "It's a copy." Handwritten on the tape was *Folley vs. Ali*.

"If you lived in the neighborhood, I'd say that your doing so was neighborly of you," Tommy said.

"Like I told you the other night," Six said, "I'm not suggesting I understand anything about boxing, and I'm not giving advice." He gestured for the ball, and Tommy flipped it to him. Six shot like he was heaving luggage to the upper shelf in a closet. Didn't even draw iron. He shook his head at his own incompetence. He said, "You got a hockey stick and an ice pond nearby?" he said. "Maybe I could show you I'm not a complete klutz." Carl Six was wearing loafers and no socks. Tommy asked if he was having a day off, and Six said, "Sort of."

"You're just kicking around?"

"Jane told me you were here."

"You didn't want to leave the tape with her?"

"That possibility didn't occur to me," he said. "Which goes to show how I wasn't thinking at the top of my game."

Tommy said, "Officer Carl Six, I get the feeling you're here for more than just the tape."

Six walked over and picked up the basketball. It had rolled under an oleander. He dribbled coming back, handled the ball the way a wingless bird might. He couldn't take his eye off it for half a second. He underhanded the ball to Tommy and said, "O. J. comes to mind again."

"How's that?"

"You watch any of the trial?"

Tommy hadn't. The man killed his wife. You had to be an idiot to think otherwise. He got off because of his timing and because rich men tell no lies. Millionaires are 100 percent not guilty.

"There was a video he made," Six said. "O. J. promoting some exercise fad."

Tommy caught bits and pieces on the news. Who hadn't? Simpson looked goofy and sounded stupid. Tommy said, "One more hero down the drain."

"You'll not get an argument from me," Six said.

"You think I did something to Jane?" Tommy said.

"In the video," Six said, "O. J. says something about blaming it on working out with the wife if she shows up bruised." He looked out over the desert. He said, "I'm not getting this right, but close enough. O. J.—you can see this on the video—he's laughing, and he is saying you can always blame it on working out."

Tommy started himself and Carl Six walking up the flagstone steps toward the patio, letting Six know Six was leaving, but doing it in a way so he could think Tommy respected him. Tommy said, "Officer Carl Six, I like to set other fighters up so I can hit them. The way I manage the ring, it's an art. It's why I do it. It's why I'm unretiring. I like to hit people. It don't come from my growing up. I wasn't one of those stories. You can see by looking around I didn't begin life in a garbage dump. I didn't miss meals. No one forgot my birthdays. I had a great mommy. I could swap you home videos. Give you footage of the family celebrating the holidays. I didn't get left out at Christmas time." They reached the patio, and Ginger came out of the house carrying drinks on a tray, which was as likely a thing to happen as the sun not rising one morning, Ginger being any kind of a host, that is. Tommy said to her, "Officer Carl Six is on duty."

She said, "It's Coke."

"He don't drink Coke," Tommy said. "It's a religious thing."

"You a Mormon?" she said to Six.

He said, "Not hardly."

Tommy guided Carl Six toward the side gate, talking, being a pal of sorts, and Tommy said, "I think you've got a fan."

Six said, "She's a pretty girl."

"In her way," Tommy said. "She's on hold. There's a guy playing basketball for the Utes, but she's not finished seeing the world."

"Wise of her," Six said. "Smart."

Tommy said, "You don't fight out of hate. It's a sport. You know how they say it's not personal. It's really that you can't let it be personal. You say, 'I'm going to kill that motherfucker,' and you end up being the motherfucker on your back." Tommy opened the gate for Carl Six and ushered him through it. Out front was Six's cruiser. Tommy said, "Carl, I don't know if you have a record of this, but I was fifteen and didn't know how to fight, except what I was born with, and one night I got drunk and I beat another kid up so bad he went into the hospital. He's still around town, and we talk. He thinks of us as friends. You know how that happens. We do lunch, like they say. He's got trouble with his hearing. My doing. He walks so he's sideways a little, which is my doing. All of it is my fault." Tommy and Carl Six brushed past an olive tree Gus needed to have cut back. Tommy said, "It's why I box. Do you see what I'm saying?"

"Because of the guy?"

"Because I can hurt someone like that."

"You wanted to hurt the kid?"

"Not the point. But no. And yes. You do that—you bring about damage—and it takes the charm out of it. Like the other fighters aren't living up to their end of the bargain. No one's supposed to get hurt too bad."

"You thinking that way and you telling me, you putting the feelings into words—is that good for getting into the ring?"

"It ain't. It truly ain't."

Six stalled. He said, "I'm doing my job—that's it."

"No," Tommy said, "you're not. You're way past doing your job."

Six stopped in the driveway and turned to look straight at Tommy. First time he had done that since Tommy met the man. This big cop—six-five, two hundred and thirty pounds, no fat on him—this was the first time he had faced Tommy dead on.

Tommy said, "We'll trade advice. Here's mine, Don't linger in the hitting zone."

"Yeah," he said, "I know. And don't retreat straight back. Take an angle."

It was then they shook hands—first time for that too, and Tommy said, "Your partner, Betty, she didn't tell you that Jane said I hurt her. I don't have to be told this. I know it for fact."

Carl Six let go of his hand and shook his head. He said, "She didn't."

"And Jane didn't tell you."

"No."

"Like I said, you don't need to tell me."

Carl Six started for his cruiser, stopped, and said, "You keep that." He meant the video Tommy was hanging on to. "I copied it for you."

"Certainly," Tommy said.

He said, "Maybe I'll see you around."

———————

Tommy and Jane were up late again, in the bedroom, Hector in his crib. No storm forecast, but they had finally wised up and unplugged the cordless whenever they went to bed now. There was the regular phone if trouble had to reach them. It was 1:00 A.M., and Jane wanted Tommy to see the movie with tap dancing and hats. Tommy was hoping for the GIs and their garbage-can lids. Jane checked the *TV Guide*, but they didn't know the name of either one. Tommy said, "Look for the star's name, the dancing-in-the-rain guy."

She said, "Maybe the description will say, *if you miss this, you'll miss something good with hats.*"

They tried the movie channels. Nothing but Elvis or biblical crap, Chuck Heston as Moses on Turner, acting a lot like when you saw him speaking up for the NRA. On AMC, Karl Malden in a toga, the man suffering through a truly bad film. More Elvis, the King and Ann-Margret hot for each other but not saying so.

Tommy popped in Carl Six's Folley-Ali video and said, "Officer Six stopped at Gus's."

Jane said, "I showed him all my bruises."

"I showed him mine."

Tommy sat on the edge of the bed, and Jane passed by. She hesitated, came back, said, "Let me give you some advice," and she cuffed him at the back of the head, lightly, a parody of a cuff. It was her Three Stooges joke. *Let me give you some advice. Bonk.* Then she was headed out.

Tommy said to her back, "He thinks I'm O. J. Simpson."

"Don't you wish," she said, and she disappeared into the hallway. Tommy heard the bathroom door close. Water ran through the pipes.

A fucking work of art. Plugg was right about Zora Folley. The butterfly-and-bee man was quick, but Folley had a hard overhand right that arrived from out of nowhere. Folley fought smart and solid. Ali circled and danced. Tommy was watching a shadow fight a boulder. Ali was going to knock him out, there was no stopping the inevitable, but you wouldn't have guessed that, not if you took account of the way Folley used the ring. No doubt about the man's equipment. Forty knockouts in his right hand.

"Don't I wish?" Tommy said when Jane got back.

"Wish?"

"Why would I wish I was O. J.?"

"Mr. Simpson has his problems, but my he sits up pretty."

"Handsome is as handsome does."

She cuffed Tommy again and said, "So your grandmother says." She stepped over to her dresser.

Tommy said, "What about you and Moss? I ran into him at the gym a few days back."

"Tommy," she said, "let it go."

"I'm trying to wipe the slate clean."

"Whose? Yours or mine?"

"Everybody's."

Jane said, "Tommy, do you really want to go there? Do you want to talk about the score, whether it's even or not?" And it was then that she, like Officer Carl Six, turned to look at Tommy, and he reached for her waist. She let him hold her. His doing that, Tommy's embrace, sucked some anger from her system, and she said, "Tommy, it's Christmas. Give me a present and don't be wiping slates clean. The past is gone. If you can't let go of it, then we're wasting our time. We're making a mistake trying again. You need to go your way, and I need to go mine." She leaned back so she could see his face whole on, and she said, "Tommy, wrap that gift up for me and put it under the tree."

"Yeah," Tommy said. "I can do that."

She stood by, and they watched Ali and Folley teach each other lessons about boxing. Smart as foxes, the two of them. But Ali. Strap one of those garbage-can lids to his foot, and it would not slow him down. Waltz, jitterbug, tango, shuffle. And punch. And ride Folley's counterpunch.

Seventh round, Ali took over.

Jab. Jab. Jab. Jab.

Made you wince. Made you want to stand up and say, *Quit it, will you?*

Made you want to speak up for Folley. The man was tired. He was ten years older than Ali. Folley waited fourteen years for a title fight, and it was not going to go his way. Something wicked was tapping him on the shoulder.

Folley ducked right, seeking an angle. Right lead from Ali. Second one. The end.

Folley's last chance. Gone.

Surprised Tommy what a blow could do to a man's legs. It shouldn't have. He had been there, done that to another man. But it did.

Tommy headed for the bathroom. When he got back, the bedroom was dark, only the TV on, AMC's host promoting the next feature. *Palm Springs Weekend*. Tommy checked on Hector, their boy charming in his sleep. Tommy worried that Hector too would grow up and produce lucid dreams, that he would be one more dreamer on planet earth in need of therapy. Tommy kissed his boy's forehead. Thought for a second, fever. But no. Hector cool as a cucumber in his pj's. Tommy heard Jane get up, and then, from behind, she put her arms around him, and she said, "I've had a brainstorm." Which turned out to be a kiss, the kind that takes your breath away, that buckles your knees. Heady. Enchanting. They held it for the longest time. After sex, Jane asleep, Tommy sat up in bed, hunting the remote to turn the TV off, and there they were, the tiny people on the screen doing truly unbelievable things with hats. It was better than the garbage cans. It *was* good to see what you could do with a hat, your feet, and an ounce of imagination.

Tommy turned to tell Jane, and she was already sitting up. She was about to say, *I told you so.*

———

McCarran airport, December 31. If this is a dream, and, given Tommy's history, it is lucid, he will soon be in control. If this is a dream, Tommy's unconscious has done a fine job surrounding him and Jane and Hector in detail. They can hear the slot machines. If it's a dream, Tommy is pointing out that in the dream all the colors shimmer, red, white, and gold. He tells her he is dreaming about streamers and bunting and flags. He is asking her what that means—what should he *put* down? Positive? Negative? It's New Year's Eve. There are gigantic neon champagne bottles outlined on the walls. Jane, Tommy, Hector—they're flying to San Diego, then driving to Bluebird, California.

They are living out Jane's wedding plan. It goes like this: They fly to California, to Bluebird, a place she heard about from a friend. Actually, they land in San Diego, rent a car, and drive to Bluebird. Spend a few hours. Buy gifts. They make themselves at home. They act like Bluebird, California, is where they are from. Then Tommy says, "Let's get married," and she says, "Where?" He says, "Las Vegas. It's open twenty-four hours." So they take the redeye back to Las Vegas, and here they rent a limo and find a chapel on the Strip. No reservations. Like it was spur of the moment. Like they truly are couple from out of town.

All this they do with Hector in tow.

Friends at the chapel? Tommy had asked.

Nobody, she said.

Not even Plugg?

Not even Plugg.

So here they are cruising through McCarran airport. One overnight bag between them, and it's hooked over Tommy's shoulder. Everything in it is for Hector's sake. Diapers, talc—all the boy needs. Tommy is holding him high in the air, and he is flying. He's charming the entire airport population, including the pilots on their way to their planes and their duties. They recognize one of their own and salute the boy.

At the baggage check, Tommy says to Jane, "You know, Bluebird is not going to be all it's cracked up to be."

She waltzes through the metal detector and waits for Tommy and Hector on the other side. The two of them pass with flying colors, and Jane takes Tommy's arm, and she says, "Yes, it is."

Tommy hugs Hector to his chest.

Coming toward Tommy and Jane and Hector, on the walking escalator, but striding along like he is determined to keep on trucking on into eternity, is Wayne Newton. The Singing Sensation is so tan you wonder if he's real. It's winter. It's the last day of December.

Jane says to him, *"Danke Schöne,"* and Mr. Las Vegas's smile lands on the three of them like the big spotlight.

Like roll the credits.

The Blues Is
about Mans
and Womans

Vegas Vic was being philosophical. Shit happens, Vic was saying. The world turns. The dog's argument was Tommy Rooke had no right to the blues, not his own, not Humpty Dumpty's, not the prizefighter's.

Take the test:

Q. *You ever walk the chain gang? (Provide documentation)*

Q. *You been shot at, directly?*

Q. *If number two is yes, was you coming in the front door or coming out the back door?*

Q. *You been drunk for so long you wouldn't know sober if it walked up, offered a hand, and introduced itself?*

Q. *A lover (specify gender and orientation) died in your arms?*

Three A.M., and the blues, Vegas Vic wanted Tommy to understand, is about mans and womans. The blues is not boxing. No, sir. The blues is not prizefighting. Fighting is fighting is all it is.

Tommy and the dog were walking the streets of Tommy's gated community. February, and Las Vegas was cold enough for jackets. Hands in pockets. A cap, if you owned one.

Not quite six hours ago, Tommy, in the ring, making a comeback, was throwing a right and stepped into that right we never see. It was the seventh round of a ten rounder, Tommy points up on every card of what had devolved into rumble. He was a step and a half ahead of his opponent, his punches timed and coming at different speeds and angles, Tommy driving the guy into the ropes, not allowing him to plant, spinning him, Tommy working in and under the guy's elbows, sucking the snap from the kid's jab. Tommy's stick and power in perfect harmony. Then Tommy caught the blow—his opponent's prayer, the kid's only real hope.

So many ways to describe a knockout.

Liston claimed it was having your dick yanked off. Floyd Patterson got poetic about it. Hey, Marciano said, the guy knocked my head out from under my hat.

———

Tommy and Vegas Vic turned the corner, and there was Las Vegas laid out across the shallow bowl of the valley. They took a cart path into a golf course, Vic slow, his choppy gait the result of back surgery. A few months ago Tommy found him out by his father's pool, Vic paralyzed. The dog's hind legs useless. He had crawled into the shade of an oleander. Gus was out of town. A myelogram showed blockage of the spinal fluid, and there was a ruptured disk. You could see it there on the screen like a smudge. Surgery gave Vic a 70 percent chance of walking again. Age didn't matter in this case. Two thousand dollars minimum, and everybody pays up front. Or Vic could be put down, and they would take care of the body. The vet's assistant held a clipboard against her chest and said, "Do you want me to call the surgeon?" The lady was not a woman you would want to spend time on a boat with.

Where the sky met the mountains, it was a deep purple. Tommy's ribs hurt, left side. Two of them were cracked, and, like the dog, Tommy gimped along, a blister the size of quarter on his toe, right foot, from throwing punches, the torque, the leverage.

All signs of Tommy's indolence. Tommy trained badly for the fight.

He ignored his bag work. He skipped workouts. He stayed in Las Vegas. Should have left the city, set up a camp in a desert. Piped in fighting music, like Liston, like Ali. He remarried his ex, all that rigmarole, and they bought a new home. All that house hunting. Tommy fiddled, and Rome burned.

Why? Vegas Vic wanted to know.

"Don't ask," Tommy said.

Someone needs to.

What was Tommy to say? That the point was gone? That his pal who had come to photograph it all died on a side street because a goofball tripped and let loose a bullet? That he didn't need any more stories about the harm he had done?

That all the stories were really only unanswered prayers.

"We're a pair," Tommy said to the dog. Vegas Vic stopped and surveyed the city. "Always wanted to know," Tommy said, "do dogs think things are funny? Get together for drinks and tell jokes? Like the one about the two poodles and a rabbi who rent a boat for a day of fishing on Lake Mead?"

Tommy's face hurt like he had been stabbed there. There was a cut the shape of c-clamp at the outside edge of his left eye.

He and the dog stuck to the cart path, wandered through spiky plants and palm trees, and exited the back nine into a cul-de-sac near the club house. Tommy stooped to pick up Vegas Vic, and the dog rocked backwards into Tommy's arms. Tommy cradled him, which hurt his own ribs. Drove a hot spike into them. No pain on earth like it. He held his breath, then hoisted the dog higher, gave Vegas Vic a clear shot at the Strip. The dog sighed. Gave up some lowdown grief. This was his hometown, and he was near the end of his long journey.

The blues, Vic meant to emphasize, is about mans and womans. The blues is forever. You know anything else can say that?

Tommy was thinking nothing lasts forever. Except death, which is one everlasting son of a bitch.

They found a bench where they sat until daybreak, Vic on the seat and asleep at Tommy's side. A full moon—sinister in its indifference, lit up the houses scattered throughout the golf course. It highlighted the unearthly white stucco walls and red-tile roofs. It shone on a lake and spotlighted three coyotes loping across a fairway and along a drainage ditch. Two more appeared, empty handed. One stalled, glanced over its shoulder. Punks of the animal kingdom. Strung-out creatures. Sinewy and lank. Heartless fuckers. Beyond sorry. They had no truck with remorse. The coyotes hunted the neighborhood cats put out at night.

The last thing Vegas Vic said before he slept was a question. Tommy, do you know how to ask?

Cryptic. A riddle. Tommy hated riddles. Rubik's Cubes. Puzzles of any kind. Toys for the real smart.

"What for?" Tommy said. "And who? Ask who about what?" But

the dog was tired, and the question was sort of rhetorical. To ask was an art. This Tommy knew. It involved the setting of things in order.

Tommy carried three items in his pants pocket. Always. Wherever he went, whatever he wore. For luck, a twenty-five-dollar chip from the Horseshoe Club. For health, a fetish bear, Zuni, black marble, a turquoise arrow inlaid into its face. For family, a silver dollar Tommy's Uncle Stuck gave him. Tommy a teenager at the time and about to step into the ring for his first bout.

Tommy sat and rubbed the bear. Felt his ribs healing. He used one thumb, then the other one. Left for the brain. Right for the body. Both of Tommy's hands were swollen. He squeezed the stone tight. Worked a circle.

Only the thumb. Mr. John Lee Hooker. *Hold your hand right there. And then work your thumb kind of beat like.*

The man, John Lee Hooker, like Tommy's friend Pete Hitchcock, was born with a shadow on.

The blues is about mans and womans.

You dig it. And dig my feet.

Tommy never had to ask. Not since he was five years old. No fear. Ever.

From day one he stepped up and took.

Now you're cooking. With gas. Yes, the pot's on now. Oh, you working now.

The blues.

Vegas Vic wobbled and his knees buckled, so Tommy took him in his arms and walked. Tommy felt dizzy.

There was enough light by the time they reached the corner down the street from Tommy and Jane's new house he could see Gus sitting on the curb out front. Gus stood and came to meet them, his arms out. He was wearing an overcoat like this was New York City. "There's food inside," he said. "Plugg's here. Jane's got peach cobbler. French toast."

Plugg would have another bout lined up. He would have spent a whiskey-and-coffee night on the phone. Selling Tommy. Selling the show Tommy had put on. Selling Tommy's stick and power and footwork.

Tommy didn't want to hear it. He was struggling with the dog and trying to locate his car keys. He tasted blood in his throat.

"Hey," Gus said, "why so glum? It's not like you mugged a widow." He dipped into his boxer's stance. Peekaboo. He jabbed, left-left-right. Threw an uppercut. Delight on him like a quilt. As if Tommy had won. As if Tommy hadn't been taken out. Gus was finding joy here in Mudville.

Tommy hurt too much to talk. He hugged Vic to him and dug for his keys.

"You didn't beat up an orphan," Gus said.

No sun yet, only a light seeping into the valley, the bluing mountains lit backside by footlights. It was too cold to be out like this, to sit on a bench all night. The dog was shivering. So was Tommy. His hand shook. Gus said to Tommy, "You're limping."

"It's Vic," Tommy said. "Something's wrong."

Gus stroked the dog under the chin. He said, "What?"

"He can't stand."

"Again? Paralyzed?"

"Different," Tommy said.

"What?"

"Get the door, will you?" Tommy said, and he flipped the car keys to Gus. Jane was in the driveway, and Plugg had come out behind her. He was carrying Hector. Tommy placed Vegas Vic on the front seat, even tried to belt the dog in. Gus hopped in the back. Tommy circled the front of the car, said to Jane, to Plugg, "Vic's in trouble."

"Should I call?" Jane said.

He said, "How about a towel?"

Jane brought him one, and he wrapped Vegas Vic in it. The dog sighed. Deeper.

———

At Emergency Vet, it was first come, first taken care of twenty-four hours a day, seven days a week. Leashes were hanging by the front door. Gus and Tommy, carrying Vic, walked into a hotel-sized waiting room. There was a posting board—lost dogs and cats and birds. A horse was missing. There were breeder ads and photos of animals that needed homes.

One of the receptionists asked Tommy to bring Vegas Vic into an examining room. A vet was on the way. Gus filled out forms, and Tommy fussed over the dog. He worked the towel under Vic, between him and the stainless-steel examining table. The only other animal this early in the morning was a kitten that wasn't going to make it. In the quiet a vet was talking to the owners. It had been dropped off at their house, and they adopted it. All went well, then it started sneezing. Now it was dying.

Vegas Vic, sound asleep, leaked urine. Soaked himself and the towel. Tommy removed it, was looking for a sink, and the vet came in, saw Tommy and said, "Should I ask what the other guy looks like?"

"It's a long story," Tommy said.

Gus had finished the paperwork and followed the vet in. Gus said, "This is Tommy Rooke."

Vet had no idea what that meant, but shifted the file he carried and shook both of their hands. His name was Weaver.

"Tommy Rooke, the fighter," Gus said.

"Boxing?" Weaver said.

"None other," Gus said.

Weaver said to Tommy, "Should I know you?"

"Only if you live on the planet," Gus said.

Weaver said, "You were the big fight last night?"

"Undercard," Tommy said.

Gus said, "He's coming out of retirement."

Weaver was already checking Vegas Vic, stethoscope to the dog's chest. He shook down a thermometer. Vic's legs reacted to the vet's touch, front and hind both. There was strength in them. Weaver pinched the dog's footpads, and Vic jerked. "He recovered okay from the surgery?" Weaver said, a hand on the dog to calm him.

"He walks," Gus said. "A little low in the butt, like an old guy with a load in his pants, but he's up on all fours."

"Eating?" Weaver fingered Vegas Vic's ears. Looked in each one.

Gus said, "Sure."

"Drinking water?"

"I keep filling up his bowl," Gus said.

"There's something going on with the lungs," the vet said. "I want to take some x-rays. See what's up." He wrote in Vic's file. He said, "What was he doing when you saw him like this?"

Tommy told Weaver about the walk, about sitting on the bench. He said he was afraid it was too cold.

"Not likely," Weaver said. "Not a cause."

Gus said, "His back again?"

Weaver said, "I'm not a neurosurgeon, but you can see his legs are okay. There's resistance." He stroked Vic's back and said to Tommy, "You out walking off the fight?"

"Singing the blues," Tommy said.

"You lost?"

"I lost."

"You got knocked out?"

"Completely."

"I've wondered what that felt like."

"You don't want to know."

"Basketball," the vet said. "Basketball is my game."

"Jesus," Gus said.

"It can get rough," the vet said.

Gus said, "Like croquet."

Weaver wanted to talk to the vet who did the surgery, and he ordered x-rays. It would be half an hour. Tommy leaned down close and whispered to Vegas Vic. "So a rabbi and the poodles rent this luxury boat," he said.

––––––––

Don't.

Don't.

Don't.

But Plugg couldn't *not* talk. Today he was not capable, come hell or high water, of putting a sock in it. More likely that the sun would burn up this minute and the oceans run dry than Plugg would keep his two cents to himself. He tapped his chest, once, twice, hard. "The heart," he said to Tommy, "not the head. The head might as well go shopping. Take a trip. Drive cross country."

Vegas Vic lay in blankets Tommy had fixed up in the TV room. Jane found an afghan for the dog.

Plugg's subject was intelligence. Where it resides. In the heart— the seat of intelligence and goodness. Not the head. Tommy's opponent had none. No smarts. Not an eyedropper's full. He had gotten lucky was all. "You know the hypothesis they say about a million monkeys," Plugg said. "A million monkeys typing twenty-four hours a day for a hundred years and one is going to write Shakespeare."

Don't, Tommy thought.

Don't.

Don't.

"Is what this kid did," Plugg said. "Punches all day long and into the night for a hundred years and he lands one."

That wasn't true. The kid and Tommy beat each other up. The kid, Jarret, broke Tommy's rib. He busted his chops. Tommy nailed him. He nailed Tommy. And then the kid coldcocked Tommy.

Tommy cross-blocked and was throwing a hook off it. He caught a jab and popped a jab. His own right was going to be a body shot. Was going to damage organs. No law of nature or physics or ring savvy could account for where the kid's right came from. Jarret was a warrior. God grant him his nerve and guts. Tommy banged him, once, twice, round after round. He hit him with punches that dislodged the kid's tattoos. Every blow was asking Jarret if he had nerve and heart, body shots checking to see if Jarret's legs could repair themselves quick enough. The kid weathered punch after punch, and he kept stepping into his own range and throwing. Tactics out the window. No showboating.

Footwork and fists.

Tommy leaned over, close to Vegas Vic. The blanket rose and fell lightly on the dog's chest. You could barely see the movement, but it was there. Once. Twice. Three times. Tommy held Vic's paw and rubbed it.

Plugg said, "Rabbi Tarfon—"

"Not today," Tommy said.

"What's not today?" Plugg said.

"No rabbi stories."

Jane had come in. She stood next to Plugg, and he looked up at her. He shrugged, and his shoulders suffered the affront. Jane held Hector in her arms, had dressed their boy in a Superman T-shirt.

Plugged tapped his heart.

"Vic okay?" Jane said.

There was a water bowl nearby. The dog had eaten some yogurt.

Plugg stood. He said to Tommy, "You don't want to hear. God forbid I should tell you. God forbid your pal takes up your time." He moved to get past Jane and Hector. He said, "Me? I thought we was talking is all. How presumptuous."

What he really wanted, Tommy knew, was to bring up the next fight, the next bout, the next purse. Game over, rack 'em.

Jane said, "Carl—"

"The scriptures say a man don't intrude where he's seen as a thief of time," Plugg said. He got into his coat. "You make a trip of hundreds of miles because maybe an omen tells you to. The way some twigs are laying or how rocks sit side by side," Plugg said. "Maybe you have a dream five times over and over. You tire your legs and you wear out your shoes because the twigs the rocks the dream they tell you your treasure is buried say in the middle of Nebraska by a certain tree looks like an umbrella." Plugg straightened his tie and said, "Your treasure, the whole time is under the stoop to your front door. All you got to do is go to the garage and pick out a shovel."

Jesus, Tommy thought.

He got up and took Plugg into his arms. Tommy Rooke gathered to him the man who taught him to keep it simple, who taught him to move forward and backwards and side to side. "Not today. That's only what I'm saying," Tommy said. "Tomorrow and the tomorrow after that. We'll talk. We'll go over the blueprints like we always do." Tommy put his hand to his own heart and said, "The brain has its reasons. The heart—"

Plugg said, "The brain says, Doctor, Doctor. Pills, pills—"

"Plugg," Tommy said.

"To the point?" Plugg said. "Cut to the chase?" Again, with the heart. Tap tap tap. He looked to Tommy for his okay. Tommy stepped back, and Plugg said, "Seven hundred and twenty good deeds, a man does. Also, he does seven hundred and nineteen bad. So, you comprehend, our topic is basic human nature. Is the fundamentals of the human brain and the human heart. Good deeds. Bad acts." Plugg paused. Then he said, "On one side of the ledger, seven hundred twenty. On the other side of the ledger, seven hundred and nineteen. In this way are the accounts kept." He held his hands as if to say *so it goes*, as if to weigh what he had placed on the scales of justice. He said, "Seven twenty good to seven nineteen bad—the man is more righteous than bad."

"The point?" Tommy said.

Plugg looked to the heavens. "Forget God," Plugg said. "God

quibbles. It's what God does best. God nitpicks. It's yourself you can't hide from. It's yourself you see in the mirror."

"Ah, Plugg," Tommy said.

Plugg, at the door, said, "The psalm says, 'There is no peace in my bones because of my sin.'"

———

Sin?

What was Tommy's sin? Against who?

Himself?

———

Late afternoon, and Tommy set Vegas Vic in a dog bed on the patio near the pool. The water was heated. The sun flashed on it like tiny fires. A breeze rustled a cluster of palm trees. Sweetest sound on the planet. Tommy slept for all of half an hour. He pulled up a chair and sat across from Gus. It was cool. Low sixties. Gus said, "Don't be too hard on Plugg. His world is small on account of his vocabulary." Gus sipped bourbon. "What does he do day and night but sit in a room on the phone. Three phones. One to his ear. One on speaker. One in his hand, and he's dialing."

Tommy reached for a bottle of Scotch and poured himself two fingers.

Gus was wrong, only you didn't quarrel with the man. To do so was to waste the letters of the alphabet. Better, Plugg himself would say, you spend your time stringing pearls for heaven. You use logic one way. You use logic the other way. All you got left is logic.

You can think yourself into a box.

Tommy hadn't trained for the fight like it was hell he was getting into. Why? There were one hundred and one answers. Each one a story. Each one correct. Each one wrong.

"A fighter fights," Gus said. "A promoter juggles the fruit."

Tommy raised his Scotch to Gus and said, "'One bourbon, one Scotch.'" More John Lee Hooker.

Gus raised his bourbon. Said, "One bourbon, one Scotch."

"'And one beer,'" Tommy said.

John Lee Hooker and the blues.

Plugg would have already cut a deal. There would be a fight on the table. Some grease to adjust the rankings if needed.

Tommy and Jarret put on a show.

One lucky punch was all. Throw one lucky punch out of the picture and Tommy would—but that's another story. Ain't no such thing as luck. Not in the ring.

> *One bourbon. One Scotch. And one beer.*
> *I ain't seen my baby since night before last.*

Woman wants to see her man real bad. So bad she can taste his absence. Man wants to see his woman bad. Real bad. Trouble lying in betwixt. They are not married. She's got a man who beats her. He's got a child up the block, one down the block, one behind. One in the avenues. One in San Francisco, Memphis, Atlanta.

Tommy had only the one boy, Hector.

But women? Was that his sin?

So many of them on the planet.

———

"Tommy," Jane said. They were standing in the foyer of their new home, and he was sending everybody ahead—Gus, Jane, Plugg. They had reservations for dinner, at the Bellagio. Short notice, but Gus's juice got them in. Tommy was asking Jane to ride with Gus and Plugg, and she said, "You are coming?"

He was. He told her she looked like a million bucks. He would be there. He held his arms wide for her to take in the big picture. Here he stood like a happy ending, dressed for dinner. He was standing here in his suit like he dropped in from a Godfather movie. An overcoat was neatly folded on the chair near the door. Shoes, shined. Jane had picked his necktie. His face had lost the beating it took. There was only the cut near his eye. He had vetoed stitches, and it kept bleeding. A butterfly bandage was holding it together. Tommy's breathing was difficult. Ribs like pick-up-sticks.

He had asked Plugg to walk Hector to the sitter's two doors down.

Jane said to him, "You won't fly to Reno or take a train to Mexico, right?"

Tommy said, "Not on your life," and touched the cut.

"Poor baby," she said. She was wearing a red dress whose top angled in from above her breasts to her throat where it tied around her neck.

Mans and womans.

Tommy wanted his woman bad.

———

Vegas Vic lay on Tommy and Jane's bed. Near the pillows. The dog snorted, got to his feet, and shook off the cobwebs. He studied Tommy. Vic wanted to know if Tommy could sing. It was a joke between them. The dog knew better. Not a lick, that was what Tommy could sing.

"Funny," Tommy said. "Real funny."

Vegas Vic wondered if they could walk down and see the city?

"You're up for that?"

Sure. No problem.

"I could carry you?"

We'll see.

Thirty minutes. Tommy would make the dinner. He phoned Gus. Caught him in traffic and asked to talk to Jane. "Going to be slow," Tommy said. "Start without me."

"You're okay?" she said.

Tommy assured her. He put a wink in his voice. He gathered the dog into his arms and they left the house.

Rabbi Hanina, Vic said.

"God, not you," Tommy said. "Enough is enough."

Vic shrugged. He admitted Plugg had been talking to him.

Tommy said, "Oy," and they had a great laugh together. They reached the street, and Vegas Vic asked to be put down. Tommy's ribs burned. He kneeled to set Vic on the sidewalk. Vic shuffled his feet, righted himself, and shook his ears into place.

The dog picked up where they left off. Asking, he wanted Tommy to know, was an art. Did Tommy know how to ask?

Tommy said, "You've got a one-track mind. You know how that works, right?"

Vic put some zip in his walk, let loose his old scoot. His swagger.

"A one-track mind," Tommy said. "So you're looking left. You're looking left. You're looking left." Tommy paced the punch line. Said, "It's the train coming the other way that nails you."

Put it to music, Vic said.

The sun had set, and the desert was cooling off. There was a pink tint to the sky. They turned a corner and there was the city. The

Strip was lit. Rubies, diamonds, sapphires, emeralds scattered across the valley floor. The moon above Sunrise Mountain was bigger than science could explain. It could have swallowed the place whole. Tommy and Vegas Vic stopped, and Tommy picked the dog up. He saw the need to. Vic let Tommy know they better hurry.

"Screw dinner," Tommy said. "I can be late."

Not dinner, Vic said. The big sleep, Tommy. The big sleep cometh. The dog scrutinized the city.

"Now Las Vegas," Tommy said, "there's something even a dog can see is funny. No way was it Bugsy Siegel's doing. A killer is not a man who can put two ideas together. Think about it. What's the future to a man who can pull a trigger two inches from your ear?"

They climbed a slope and sat on a bench at the seventeenth tee. A par three, one seventy from the back box. A six iron for Tommy and the high fade he hit when the pin was tucked in behind a sand trap. His ribs were killing him.

Vegas Vic was going on about Hollywood making a movie, about how Hollywood gets hold of a story and the world weeps. He was hung up on Bugsy Siegel. The dog shook his head, declaring it all a crock. Saying, A killer, and the world cries about his dying. Entertainment? This is the American dream?

"No one said that," Tommy said.

Vic wanted Tommy to understand it was the Jew.

"Who?"

It was the Jew Lansky. Not Bugsy Siegel. Meyer Lansky thought Las Vegas up. It was a good bet to say he even imagined the embarrassment it had become. He saw it all.

"Something tells me you have a point to make."

Lanksy saw the day Tommy would walk into Jarret's right hand.

"You're telling me Meyer Lanksy is God."

You don't have to believe in God to believe in God.

More riddles.

To ask was an art. Had the dog had arms he would have waved them at the city. He would have dismissed what it had become. A roof on Fremont Street. Such stupidity. Rollercoasters on the Strip. The fucking Statue of Liberty in the middle of the Mojave Desert. Vegas Vic told Tommy that Lansky knew how to ask. He combed his hair. He whitened his clothes. He put rings on his fingers and he carried a walking stick. Deference, even if it was faked, carried the day.

Meyer Lanksy used the words *atonement,* and *day of*—day of judgment, day of salvation, day of repentance. He said, *Divine.* He said, *Everlasting.* Big gangster that he was, Meyer Lanksy understood fear.

Tommy couldn't afford fear.

Not a fighter.

Vegas Vic was tired. He lay down on the bench, head on Tommy's thigh. He took a deep breath like he was sucking on life. Would have asked for a hit of oxygen had the damn vet thought ahead and given him a tank. He was only a dog. Who provided such care for a dog? A dog should be toting around one of those tanks on wheels? Oy. Vic went on. Lansky comprehended enough to sing God's praises—*before* he asked, not during, not after. Fear God and rejoice, Vic said. You don't ask first. Number one, Lansky gave credit to God for the sun and the moon and the heavens. He acknowledged the creator of the oceans and the deserts and the polar ice caps. Craftsman, as the poet would have it, of the snake and the bird and the armadillo. The mover and the shaker. Creation in a nutshell. *What* declares the glory of God? The toads, the rodents, the bugs, stones and twigs—all of creation, high to low. Vegas Vic said you don't ride in like a one-eyed, one-armed buckaroo and ask for oxen because you don't like the oxen you have.

"Oxen?" Tommy said.

Vic faked perturbation. As if the last straw was on its way. The dog let Tommy know it was biblical. It was a metaphor. It was words where one thing is standing in for another. For clarity's sake. It was the language of the heart, not the head.

"Still," Tommy said. "Oxen?"

Another great laugh.

Tommy, Tommy, Tommy. Had Vic hands he would have gently slapped Tommy's cheek. Tommy, always the jester. The banger who could jab-a-jabba. Who could peck you to death. Vic let Tommy know you ask, with genuine concern, after the shank of the oxen, you ask sincerely after the silk and luster of corn, you ask after the firmness of the grapes but speak first of their roundness.

"Oxen? Corn? Grapes?"

There is the throne of judgment. There is the throne of mercy.

Tommy said, "A two-year-old can tell you this. This is the crap they bring you up on. Riddles. Puzzles. Conundrums."

Can a two-year-old, Vic wondered, tell you how to move God from the one to the other? Had he arms and hands the dog would have shown Tommy what he meant, the urging of God from the throne of judgment to the throne of mercy. From hand to hand, his point would have been, the wicked shall not be unpunished.

The wicked? Sin? Tommy?

Tommy studied his own hands. Still swollen. Someday he would be able to use them to predict the weather. He touched where his ribs bit him. "For boxing?" Tommy said. "I'm to be judged for boxing?"

Tommy, Tommy, always the innocent. So naive.

Tommy said, "Because a boxer shows no mercy?"

Tommy, Tommy. Had he arms and hands the dog would have thrown them skyward. He would have gathered Tommy to him. Would have hugged him.

Would have left all of it at that.

Tommy picked up Vegas Vic and started walking, and the dog fell asleep in his arms. At the house, Tommy laid him on the bed and covered him with the afghan. The phone was ringing. It would be Jane. Gus. Plugg.

The big sleep, Vegas Vic said.

Tommy sat next to him. He held his hands open, palms up, like he was weighing steel balls. The dog's chest rose and fell.

Once.

Twice.

Three times.

Tommy touched it. Could feel Vegas Vic's heart, like a fist squeezing a rubber ball.

Tommy didn't know what to ask for.

For forgiveness. For Pete Hitchcock's life back. For one big trade, his life for Pete's.

Or forgiveness for all the hurt he had done.

For all the harm.

For the dog's heart to stop. For the dog's heart to continue.

———

Close to eleven, and Jane sat next to Tommy on the end of their bed. No real sleep for him. Not yet. Behind them Vegas Vic lay with his head on a pillow. Jane had to hike up her red dress to sit down.

She had taken a cab home. Gus and Plugg stayed on to gamble. Tommy saw the cab pull in and met Jane at the door. God, was he sorry. Vegas Vic had wanted to see the city. Time got away.

Jane walked into his arms. "World-class cuisine is highly over-rated," she said.

Here, on the bed, she said, "How's Vic doing?"

"He didn't eat tonight." There was a bowl of yogurt on the floor. Jane turned to look at the dog, and Tommy said, "The big sleep."

"Tommy," she said, "you lost a fight. Not an arm or a leg. Not Hector."

"Not you?"

"Not even me." She showed him, her gesture saying *I'm sitting here big as life itself.*

Tommy said, "You sure?"

She said, "Time will tell."

He said, "It's not the fight."

"I hear from the TV it was a lucky punch."

"No such thing."

"Whatever you say."

She took Tommy's arm and got the two of them to their feet. "Let's go get Hector," she said. "There's a moon out there you've got to see."

"I saw it."

"You didn't really look at it."

"You think so?"

"It'll trick you."

"Into?"

"Dancing."

"Can't. Two left feet out of the ring."

"Into singing?"

"Not a lick. Ask the dog."

ACKNOWLEDGMENTS

Grateful acknowledgment is made to the editors of the following journals, in which these stories previously appeared: *American Literary Review* ("Death Care World Expo, Reno, Nevada"); *Ascent* ("i.e. God," published here as "Bring Your Legs with You"); *Epoch* ("The Sweet Science"); *High Plains Literary Review* ("Five Times for Disorderly Conduct" and "Until Liquor Is Made Legal"); *Quarter After Eight* ("How Would You Play This?").

I want to thank those who read these stories for me and offered kind and exacting suggestions—Kate Spencer, François Camoin, Rob Roberge, and Brady Udall.

I also want to thank Ohio University, where I am a professor in the English department. The school's generosity has provided me with support and time that I greatly appreciate.

I am particularly indebted to three books I read as a way of returning to a world of storytelling that I once knew only as an outsider. They are Abraham Cohen's *Everyman's Talmud*, Martin Buber's *Tales of the Hasidim*, and C. G. Montefiore and H. Loewe's *A Rabbinic Anthology*. Growing up in Las Vegas, at ballparks, around swimming pools, in living rooms, I heard stories, anecdotes, tales, and teachings similar to and variations of those that infect *Bring Your Legs with You*. Carl T. Plugg gives them voice. The three books created again, for me, an atmosphere I was familiar with, and they provided specific details, such as Rabbi Tarfon, one of the sure-footed and unsung heroes and philosophers of the stories.

And, of course, I want to express my thanks to Mrs. Drue Heinz for originating and supporting the Drue Heinz Literature Prize, Michael Chabon for selecting *Bring Your Legs with You*, and the members of the staff at the University of Pittsburgh Press for their generous and excellent assistance with the manuscript.